"Hmm, a proper greeting first, eh? And a thank you, mayhap?"

"Of course, my lord, I am sorry," Penelope said, aghast. *Gor, how could I have forgotten my training so easily?* Leaning up, she brought her lips to his in a gentle kiss. "Welcome, 'tis lovely to have you here with me."

"All is well, Pen. I was teasing you." Michael smiled. "But I would not be upset by you removing one article of clothing to thank me." He arched his brows in hope and took one step back, releasing her.

"Oh!" She considered, tilting her head. Then, with a small smile, she bent and removed a slipper.

"Will that do, my lord?" She slid him a sidelong look. Internally, she berated herself. *I should be thinking of these games. But I like that he created this one. I like playful Michael a lot, I shall do better in the future.*

He strolled over and fingered the bread peel, his lips pursed.

"At the very least, the pair is really one article of clothing as you always wear them together. Beyond that, I can see I will need to be more specific. Fair enough, young lady."

Penelope's Passion

by

Maggie Sims

School of Enlightenment,
Book Two

This is a work of fiction. Names, characters, places, and incidents are either the product of the author's imagination or are used fictitiously, and any resemblance to actual persons living or dead, business establishments, events, or locales, is entirely coincidental.

Penelope's Passion

Cover Art by *Lisa Dawn MacDonald*

The Wild Rose Press, Inc.
PO Box 708
Adams Basin, NY 14410-0708

Publishing History
First Edition, 2022
Trade Paperback ISBN 978-1-5092-4595-6
Digital ISBN 978-1-5092-4596-3

School of Enlightenment, Book Two
Published in the United States of America

Dedication

For Julie J—my confidante, unofficial book therapist, idea generator, and first beta reader—and most of all, a great friend

Acknowledgments

First and foremost, I must thank my amazing and patient senior editor, Diana Carlile. Despite several other roles including managing the Scarlet Rose line for The Wild Rose Press, she took me under her wing and has taught me so much. Sophia's and Penelope's books have benefited greatly from her guidance.

So many multi-published authors continue to help me—especially Annabel Joseph, Marie Tuhart, Desiree Holt, Cecilia Rene, Robecca Austin, Melanie Rose Clark, and Courtney McCaskill.

The Passionate Ink organization is the most supportive group of people I could imagine, all while providing excellent immoral support. I live in hope for an in-person conference.

And I must take this opportunity to thank my fellow 2022 Wild Rose Press authors who formed a support group with me—Avis M. Adams, Lis Angus, Corinne LaBalme, Amy Bernstein, Cara Bertoia, Janie Emaus, Terry Segan, J L Sullivan, S. Hilbre Thompson, and Sandra L. Young.

And always, thanks to my very own real-life romance hero, my husband. He respected my writing as work for two years before a publishing contract promised a future return and has adapted admirably to the fact that this is consuming a lot more time than either of us expected.

Chapter One

Winter 1816, Mansfield Manor

Lord Michael Slade walked into the dining room of his family's country home after an early morning ride, having taken advantage of an unexpectedly clear winter day. His parents, the Earl and Countess of Mansfield, had just sat down for breakfast. During the winter, with him home, they ate cooked breakfasts in the dining room. At least they did when his father's health permitted.

"Good morning, Mama, Father." He kissed his mother's cheek and patted his father's shoulder as he rounded the table to select a few bites of eggs and a small pastry. "How are you feeling?"

"I am well, thank you. The drier days help."

His father had developed a persistent cough and shortness of breath two Seasons ago in London, and it had worsened in the last year. The Season would begin again in two short months, with the earl's presence needed in the House of Lords.

"Good, good." Michael nodded and ate quickly as a servant poured tea for him. He was anxious to get through paperwork while his father felt up to it. "We can go over the estate books then, mayhap. I have several documents I need your final approval on, but I've made recommendations for action."

"Excellent."

"I'll remind you I am also happy to go ahead to London and read the first round of Parliament drudgery on your behalf. The first several bills are always budget and funding anyway. And I'll take your delegation of voting authority to one of your cronies."

"As today is a good day, I'm loathe to decide now. Stop harping, son." His father smiled to take the sting out of his words.

"I only want what's best for your health." Michael waved his last bite of pastry toward his mother. "And Mama worries."

"I know, I know. And it may very well make sense for me to travel when 'tis a tad warmer. But Matilda's pregnancy will also drive our timing."

Michael's sister was expecting her first child toward the end of the summer.

"Right, then." Michael pushed back his chair after a last slurp of tea. "If you'll excuse me, I will change out of my riding clothes before joining you?"

His father nodded, and Michael headed for his room. As he cleared the doorway, his mother said something in an undertone to the earl, and her chair scraped.

"Michael! A moment, please?" His mother's voice stopped him in the hall.

"Yes, Mama?"

She stepped close to murmur, "You can see your father's health declining. This winter has been especially hard on him. What he doesn't say is that he'd dearly like to see you settled and to hold a future earl in his arms."

"Mama." He extended the word into a groan. "Are you sure you're not speaking of your own wishes?"

She laid a placating hand on his sleeve. "Of course, I would love naught else. But I am being forthright with you regarding your father's wishes. I know he *says* that he wants you to enjoy your freedom and youth whilst you can. And that you should make your own decisions. I only hope those will include a betrothal sooner rather than later. With a suitable young lady, that is."

"Yes, Mama. I appreciate your concern. I shall consider it."

"The doctor told him he mustn't travel to London anymore. The air there is bad for him. But he feels duty bound to vote in person in Lords. Even if he didn't, this year he'd go if only to see your sister and his first grandchild."

"See? He can hold a grandbaby in a few months." He smiled, hoping to escape.

She tilted her chin down and stared at him from under her brows. "You know that is not the same. He wants to ascertain that the line of succession will continue. He has put so much work into maintaining the earldom and the estate, despite hurdles that you cannot imagine."

His mother's past as an actress had always haunted her and colored their family life. Both his parents had tried to shield him and his sister from the Ton's malicious gossip and unkind behavior. But Michael had overheard enough conversations between his parents to understand the spite and cruelty directed at them. "Decorum—respectable, acceptable behavior," was her constant motto, even after he teased her that he had no desire to be "drab." She had drilled the concept into her children from a young age.

"Right, Mama. Only a 'drab' young lady for me.

3

Sooner rather than later. I love you." He leaned in and kissed her. "Now, finish your breakfast with Father and let me go change clothes."

"I love you, too, Michael. I am so proud of you." She beamed at him, and he returned her grin before turning to run up the stairs.

His mother's "drab" motto was ingrained. After fielding scorn from some of his peers at boarding school, he understood more why she pushed so hard. She wanted them to work within the narrow rules of the Ton, believing their lives would be happier with less conflict.

Wanting to pay tribute to his mother, and mayhap in part because it was a subtle way to thumb his nose at society's rules, he had bought a theatre a few years ago. Beyond it being a sound investment, he thought she'd be flattered. Her resistance had surprised him, but after much debate, she'd demurred to his father's support of the purchase.

Father is ever the romantic, but I won't have that choice. I am out of time.

****

Spring 1816, London

Leaning forward, Penelope Wood stared out the carriage window as they rolled into the outskirts of the city. At eighteen, this was her first visit to London. Her sewing lay forgotten in her lap as she gazed wide-eyed at the pedestrians, horses, and hacks in the streets, intersecting at haphazard angles.

Her companion, a woman of forty, snickered at her astonished expression.

Penelope's dark hair swung as she turned. "Mayhap school should have covered navigating

London streets."

Peterborough, where she'd spent the last six of her eighteen years, was a city, but a much smaller one in Northern England, and she could walk the length of it in less than two hours.

The snickers became an outright laugh. Leah Godwin shook her head. "I doubt they could do London justice. 'Tis something you'll have to experience for yourself, like the rest of us."

"One more overwhelming new adventure." Penelope's smile faded, her hands fisting on her lap. She'd been nervous enough about her decision before she realized how vast this metropolis was.

What if I hate the city? Or I can't do the job? No. I can. I know I can. School prepared me for this. Gor, what if the men are all ugly or, worse, cruel?

Leah leaned forward to pat one clenched set of knuckles. "Pen. Be sure about this. You can change your mind at any time."

But then what would I do? There aren't jobs in Peterborough for me. An internal voice argued, *A governess would be more respectable. You'd have a chance at a good marriage.*

Her practical side asserted itself again. *Not necessarily. Leah's friend Mary is proof there are as many risks to being a governess, and it pays less. And why assume I'll want to marry someone?*

She shook her head. "I'm sure, thank you. There are risks in every profession for women, and this has the greatest reward—the ability to send more funds home to David and Matthew right away." Her stepfather and half-brother, who was only three and a half, remained in Peterborough. "I miss Mama so much, but she and I had talked about me finding my own way. I know she'd support this, strange as it may seem."

"From her visits to my house, I'd agree." Leah nodded. "However, there is still time to reconsider. No matter what advanced courses you took at the School of Enlightenment, this is a big step."

"I want to make David's life easier, as he did mine these past six years when Mama was alive. And besides, this is the fastest way to gain the savings I'll need to start a bakery."

"Right, then. We have a fortnight. Prudence, the theatre manager, and I will both be available. Please come to either of us if you have concerns. While I am your sponsor, you can ask her anything as well. She ran the auction last year."

"Thank you. I suspect I may have more questions afterward. For now, I may be nervous, but I am ready to become a courtesan."

****

A shiver of anticipation ran through Penelope.

Tonight, I'll be auctioned on this stage. Will many men bid on me? Am I ready to become some man's mistress? Well, even if not, it'll likely happen tonight.

She dunked the mop in the bucket and made another pass of the boards.

Gor, what if no one bids? The whole idea of participating was to help David and Matthew and save for a bakery.

Unsure if multiple offers or no offers would be worse, she lowered her head to finish mopping the stage. As she did, she chastised herself for her language, recalling her lessons. *Remember to speak like an aristo. A nabob will only take you places if you can blend.*

She paused downstage, near the left stairs leading to the audience floor to admire her handiwork. She had developed a knack for making the wood gleam. This time she had pushed all her nervous excitement through the mop, her focus on the next time she'd tread the boards. Sewing for the theatre had kept her mama's memory alive, and the rest of the work had given her pocket money, so she didn't mind. The night would bring different work, a new beginning. Hopefully.

Bootsteps rang across the stage. A man had entered the theatre through the side door near the stairs to stage right. He ascended the steps and strode across the freshly washed stage floor as if he did not care that it had been raining and he was leaving muddy footprints.

He caught sight of her, opening his mouth to ask her a question, but Penelope cut him off with a growl. "Did you not see the clean stage ready for an event tonight? How dare you prance across it as though you own the place. Did your mother not teach you to wipe your feet when you come in from the rain?"

His blue eyes widened, then narrowed.

"How dare I?" he ground out, advancing.

She realized she looked like a young servant in her mob cap and shapeless work dress, but she stood her ground.

"I assure you that the Manageress of this theatre will hear about you yelling at me," he bit out.

She rolled her eyes. "Aye, she will. From me!"

Then she gulped as she took in his frock coat, breeches tucked in those shiny, fancy boots, and a fancy cravat.

A fancy nabob.

"Why, you little brat. You do not realize one key fact—I do in fact own this place. And let's dispense with involving Prudence. I've a mind to punish you for your insolence right here and right now."

He owns the theatre? She hadn't given any thought to the owner. Leah and Prudence and two other women were hosting the auction.

His hand snapped out and grabbed her wrist to haul her down the steps to the first row of theatre seats. He sat, then used his hold on her arm to pull her across his body, plunking her face down across his lap.

Penelope was staring at his Hessians when she finally found words to fight. "Unhand me!"

She assimilated the risks of being manhandled by this stranger. He knew Prudence. Anyone allowed into the theatre today was privy to the nature of the evening's event.

Not only was he tall, fit and handsome, with Brummel-style chestnut curls and his fancy clothes, he smelled delicious. Sandalwood and a slight musky note teased her nose. Odds were he'd do nothing more than spank her a few times.

Then his words sank in. He owned the theatre? She gulped. She couldn't jeopardize her place in the auction.

Resigned, she let her fear go. She knew what to expect from a spanking, albeit she'd prefer one not administered in anger. After all, advanced classes at the School of Enlightenment had included a brief trial of various spanking implements, so she was innocent but not ignorant. She stopped fighting and relaxed her back, draping her limbs more comfortably over his legs.

The eccentric would-be nobleman kept one hand

where he had pressed it to her back. The other flipped her skirt over her legs.

Her calm disappeared. *How dare he!*

Ignoring her legs kicking, he bared her bottom and sucked in a sharp breath.

His free hand skimmed her cheeks with a feather-light touch, raising gooseflesh in its wake. The draft of the theatre air over sensitized flesh caused a shiver, and her nipples pointed against her dress.

His hand lingered for a moment, caressing the silky globes, before it withdrew, then slammed back in a hard spank.

"Enough. Clodpate, let me up," Penelope wailed. *Devil take him, that bloody well hurt.*

Thwack! Thwack! Thwack!

With each blow, her anger sparked higher. "You arrogant arse. You'll be sorry." She had no idea how she'd make him pay, especially if he owned the theatre, but she'd find a way. She really must stop swearing, though.

"Your lordship? Michael?" They both started at Pru's voice. "Did I hear you come in? Where are you?" Light footsteps sounded from the rear of the theater, approaching the stage from the hall leading from dressing rooms and offices.

The man helped her up, adjusting his clothes over a noticeable lump in his trousers.

Distracted by the metamorphosis of the pain into a more pleasurable heat—*so that's what the instructors meant*—she brushed her cap back from her face and smoothed her skirt down, only to encounter his hand lingering on her hip.

It flexed once, fingers digging into her

momentarily before releasing her.

Her skirts falling over her tender flesh pushed the heat from her bottom forward. Blood pooled in her core, cords of pleasure weaving through her belly, buttocks, and nether lips. At school the lessons had been fun, lighthearted. This was darker, thicker, giving her a deeper understanding of why some men and women enjoyed spankings.

His looks, scent, and gentle caresses before the spanks also may have had something to do with it.

"You're lucky we were interrupted. I hope you learned your lesson," he snarled at her under his breath before turning his head toward the stage.

His voice revived her anger, and she frowned back.

"I just arrived, Pru. I shall be right with you," he called louder, even as his gaze strayed back to Penelope, assessing and roaming her figure.

As he stalked away, she returned the favor. His thigh muscles were still imprinted on her stomach, his arse above them the perfect roundness of a frequent horseman. A narrow back tapered out to broader shoulders than most gentlemen she'd seen.

Delicious. Of course, his arrogance detracted from his good looks, but she knew enough of the sensual arts to appreciate his physique's effect on her. However, she wouldn't want him to bid on her given his hauteur and disdain for her hard work.

Her nipples and nether regions didn't care about his vanity. They wanted to play with those muscles. Eyes on his derriere again, she licked her lips.

He glanced back, catching her. When her gaze rose guiltily to his, he raised a brow.

****

After checking in with Pru on preparations for the auction, Michael returned home for dinner and a change of clothes. Back at the theatre a few hours later, he lingered in the lobby, waiting for his two closest friends to join him. Handbills describing each girl up for bid lined the walls. The core elements of the sale mirrored the first auction, held the prior summer. All girls were untouched but educated in pleasing a man, and bids were a one-year exclusive commitment, with an astronomical sum split between the organizers and the girl chosen.

The young women had been educated for a wide variety of tastes, and the auctioneers understood that personality, accommodations, and even hobbies and interests were important to a successful relationship. Therefore, they had summarized each girl's attributes on a profile sheet for review before the auction.

As the owner of the hosting venue, Michael knew more details of the process than his friends did, despite not being directly involved. Mrs. Sarah Potter's Spanking Club, their favorite evening destination, advertised to potential bidders who were then vetted by the organizers. All bidders had been required to submit answers to questionnaires and provide personal references two days prior.

Bids would be submitted in writing as each girl was presented on stage but would only be considered if the hostesses had the requisite background paperwork, and the winning contract would be based on more than the highest amount.

The young women came from a secret school that taught girls of all stations—members of the aristocracy and servants alike, as well as those in between, the demi-monde. Qualified girls from the demi-monde classes had been invited to participate in the auction after being educated in reading, math, financial management, deportment, and sexual acts.

Although he had no idea how that worked, if they remained chaste. Nor was he likely to, as specifics were strictly prohibited from being discussed.

The organizers included Prudence, Sarah from the Spanking Club, the School of Enlightenment's headmistress, and a retired courtesan somehow involved in the school.

"Slade!"

He turned and beckoned Evan Gardner and Robert Orford to join him at the end of the row of handbills. The men had attended boarding school and Oxford and traveled the Continent for much of their Grand Tours together, competing to find the most outrageous activities country by country. Having returned home before the start of last Season, they had been enjoying bachelorhood and avoiding the marriage mart.

Evan, labeled "Bags" by the other two at university, was already the Earl of Cheltenham. Robert was the second son of an earl while Michael was heir to an earldom. At twenty-six, none of them were in a hurry to marry, despite their mothers' requests for heirs and grandbabies. But while his friends were eagerly anticipating this auction, Michael's family history precluded him from participating, even as he provided the theatre to host it. Worse, his father's health was declining, which had prompted his mother's exhortation to find a wife this year.

"Have you changed your mind yet?" Evan ribbed Michael as he had done for the first several sennights of the Season. "Mightn't an exclusive mistress set up quietly in her own house be as discreet as the Spanking Club?"

Michael shook his head. "Bags, we've been over this. You know as well as I do that talk is rife among the Ton."

He referred to the fashionable set within the aristocracy that was the source of most gossip. "My mother would hear about a mistress within a fortnight. I can't do it."

Despite his words, he could not stop picturing the young woman he had encountered earlier. Dark liquid eyes, smooth caramel skin, a hint of midnight hair peeking out from her cap at her ears and nape. The memory of her bottom still warmed his hand, and he had the sudden wish that she was part of the auction and he had the freedom to bid on her.

"We shall have to find someone willing to share then," Evan exclaimed as he turned his attention to the first handbill along the wall. The men had shared a few women in university and at Evan's wilder parties. Bags had never allowed his Parliamentary and other responsibilities to interfere with his fun and often had more energy than the other two combined. They strolled along the row of posters, each lingering over different names as the listed attributes appealed to one man or another.

Evan stopped in front of one, reading aloud to the others, "Beth—energetic and playful, requires strict oversight, full-time residency recommended." His voice rose in surprise. "Oh, gentlemen *and* ladies interested should speak to the auctioneer. She sounds a bit high-spirited, but at least she's open to various forms of punishment, based on the 'strict oversight.' I am not interested in full-time residency, though." He shuddered. "And this sounds like she'll get up to no good if left alone too long. Hmm…"

They continued down the row, reading and dismissing a few other profiles based on the encoded phrases that invitees knew how to interpret.

"Here, then, Robert." Evan stopped by another profile. "A more malleable one for you. Caroline— quiet and respectful, minimal oversight needed, schedule is flexible, interested gentlemen should speak to the auctioneer."

"I don't want someone quite that timid, thanks," Robert said with a sniff. "You know I need a bit of fun and fluff along with the obedience."

"There is simply no winning with you, I think," Michael said, and Evan grinned at Robert in agreement.

Evan stopped in front of one of the last posters along the wall.

"There might be, gentlemen. Listen to this. Penelope—dramatically beautiful, requests access to a kitchen and garden, and makes friends easily. It seems she's open to role-play, might cook for me, and based on the 'makes friends easily' may even be willing to be shared. I'd be doing us all a disservice if I did not bid on this one, boys."

"Leave me out of this, if you please." Robert shook his head at his friend. "But Michael here could use the discreet access, especially if she likes to cook. You know how he likes to tinker in the kitchen."

An usher interrupted their debate as he walked through the crowded lobby, ringing the bell for everyone to enter the theatre.

"Who else is here tonight, then, from the Club?" Robert asked. "I expected to run into Mordaunt at least."

Michael cocked his head. "Haven't you heard? He's Peterborough now. And newly married, besides."

"The devil you say." Robert frowned, but then Evan nodded as well. "You'll have to tell me more, but now is not the time or place."

After waving to a few other acquaintances, the men made their way to the owner's box, which hung almost directly over the stage with one of the best views in the house.

Chapter Two

Penelope's hands shook as she rushed to dress for the auction. The reality of being on a stage in front of dozens of people was quite different than discussing it in a classroom miles away.

She watched the other participants from the corner of her eye. Girls with enough funds had tried to make themselves appear older or more worldly with makeup and elaborate dresses while the less fortunate wore what they had. Still others dressed to tout their charms and wore gowns that belied their innocence.

The same concern had plagued her all day. Would her outfit—or she herself—attract enough bids to fund her bakery?

She had chosen a simple cream dress to offset her dark coloring. With a modest neckline and a straight fall from the empire waistline, it was a playful contradiction of purity and mystery, a tease on the night's theme. In lieu of tuition, terms of her scholarship had included labor. Gardening and cooking had paired well with her epicurean pursuits, and she loved learning more about pastry and seasonings and growing her own herbs and vegetables.

With that in mind, she'd pinned an apron to her auction dress. She'd also made a ginger candy stick to take on stage, to demonstrate two of her learned skills, cooking and otherwise. It was eight inches long and a half inch in diameter, and she had practiced sucking on it until her lips could meet her fingers where they held the end.

Searching for a friendly face, she scanned the dressing area again. She'd spied Beth earlier, a friend from her class at school, and chatted with her briefly. Penelope had been surprised to see her friend there, as some of Beth's comments had made it sound as though she had more experience than the auction allowed. But Beth had been excited about the auction, and Penelope wished for her friend's cheerful outlook to calm her own nerves.

Looking again at the other young women, she worried that her plain muslin shift would fade into the background and, at the last minute, slipped out of her chemise and petticoat. The muslin rubbed her chafed bottom, and hot sparks raised gooseflesh on her arms and legs, tightening her nipples and the sensitive flesh between her legs. Energized, she straightened her spine and lifted her head as bravado returned.

****

The auction began with all the women up for bid promenading onstage, forming a semi-circle facing forward, then spinning to face the rear. They turned again and stepped back to become a backdrop for each woman's solo turn in the spotlight.

As the girls circled, Michael glimpsed one young woman at the rear of the stage who looked younger than most. Peering down, he waited for the stage lights to hit her face. When they did, he reared back in surprise. She was the theatre cleaning girl he had spanked earlier. He knew from his relationship with the Spanking Club and the auctioneers who rented the theatre from him that only individuals eighteen and older could participate in this auction.

I thought she was a bit younger. Although 'tis probably good she is older than I originally guessed, given the spanking and how aroused I became. Now, she'll belong to someone else? The idea rankled. *No. Blast, as much as I'd like to bid, I cannot.*

One by one, the women walked solo downstage as the auctioneer read the attributes on their profiles. Some dressed to provoke, others dressed to help the men remember their preferences, and still others kept their clothing simple. After what felt like dozens of girls, the auctioneer called, "And here is Penelope."

Evan leaned forward in the box.

Michael's jaw dropped as the servant girl from earlier sauntered on stage. She wore a simple sheer muslin dress with an apron pinned to it. Barely covering her nipples, the apron tied around her waist and fell to mid-thigh. Her thick, straight ebony hair swung free at the top of her decolletage, and her eyes were dark pools in her face in the stage lights. His lips pressed flat in consternation. His theatre girl was Penelope, the young woman Evan wanted to bid on.

The pale dress over her honey-toned skin showed that she did not appear to wear underclothes, which seemed to be a habit, at least based on this afternoon. Remembering that her skin was the same color all over, he realized it was not a tan. Most shocking, she had a ginger candy stick in one hand that she licked as she strolled to the front of the stage, where she sucked it deep into her mouth and hollowed her cheeks.

The audience emitted groans, and Evan swore. "God's blood, she just doubled her asking price. I shall have to re-think my bid."

Evan's investing skills had multiplied his friends' savings from their quarterly allowances, and was the reason Michael had been able to buy this building. None of them had to worry about affording a mistress. But Evan prided himself on not over-paying.

As she turned to promenade offstage, the audience received a view of her bottom cheeks jiggling with each step through the muslin, verifying Michael's guess that she wore nothing beneath the dress. A collective sigh rose from the crowd. His gut twisted. She was his. He'd already claimed her with a spanking.

How could he keep her? Where would he have her live? How could he hide her? Too befuddled to settle on solutions, he kept circling back to the fact that he could not watch her go to someone else's bed. He had never thought he'd care if a bedmate—aside from mayhap a wife—was a maiden or not. But knowing auctionees were untouched further fired his need to possess this girl.

"What do you think will suffice to win her?" Evan's voice stopped Michael as he stood to leave.

As the owner of the theatre, he knew the prior year's bid ranges, the first ever of such an auction. He considered last year's crop versus this year's and the growing popularity of the auction, given the breadth of the community privy to it.

He hesitated at the curtain. "What are you thinking you'll offer? What's she worth to you?"

Evan tapped his lips with a finger. "I do like the convenience of someone at my beck and call, but for the blunt it might take, I may save it for the Spanking Club and my famous parties. You warned us what the high range was from last year. I figure I'll wager that for her and see what happens."

Robert snorted. "Only you'd think of it that way, despite being richer than Croesus."

"'Tis all about the return on investment, old chap."

Michael laughed with them. "If you'll excuse me, I have to help the auctioneers coordinate the logistics of getting the girls placed."

"We're heading to White's. We shall look for you there later."

With a wave, Michael flew down the stairs to find the auctioneer and request special dispensation to bid without pre-approval before Penelope's bids were evaluated. As the host, mayhap they'd make an exception for him.

Please make an exception.

Then he'd have to ensure his bid was the highest and procure a house within a matter of days or possibly sooner. The girl might not have suitable living arrangements beyond tonight.

He was determined to win her, even if he hadn't a damned clue what he would do with her.

He grimaced. Then he'd need to find a way to explain his actions to one of his oldest friends.

****

Penelope had loved her time in Peterborough before being sponsored to the secret school for young ladies. Rumors abounded regarding the four spinsters who shared a house at the north end of the city. When they took her under their wing after the death of her mother, she had discovered at least one of the rumors was true. They were in fact retired courtesans. One was Leah Godwin, a recruiter for the school, who had become her sponsor.

The school's initial curriculum was broad enough to prepare Penelope to choose among career paths. After the introductory session, Leah and Mrs. Montague, the headmistress, had sat her down and discussed her options, among them, governess, actress, or courtesan.

Penelope had wanted to go to London but worried about her family. Her goal was to earn money to help them as well as ensure a comfortable life for herself. With the ultimate goal of saving for her dream bakery, she had also been tempted by the financial independence Leah and her housemates portrayed. The first classes had been energizing, teaching her to manage her finances and to appreciate the beauty of her body and those of others. They also provided her first glimpse of sexual pleasure. Thus, becoming a courtesan held an appeal beyond the highest wage. It also was more likely to result in some delicious-sounding activities. In the end, her decision was easy. She continued to explore the school's advanced offerings.

After she had completed the courtesan classes, she was called back to meet with Leah and the headmistress again.

"Penelope, have you ever been intimate with a man?" Leah asked, her voice matter-of-fact.

She shook her head.

"Good," Mrs. Montague replied. "Miss Wood— Penelope, I've watched you, talked to Leah, and spoken to your instructors. We have an opportunity that might interest you, which would provide a lovely start on your savings."

Penelope glanced at Leah, who encouraged her

with a nod. "There is no pressure to do this, though, Penelope. 'Tis only one of the paths available to you. Listen to the idea, consider it, and come back after you've taken that time, and ask us questions. We do not need an answer today."

Mrs. Montague explained the premise of the auction, the first one having been held the prior Season. Discreet though it had been, the advertisement of the girls as untouched brought very high bids, and the girls kept half of that amount if they remained in the relationship at least six months. She also reassured Penelope that bidders were required to pass a safety screening.

"Even after such selectiveness, final bids must be approved by me or someone who knows both parties before we accept them. In your case, Leah. After we place the young ladies, Leah or I will visit you several times to ensure you are safe and happy. Bidders must agree to unscheduled visits. No one can be spirited away from London, or hidden away."

The money sounded alluring enough, and the idea of being auctioned exciting enough, that she had agreed.

****

Nervous, she sat backstage as the rest of the girls returned from their time on stage.

When she'd taken her turn to stroll forward under the spotlight, her grip on the candy had been so tight it stuck to her palm. She'd lowered her lashes to avoid the avid stares and pulled the rod deep into her mouth, sucking hard in her distraction. At the chorus of groans, she'd jolted in surprise.

Were they disgusted, or did it work as I was taught

it should? Bids for earlier walkers were coming in, and she still worried that none would be for her. The auctioneer ladies remained behind closed doors in a back office where they received bids from the audience via runners and matched them against the girls for approval.

The organizers knew their audience as well as their auctionees, and many bids were approved without fanfare, bank drafts accepted, and girls sent out one by one to meet their clients. Penelope said goodbye to friends, waved farewell to others she knew less well, and watched as their number dwindled.

A sudden commotion rose in the hall leading to the office from the stage wing. At the sight of who caused it, her brows drew together in annoyance. The arrogant theatre owner was striding past her, when no men were allowed back here in case girls were changing to leave for their new residence. He stomped past the runners and thumped hard on the closed door of the office.

****

Michael held his breath waiting for the organizers to respond to his knock. When Pru opened the door, she froze, eyes wide with shock. Taking advantage of her stillness, he pushed past her into the room. The other ladies turned to the intruder.

Helen Montague stood. "Lord Slade, what are you doing here? These bids must remain confidential." She shifted to stand between him and the desk the women were gathered around.

"I know, I know, I am sorry to interrupt. I know this is highly irregular, but I need to make a bid."

Helen blinked. "But, my lord, you were not pre-approved."

23

"You ladies know I am good for the blunt," he replied, cocking his head, willing them to recall who owned the building they were using.

"Do you even know what accommodations you will provide for the young lady?" Sputtering, Helen continued, "You do not have a signed bank note…"

"No, I do not yet have a house set up. I had no inten—" He cleared his throat. "I am requesting a favor. I'd need the girl in question to remain where she has been residing for a few days, whilst I make the necessary arrangements. I will do so with the utmost speed."

He met each woman's eyes in turn. "You all know me. You know my circumstance. I would not do this if my interest was not serious. Please."

"To whom are we referring, my lord?" Leah stood. An investor in the theatre, she was unphased by his title or wealth.

"The young lady with the candy stick, Penelope."

"Ah." Leah smiled. "I am happy my protegée inspires such passion."

The roaring in Michael's head to *bid, bid, win her* barely allowed him to process his lack of surprise that Leah had mentored this student.

"And what were you thinking of offering? There is no guarantee that your bid will win her." Sarah Potter shuffled some papers before her on the desk.

He narrowed his eyes. "Mayhap I was not clear in my request for your forbearance. If you will provide me with the highest bid for her, I will match it—no, I will double it."

The women glanced at each other. Leah gestured them to the far corner of the room.

He heard snippets. "Peers of the Realm…accustomed to getting their own…But he owns the…No exceptions…must be a fair bidding…"

Turning back, Leah's voice was gentle. "Sir…my lord, I am sorry, but we cannot permit that, even for you. However, my partners and I have agreed to consider your bid for Penelope, to be submitted and compared to any others. Happily, she has a place she can stay for a few extra days."

Gritting his teeth, Michael ran over the bids he remembered from the prior year and what Evan had told him he planned to offer. An image of the candy stick disappearing between Penelope's lips flashed in his mind, and his palm twitched with the memory of the mounds of her arse. His mind raced. He added a significant sum to the highest bid from the previous year's auction. The figure was higher than Evan's bid by a wide margin.

He took a deep breath, stated it, and closed his eyes, hoping that was enough.

Leah nodded and wrote it down on a piece of paper. She pushed it across the desk to him. "My lord, can you please initial this for our records as we finish sorting all the bids?"

He borrowed her pen, scribbled his initials, and stepped back. One hand behind him on the door handle, he nodded to the group.

"My sincere gratitude, ladies. I will wait in my box." He sketched a shallow bow before stepping through the door and whispering it shut behind him.

****

After two days of nervous worry sliding into nervous anticipation and back again, Penelope followed

25

Leah into what was to be her new home. Her mentor had explained that Penelope's winning bidder, a Lord Slade, needed time to arrange her residence.

An older couple emerged from the rear of the house when Leah called out, and she introduced them as Mr. and Mrs. Thorpe, Penelope's butler and housekeeper. Never having been the mistress of a household, Penelope was unsure how to read their stoic expressions.

Leah provided more details. The house next door offered stable-sharing for a horse, if she wished to obtain one. She now possessed an account at the Bank of England with her portion of the auction proceeds in it, but she should not need that for living expenses. Her initial budget was set per the bid and allowed for a horse and curricle this quarter, as well as a few pieces of furniture if she desired any changes to the decor. The house, food, and servants were paid for by her benefactor, and her money was for clothes and other entertainment. Some patrons even set up accounts at a clothier.

The less she spent on fripperies, the more she could save for her future.

They walked through the downstairs and found Mrs. Thorpe back in the kitchen putting a cold plate together for them with tea.

"I shall bring this out to the parlor in a few minutes, Miss, and then we can discuss what you'd like me to prepare for dinner. Will his lordship will be joining you?" she asked pragmatically.

Penelope's distraction with logistics fled as her nerves flooded back. She looked at Leah, who shook her head to indicate a lack of any information.

"Er, no. I am not sure. Mayhap he will send a note 'round later," she stuttered.

Leah led the way back to the front hall and upstairs. There were two bedrooms—a smaller front room and the master with its own sitting area in an alcove and a dressing room attached. Deep gold tones in the upholstery, drapes, and bedding were accented with burgundy pillows and trim.

Gor, this place is five times the size of our cottage in Peterborough. On the other hand, by Ton standards 'tain't—er, it isn't—a house for a family. 'Tis the size I was led to expect for my circumstances, complete with a small staff.

With each room, her situation became more real. Even as she admired the house, she worried about the next step—meeting her new employer.

In the parlor, she and Leah settled into matching Hepplewhite chairs, and Mrs. Thorpe bustled in with the tea trolley.

Penelope gestured to the settee. "Please sit with us a minute. We shall need less time to become comfortable in the house if we get to know one another, and I dislike formality. I grew up as the daughter of a housekeeper." When Mrs. Thorpe hesitated, she gestured again, "Please?"

"Thank you, Miss." The woman perched on the edge of the settee cushion.

Thankfully, there were three teacups on the tray. Penelope poured, first for Leah, then Mrs. Thorpe, asking how she took it and doctoring it accordingly.

"Leah told me she'd been by yesterday to help you settle in. I've never had servants. Nor have I had a benefactor." Penelope looked down and blushed. "I am not sure if you are aware of my circumstances?"

"My lady explained." Mrs. Thorpe dipped her head at Leah. "We are happy to help you adjust and get settled."

"Thank you." Penelope let out a sigh of relief. "I realize there is often a separate cook, but in such a small household, I prefer to keep things simple. If you are willing, I'd be grateful for your assistance in the kitchen, please?"

"Oh, yes, dear. I may not be the most imaginative chef; I've always made do with what was at hand and what we could afford. I am not big on making fancy dishes, mind you, but I can create plain hearty fare."

"Excellent. The reason I ask is that I also enjoy cooking. So I should like to join you sometimes, or request preferred ingredients occasionally. While I can prepare main dishes, my greater love is pastry and baking. Mayhap we can blend our skills into some excellent new ideas."

Mrs. Thorpe's eyes sparkled. "I look forward to it, Miss. For tonight, mayhap a simple beef and vegetable roast? Large enough for four should his lordship come, or with leftovers for a pie tomorrow?"

"Lovely, thank you. We shall work the rest out as we go. Until I talk to my benefactor, I cannot set a schedule."

Mrs. Thorpe excused herself, and Leah turned, one side of her mouth curled in a half-smile. "You really must start calling him by name, you know. I gave it to you, and I am certain he doesn't want to be 'Lord Benny Factor.'"

They both laughed.

"Right, then. Lord Slade." Penelope nodded. "I

think 'twill be easier when I have a face to go with the name. Can you describe him a bit more please, Leah?"

"I have told you all I know, dear. He is quite handsome and wealthy besides. He has always been supportive and courteous to women, and he likes inventiveness between the sheets. I was surprised he took a mistress when he never has before. In fact, he's never been associated with any indiscretions, despite owning a theatre."

Penelope sat forward, alarmed. "What? You did not mention before that he owns a theatre. Not *the* theatre where the auction took place, surely?"

Leah cocked her head. "Why, yes, that's the one. I did not realize it would matter. What is your concern?"

Penelope gasped. "Michael? Is his name Michael? Tall, curly brown hair, piercing blue eyes?" Her hands fisted in her lap and her heart pounded.

Leah nodded once, still looking perplexed, her brow wrinkling at Penelope's choice of words to describe him.

"Oh no! No. I shan't stay. Of all the high-handed arrogant lords to—" She took a deep breath to slow her heartrate and her thoughts. She had come so far. There really was no choice. The reason she had participated in the auction was to build her savings for her bakery. And she'd accepted the money. She uncurled her fingers and pondered the spanking again. No permanent damage occurred, and she had been trained for it, mayhap even come to enjoy it, although she'd never admit that to his lordship.

Leah's eyebrows rose at her extended silence after such a strong start.

Penelope gazed into the distance. He must have

known who she was to bid on her, so he must have enjoyed spanking her as well. She shrugged mentally. Her training had prepared her for a wide variety of tastes. She could manage him. She nodded decisively.

"Apologies. I ran into him—Lord Slade—before the auction. He stomped across the stage I had just mopped wearing muddy boots, and we had a minor disagreement." Penelope found her voice to explain. "It seems he has forgotten it, so I simply must do the same." She smiled, albeit a bit grimly, at her friend and mentor.

"He may call this evening, as he is aware of your arrival." Leah arched a brow. "To my knowledge, he has not taken a mistress before, so he may not think to send a note 'round. Plan how you want to greet him. And remember—"

"Yes, yes. Do not, whatever you do, fall in love," Penelope interrupted to finish the school's maxim. "I shan't. You know my goal is a bakery or at least financial independence."

The women exchanged grins at the oft-repeated mantra from class.

Chapter Three

Michael paced his study, swishing the Scotch in his glass, his thoughts circling as fast as the whisky.

Is she at the house yet? Should I send a note around? Should I go for dinner? Later? Am I ready for a relationship, even one in which I dictate the terms? What if someone sees me arrive? Blast, my mother can never hear about this.

He had spent the morning on estate correspondence and wading through the pile of Parliamentary bills he needed to review. But as the day progressed, his ability to focus diminished by the hour. Finally, he'd abandoned his desk and fetched a Scotch to sip as he strategized. He wondered if she knew the man who had spanked her only hours before the auction had won her for a year.

What will her response be? Will she recoil in fear, or worse, anger again? What then?

But the program's reputation made that unlikely, and her profile had represented her as open-minded. He turned again and drained his Scotch. As he considered another, a servant entered to announce that dinner was ready.

Well, that solves that, doesn't it? His lips quirked. *My cook will serve me cold dinners for a sennight if I miss a meal without notice.*

As he picked at his meal, his reflections turned to

his parents. He smiled, as he always did at images of them. Well, almost always, mayhap.

How ironic that he'd encountered Penelope in much the same manner his father had met his mother—in a theatre, by propositioning her. A curl of hair flopped onto his forehead as he shook his head.

This is not a love story. I'm not asking for the girl's hand in marriage.

His fork clattered to his plate as he contemplated what his mother would say about Penelope, particularly given her push a few months ago regarding heirs. He had a month or so before they arrived, though, and planned to make good use of it. After that, he'd see.

He loved his parents enough to want to fulfill their hopes and dreams whenever possible, so it would not be a hardship to find such a match…whilst he spent time with his new mistress.

Thinking of her brought him back to his dinner and impending visit. He attempted to concentrate on his excellent roast lamb. He could not help feel a little cheated, though. His mother had made a successful countess, despite humble beginnings. His father had found a way to keep the woman he wanted by his side. Admittedly, a courtesan was a degree further than an actress, rather beyond the pale, but he wasn't marrying the chit. He only wanted her in his bed.

He sighed. His new motto would be "drab" by day, discreet visits to Penelope's little house by night.

****

The day was dreary, so while the hour denoted dusk, the streets were quite dark, minimizing the risk of being sighted. As Michael rode, he reviewed his conversation with Bags. He hoped he had successfully repaired that relationship. After receiving the auctioneers' acceptance of his bid, he'd gone at once to meet his friends at White's to resolve the issue.

He joined them in their usual corner later than planned, and they questioned him.

"Slade! Where have you been?" Evan asked, passing him a Scotch and gesturing to a leather club chair. "I have not had news about that little dark-haired wench I bid on yet."

"Er, right. I need to speak with you about that, Bags."

"*And* you are." Evan laughed, and Robert snickered.

"I put in a bid. And, ah, I won. I have already begun setting up the house for the girl."

Both men's brows rose, knowing his family. "Have you devised a way to keep your parents from finding out? Or did you simply stop caring?" Robert chimed in.

"Neither really, although I guess more of the latter. But Bags, let me explain. I need to tell you—" His lips twisted. "—I won…Penelope."

Evan straightened from his usual loose-limbed lounge in his chair. Both men's faces sobered. Given their years of camaraderie, they were willing to let him explain, but their solemn expressions told of their view of his actions. He had transgressed the lines of friendship, and they required a good reason.

"I met her before the auction…" Michael explained their encounter. "When I saw her on stage, I had to have her. I was so busy thinking about logistics and how to hide her from my parents that I did not take the time to explain. I should have, and I'm sorry."

Evan nodded slowly, looking thoughtful. "I can see

that. 'Tis not as though I was emotionally attached. Hell, I mentioned sharing. Mayhap you will embrace that idea." He returned to his sprawl, sipping his whisky.

Michael flipped an evasive hand, not ready to hurt his friend any more than he had.

"You do me proud, old man. Spanking a wench you have never seen before because she yelled at you." Evan chuckled. "I wish you'd told me then, though. I might have made a bid on a second choice." He cocked his head before shaking off the lost opportunity and saluted Michael with his drink. "Ah, well. May the best man win, and all that."

"Thank you, Bags. I owe you one." Michael sighed and raised his glass to cheer the other men in gratitude. "I truly am sorry. It all happened so fast. I was not even sure they'd accept my bid, as I had not been pre-approved."

He sighed again in relief at Evan's magnanimity as he arrived at the little house he had rented for…his mistress. That word still felt foreign, as did the anticipation that elevated his pulse. He tied his horse and stalked to the door to the little house. Hand raised, he questioned whether he should knock or enter unannounced.

I own the place, devil take it.

But for this first unplanned visit, he knocked—hard, the raps sudden and echoing within.

The butler appeared after a moment and bowed his head. "My lord, please, come in."

Michael's shoulders lowered, and he realized he had half-expected to be turned away.

"Has the household eaten supper? I'm not

interrupting?" he asked as he stepped into the parlor. The Thorpes had come highly recommended, and he wanted to remain circumspect until he and Penelope established a routine.

"Miss Penelope supped some time ago, my lord." The butler returned with a shallow bow. "I will inform her of your arrival. Shall I take your mount around back?" At Michael's nod, he hurried through the open door toward the stairs.

Michael registered the butler's reference to the lady of the house by her first name, and his eyebrows rose. One more thing he looked forward to learning about "Miss Penelope."

*****

Penelope stepped daintily down the stairs, tossing a hard ginger candy into her mouth to ensure her breath was fresh. She wished to make a good first impression. When Mr. Thorpe told her that Lord Slade had arrived, she was torn between surprise and resignation, again fluctuating between anxiety and nervous anticipation. After all, she had learned about and even experienced sexual pleasure, albeit by her own hand.

Gor, aside from that one time with Beth.

Once she learned what her benefactor liked, she hoped they could find mutual satisfaction together.

She shivered. *'Tis only fear of the unknown.* It had become a mantra these past few days. Reality was proving a much bigger challenge to her self-confidence than she had expected.

Mayhap it was the way we met. Either way, I need to find my bloody backbone.

Her lips firmed with determination, even as she called to mind her elocution lessons again. She must be careful. Her childhood mode of speaking could too easily slip into conversation.

Her simple day gown was presentable at least, and she was glad of the illusion of armor it provided for their first real meeting. She had let her hair down for the night, though, and was reminded of this when the thick dark curtain swirled around her arms as she descended.

As she rounded the newel post, she caught sight of her new benefactor standing by the unlit fireplace in the parlor. Should she call him Lord Slade? Michael?

Eh, time enough to determine all that. In my head, he is Michael, as that is what I first heard him called.

The rather dainty pale-colored furniture looked even more feminine next to his tall, broad form.

Her gaze was steady as she entered the room, but her fingers twitched in the folds of her skirt.

Holding his hand out for hers, he drew her toward him and kissed the back of her hand. His touch and sandalwood scent ignited her senses, her memory of their unorthodox first meeting causing an internal shiver.

"Hello, Penelope." His deep voice sent a not-unpleasant quiver down her spine. "We meet again, this time without me being harangued over muddy footprints."

"My lord." She dropped a quick curtsy in deference to him, brushing aside his reference to their first meeting. "Thank you for the lovely house. It is perfect, and the Thorpes are excellent company."

Michael led her to the pale blue settee. He waited until she sat before settling across from her in the chair Leah had occupied earlier.

Popping up, she exclaimed, "Oh, er, I should offer you refreshment. Have you eaten? A drink? Scotch? Brandy? Sherry?" All her training in poise and hospitality deserted her.

He rose as well, reaching for her hands as she wrung them.

"I had Mrs. Thorpe stock the house with several of my favorite liquors as well as sherry and wines. They are on the sideboard." He nodded to a corner of the room. "However, tonight, I thought we'd have champagne, if you enjoy it, to mark the start of our time together?" His head tilted.

"Oh. Yes, please," Penelope exclaimed. She had tried the sweet bubbly beverage only once, at her graduation ceremony. She'd loved it, although the one glass had affected her reasoning a little.

When they both held gently fizzing glasses, Michael resettled in his seat. He cleared his throat, then opened and closed his mouth several times, frowning, before blurting out, "I must say, after what I have heard of your School of Enlightenment and your presentation at the auction, I was not expecting you to be in a simple day dress."

Penelope straightened in her chair, stung, and her retort was tart. "My lord, if I had known you were visiting tonight, I *might* have chosen something different."

His eyebrows raised, and she swallowed the last of her ginger candy in a gulp, surprised by her own audacity. She guzzled the remaining liquid in her glass, the lingering ginger residue on her tongue adding a pleasant bite. When he gestured for her glass, she passed it to him for a refill.

Michael grimaced. "You are right, madame. That was not well done of me." He leaned back and propped one ankle over the other knee. "I realize we do not know each other well. I should like to remedy that. Of course, that shan't happen overnight, so we will traverse it together. For now, I'd like to understand your training, share my expectations for you, and then we can proceed upstairs."

Penelope took another gulp of champagne, the bubbles nearly choking her. She nodded mutely, hoping he would continue to lead the conversation. Her lessons played in her head—a courtesan deferred to her benefactor's wishes. When in doubt, stay quiet and let him lead. Present yourself attractively.

She turned her shoulders to him and arched her back to present her breasts to their best advantage. Surreptitiously, she caught her skirt in her hands and shifted them on her lap, drawing the hem up to expose a few inches of leg, and waited for his next words.

****

Michael stared at Penelope, at a loss. He had hoped she would respond with some indication of her training. He was struggling to understand the line between her lack of experience and what he understood to be rather more advanced knowledge than many women possessed from multiple lovers. After starting with a faux pas, he was reluctant to show how awkward he found this new situation.

She smelled of ginger, and it distracted him, reminding him of the candy stick disappearing between her lips onstage. Tired of tiptoeing through the conversation and having trained all his life for an earldom, he was accustomed to leadership. His inherent dominant nature asserted itself. "Tell me a little about your experience at school. I understand there are a variety of courses available?"

Penelope tilted her head and fidgeted her hands as she considered her reply.

"They taught us to manage households and our own expenses, so I shan't bother you about such things. Although I've never actually handled those things outside of the classroom—" She shook her head as if aware she was babbling. "I also cook and I learned to grow some of my own vegetables and herbs, which Mrs. Thorpe has offered to help with."

He arched a brow and trailed his gaze down her form to the delicate ankle bone and slippered foot visible. Drawing it back up her body, he met hers with a sardonic look to convey that these were not the subjects that interested him. He sighed and let it go, understanding her nervousness. Training or not, it would still be her first liaison with a man.

"Mmm, that is good to hear. I like to dabble in the kitchen myself when I have the time," he commented, hoping to put her more at ease before returning to his original question. "I know you are untouched but educated in sexual intimacy between men and women. What did you learn?"

There, that should get me a useful answer. Direct is always the best approach.

"Er, well, I understand the basics of your physique, my lord," Penelope stammered, blinking blearily. "And, er, the basics of the act. Well, ah, a few acts."

"Yes? What *acts* then?" He leaned forward, dropping his crossed leg so both feet were planted on the rug.

Penelope fidgeted.

However difficult he found this conversation, it was likely harder for her to sit and discuss these things with a stranger who was going to strip her naked and engage in intimate behavior.

She sipped the last of her second glass of champagne. Her hand raised to cover a small belch before holding the cup out for more.

"What did you have in mind, sir?" Sitting back, she took a swig of her third serving.

He grinned, impressed despite his discomfort by her ability to turn the question back on him. "I quite enjoyed spanking you in the theatre. I plan to do more of that."

She smiled, her grin lopsided from the wine. "That seems doable. What else?" she asked and promptly hiccupped. Raising her hand to her mouth again, she bent her head.

He thought he heard, "I beg shur pardon."

His focus narrowed on her. Reaching for the half-empty champagne glass, he eased it from her grasp and set it down. "Hmm. I think that is enough wine and words. I can show you the rest."

Standing, he held out his hand for hers and pulled her to her feet. She stood, swaying a little, and reached for his arm. He led her from the room with both of her small hands clutched around his bicep. As he turned to the stairs, her face went pale and her lips pressed into a flat line. Wrenching away, she ran through the kitchen to the back door into the garden.

He followed to see her fall to her knees on the path, gather her hair as best she could in one hand, and lean on her other hand in the dirt, retching.

He returned to the kitchen and grabbed a cloth, and wet it and his handkerchief from a pitcher of water on the counter. Upon his return to the garden, he gathered her hair into one of his hands and pressed his handkerchief into hers. The other cloth he slid across her brow, down her cheek, and under her makeshift ponytail to the back of her neck, hoping to calm her racing pulse.

After long minutes, Penelope's stomach finished emptying itself, and she sat back on her heels, holding his handkerchief to her mouth.

Tears sprang to her eyes as she looked up at him, and Michael stifled a groan.

No drunken tears, please.

"Mayhap champagne was not the best choice, eh?" he said softly, a light chuckle in his voice.

She managed a wan smile before dropping her head as far as his hold on her hair would allow.

"Come, let's get you to bed." His gentle words came with a hand under her arm to help her stand. "Can you walk? Never mind, hold on to me. I daren't jostle you too much, or your head will spin again." He slid one arm around her back and bent to sweep the other under her legs and raise her smoothly into his arms.

He climbed the stairs, careful not to bump her head as he turned on the landing. Looking for her room—*their room?*—he wished he'd had time to walk through the house rather than renting it unseen. He bent his neck to ask Penelope, only to find her head lolling against his arm.

He sighed.

Entering a room with a candle lit, he made his way to the bed with his burden. As he lay her on it, she emitted a short feminine snort and rolled away from him, still clutching his handkerchief.

Now what? Not the end to the night I expected.

Stifling an impatient sigh, Michael perched next to her hip to unlace her gown. An earl's son did not finish university without a similar rite of passage, and he hated waking up in last night's clothes.

He peeled the dress away, untied her petticoat ribbons, and unlaced her stays. Noting the plain muslin undergarments, he envisioned silk and lace in their place. He hadn't had a chance to tell her about the account he'd created at an exclusive clothier's known for her discretion.

After rolling Penelope to her back, he dragged the gown downward, taking the petticoat with it. His fingers reached for her stays, only to pause in the act. The mounds of her upper breasts above the edge of the garment made him itch to pet them, cover them, squeeze them. He groaned quietly, then fisted his hands momentarily as he checked his desires.

A gentleman would never take advantage of an unconscious girl.

His mind and heart knew that. He'd simply have to wrestle his cock into obedience later.

He made short work of removing her stays and stood. He adjusted his unruly cock for comfort and pulled the covers over her to remove temptation.

Loathe to leave quite yet, he told himself it was in case she needed him, rather than not being able to relinquish time with this mysterious young woman who would be in his care for months. He decided a tour of the house might be in order, even without a guide. With a brief glance back, he closed the bedroom door and wandered.

In the kitchen, he perused the table, counters, and assorted implements hanging. He considered what he knew of the School of Enlightenment and Penelope. A plan took shape. He found a pencil and paper and began writing.

Chapter Four

Penelope woke with a mouthful of cotton and a headache. Groaning, she tried to recall her first night in this bed or bedroom. The events of the prior evening returned in a rush—running to be sick in the garden, Michael lifting her. Looking around for him, she found the room blessedly empty.

Glancing down, she discovered her chemise. Had he undressed her? *What else happened? Did he take my virginity? Perdition, what if we were intimate, and now he bloody well expects me to know what to do?*

Scrambling out of bed, she checked the sheets. No blood. Thanks to her enlightened teachers, she had at least learned that the first time would sting and she'd bleed a little. Her shoulders relaxed. Pinch of pain or not, she'd have hated to miss her first time. She sighed in frustration. One glass of champagne was clearly her limit.

A folded note on the nightstand next to the bed caught her eye, her name printed in a bold hand on the outside.

She opened it, reading, "I recommend toast and plenty of weak tea with honey—" She wrinkled her nose. *Gor, did anyone like weak tea?* "—for the morning. I look forward to seeing you tonight around the same time. Sincerely, Michael, Lord Slade."

Mrs. Thorpe knocked. She had a tea tray with toast

and set it on the desk in the sitting area. Penelope guessed there had been more than one note left and that the tea in the pot was rather weak. Oh well, there were worse things, and it was certainly thoughtful of him.

"A bath, mila—er, Miss Penelope?" Mrs. Thorpe asked.

"I still wish you'd drop the 'Miss,' and no, not right now thank you. I would like to see what vegetables and herbs we can find at the West London markets before it gets any later in the summer." She halted, recalling, "Oh, and I need to clean up the garden before we go. But I should like a bath later, please? Mayhap before dinner, if that does not interfere with meal preparations?"

After a day obtaining a mix of seeds and vegetables to start planting, she relaxed into her bath and pondered what she might wear for Michael that evening. Her nerves were elevating again, upsetting her still-raw stomach. He made her blood sing, and he'd been very patient with her, but she worried about her ability to perform what he was paying an exorbitant amount for. This first time must be done. Then she'd have more confidence in her position, even as she learned more about him and his expectations.

What did I learn about enticing a man? He'd glanced at her exposed ankle last night. Yes, she'd let hints of her cleavage, ankles, something, show to enhance the mood.

After her bath, she dug through her dresser and withdrew her skimpiest nightrail. It boasted a lowcut neckline, open flowy sleeves, and a shorter length than the norm as she had remade it from scraps of a few sewing customers' petticoats back in Peterborough.

This would do. As she turned toward the mirror, the light behind it shone through the fabric, showing her how sheer it was. Shrugging away her lingering modesty, she tugged it over her head.

He's going to see me naked soon enough anyway. But she added a robe for warmth.

With the bath cleared, she dismissed the servants for the night, opting for a light supper of bread and cheese. She wandered through the house, nerves making her restless. Contemplating sherry, she shook her head. Drinking anything stronger than tea was not a good idea after the disaster of the prior evening.

As had become her habit, she ended up in the kitchen baking, which always calmed her. She had just finished mixing and forming a loaf of bread when a knock at the front door sounded.

After wiping her hands on a towel, she hurried through the house, making a quick swipe down her front for any flour dusting on her robe.

"My lord, welcome." Her voice was subdued as she held the door open in welcome.

"I trust you feel better, madame?" he commented with a quirk of his lips.

"Yes, thank you. I must apologize for last night. My nerves got the best of me." Penelope clutched her robe at her sides in unease.

"Hmm. I thought it was the champagne, but never mind." His smirk grew into a grin, his eyes bright as he challenged her to share the joke with him, even at her own expense.

Penelope smiled back. "Yes, well, that too." Turning down the center hall, she hustled back to the kitchen, calling over her shoulder, "If you'll pardon me,

I need a minute. I had made bread dough, and I need to cover it for it to rise properly overnight."

Michael strolled in her wake. "Sounds like a tasty breakfast. I am glad I will be here to enjoy it."

At that, her jitters from the prior night returned.

"I was thinking about those nerves." He wandered over to the large kitchen fireplace. "Tonight, we shall progress to the entertainment portion of this visit sooner rather than later."

Her stomach calmed when his words mimicked her tentative plan formed during her bath, only to spike again at his next statement.

"We can discuss expectations afterward. But first, a punishment is in order." He reached for the long-handled wooden peel used for the brick oven.

Penelope stared, aghast, before she found her voice. "But... Why, my lord? Last night was a mistake, certainly, but you were the one pouring." Her jaw firmed. "And the bread must sit overnight before it goes in the oven," she added, gesturing to the kitchen tool in his hand.

"Yes, I know," he replied, hefting the peel. "I do not know your limits for wine, Penelope, but you should. One of my expectations is no drinking to the point of slovenliness or illness. And that is why you shall be punished." Reaching his hand to her, he gestured. "Come here, now, please."

She sidled over to him. She supposed he'd spank her again, and while it had hurt the first time, the curl of heat through her core had been a delicious distraction. Hopefully, she'd respond the same, and it would center her mind for the act yet to come.

He took her hand and tugged her in front of him,

then pressed between her shoulder blades, his voice as unyielding as his actions. "Bend and hold the far edge of the table."

As she did, he gathered the bottom of her robe and nightrail in his fist and raised them to the middle of her back. His hand remained there, its weight holding her in place. The other raised the peel, his hand partway down the long handle given his proximity to his target.

"Ten, Penelope. If you squirm or cry, there will be more."

Thud! The peel hit her bottom dead center, catching both cheeks soundly. She jerked in shock and gasped, clutching the table edge tighter.

Each hit reverberated through her. She was grateful for the table height. Her hips were a fraction above the edge, or it would have dug into her with the impact of the strikes. These were not the smarting pain of hand spanks. They were broader, somehow duller, but harder, stronger, and left a lingering soreness and heat that built with each blow.

While he aimed for different spots each time, the paddle was large enough to cause frequent overlap. She felt more than a little bruised by the tenth wallop, despite knowing he hadn't done any serious damage.

Only after he leaned the peel against the table and caressed her bottom with both hands did the heat expand from her bottom to the rest of her body, engulfing her womanly parts in warmth. Her breasts swelled against the table, her nipples contracting into firm points, making her want to rub them against the wood for more friction. None of her orgasms at school had come close to the fire his simple touch evoked. Even her feet felt hot. She arched onto her toes, effectively raising her bottom into his caress.

The result was a strangled groan, and Sophia smiled, pleased that he, too, was aroused. She straightened and turned, too focused on the sensations running through her body to remember any fear.

Michael swept his hand toward the hall door, saying simply, "Shall we?"

"Yes, my lord." Leading the way, Penelope ascended the stairs and entered her bedroom, where she had left several candles burning. Her nerves humming from the paddling, she did not need to think about the next steps. She untied her robe, letting it fall from her shoulders, and turned to face him. "How may I please you, sir?"

****

Penelope met his gaze and waited while Michael studied her form, her silhouette clear through the sheer fabric with the candles behind her. His face, already taut with desire in the kitchen, tightened further into a grimace of need.

"We shall cover the niceties of undressing each other another time. I need you too much right now. Take off your nightrail and lie back on the bed."

Wrenching at his own clothes, he was naked to the waist by the time she had removed her own clothing. She could hardly tear her gaze from the slabs of lean muscle exposed to climb onto the bed. As she lay back, his second boot went flying, and he stripped off his breeches and hose before striding toward her.

Gasping, Penelope gaped at her first aroused man. He appeared huge. His cock rose from a nest of curls at his groin and was a dark plum, rosy, and glistening with need. Several substitutes had been provided for the advanced sex classes, from cucumbers to leather-covered dowels, but…

I think they underestimated size! That ain't gonna fit.

She had also only ever had those items in her mouth or hand. Only her fingers had entered her womanly passage.

At her startled stare, he slowed his last few steps, his jaw softening. He set a knee on the bed and stretched out by her side, propping his head on a bent arm. His free hand smoothed from her shoulder down over the stiff tip of one breast and farther to her hip before repeating the action.

Not being able to see his jutting cock helped calm her. She focused on the strokes of his hand. The caresses soothed at first but left pebbled skin in their wake as her senses awoke to his touch.

When she sighed in pleasure, he swooped in, taking advantage of her open mouth to seal his lips to hers. His tongue licked at the inside of her lower lip, then tested the edge of her teeth before finally moving beyond to tangle with her tongue as it tentatively met his. The heat from his mouth coursed through her, igniting her core, and she rolled toward him.

Like downstairs, these coils of pleasure were familiar yet magnified a thousand times from her training. She felt her nether folds swell and dampen.

The new angle allowed his hand to roam farther on his next pass along her side. Grabbing behind her knee, he propped her bent leg over his thigh and palmed her bottom, rekindling the fire of the paddling.

Penelope puffed a breath and clutched his hair.

He scanned the length of her then centered on her

face.

Arching, she unknowingly provided the perfect opportunity for his hand to slide over her hip to her belly and slip into the damp curls between her legs.

Her nerves jumped, and she froze as his fingers probed in gentle exploration. Her own fingers and the one experience with a classmate had not prepared her for the strangeness—the vulnerability—of having a virtual stranger touch her so intimately. She could only hope that he would care to ensure her enjoyment and be knowledgeable enough to provide an orgasm.

Two fingers stroked lower to dip into the pool of liquid then dragged leisurely upward. Her pulse leaped in pleasure this time.

She watched him, barely breathing for fear of dislodging his touch. Michael's gaze remained locked on hers, searching for something. His slick fingers slid over her hardened nub just above her channel, and her hips jerked toward him in anticipation.

"Ah," came a masculine groan with a pleased curve of his lips. "There, eh?"

Penelope nodded, unable to speak. *Yes, please! Gor, he found that much quicker than I did.*

Then she could not even think as he rubbed back and forth in tiny increments, slow at first, then faster. She promptly forgot all her training to ensure the man's enjoyment, unable to focus on anything but her own.

Falling backward, she braced her feet and raised her hips to meet the motions, little pumps becoming a full-on arch with her bottom off the bed as she pushed into his touch.

"Oh, oh, please don't stop," she wailed, panting. Her eyes slammed shut to give all her attention to where they were joined. Every muscle in her body tightened as she poised on the cliff of ecstasy. She hung there, pelvis held suspended for long seconds. Then everything coiled inside and exploded.

"Aaoohhh, Michael," she cried as her lips parted on a wordless cry, hips undulating wildly in the air.

Penelope's eyelids fluttered open to find Michael staring at her, one side of his mouth curled in satisfaction but with his brow still furled. Drifting back to awareness, she belatedly remembered her training.

"Thank you, my lord," she gasped. "That was marvelous. How may I please you?"

****

Michael was drunk on Penelope's feminine scent, musky and sweet. He wanted to bury his face where his fingers still rested and send her soaring again. Every woman had her own unique scent and her recipe of internal and external pressure, rubbing, and speed to bring her to ecstasy. Penelope, whether by training or nature, had been easy to read and responsive enough that he had quickly learned her pleasure points.

However, he was not sure he could move without exploding. Watching her reach orgasm had spiked his own desire to the point of need. Hearing his name on her lips had only added to the craving. His cock pulsed, liquid leaking from the tip. His hip was sticky from it. He worried that if his cock brushed her silky thigh, he might embarrass himself like a callow youth.

"I am glad. 'Tis meant to be marvelous if done right." His voice was hoarse, with every muscle locked to refrain from pouncing on her. "They warned you it will hurt a little the first time, right?" he asked, even as he rolled to hover above her on his elbows, his hips pressing hers into the bed. His gaze sought hers to check for any residual fear, but there was only sexual satiation, with mayhap a hint of latent curiosity.

At her nod, he growled, "Hold on then. I cannot bear to wait any longer."

He shifted his weight to one side and lifted her leg to place her foot higher on the bed with her knee bent to cradle his hip. Then he slipped his hand between their bodies and gripped the base of his cock, squeezing for a moment to ensure he did not erupt before he was even inside her. He rubbed his hot hard length against her, grazing her hypersensitive bundle of nerves and making her jerk. The head of his cock brushed from her swollen knot to her opening twice more. She twitched as the embers of her desire rekindled, and her arms tightened on him. Finally, he notched the tip at her opening.

Gritting his teeth, he braced against rushing. He preferred not to hurt her, but more, he especially did not wish to cause pain without pleasure by finding his own end too soon.

His hips surged forward, his cock slipping inside her only to be stopped by her virginal barrier. Her bent leg tensed against him as the pressure built. Was he hurting her more by prolonging it? He'd never been a woman's first. He wanted to be gentle. But her leg muscles tightened further, and her whole body stiffened. Gentle wasn't working. He reared back and plunged forward, sinking to the hilt.

"Oh!" She squirmed but stilled when he gripped her hip with one hand.

"Shh, it will subside in a moment." He stroked her cheek. "But if you don't stay still, I shan't be able to either."

She panted, her focus on him.

Returning his elbow to rest beside her shoulder, he bent his head and kissed her. His tongue plundered, distracting him from his urge to pound into her.

He was lost in this woman, this moment. Knowing he was her first and only lover gratified his mind as it shot a hot arrow into his cock. His hands tangled in the soft skeins of midnight hair, and he attempted to rein in his desire to drive deep.

Penelope's knee rose from beside his hip, and her heel dug into in the small of his back, her leg pulling him to her as she rose to meet his thrusts.

She was perfect—responsive, eager to learn and to please him. He yearned to hear her dreams, both sexual and non-sexual, not something he had ever contemplated, much less during sex.

Unh. His brain stopped functioning as pleasure swamped his senses.

"Aaahh, I cannot—" He gasped. He raised up on his hands, his hips shoving in and out in an uncontrolled rhythm. "Hold on."

Gritting his teeth hard, he thrust hard once, twice, a third time, and plunged forward. He groaned in pleasure and relief as he ground his pelvis against her, hot spurts of liquid jetting into the scalding channel tight around him.

Her arms wrapped farther around him as he sank onto his elbows, resting more of his weight on her.

"If that was anything like what I experienced, this will work out well, my lord," she declared with a smirk.

"Imp," he rasped in her ear. "And as you called me Michael at one point, I think we can dispense with the 'my lord.'" He arched a brow at her to remind her that she'd used his given name as she reached her pinnacle of pleasure.

She blushed and tried to tuck her face under his chin.

He withdrew carefully, watching her face for signs of pain, then rolled them to their sides still facing one another. He ran a palm down the satin of her side. "Are you all right? Did it hurt overly much?"

"Only at the start. But then it was lovely. I can see why you want someone to have around for it regularly."

He laughed.

She grinned in response.

Hugging her into his side as he rolled to his back, he said, "We shall discuss going forward over some of your delicious-looking bread tomorrow."

Chapter Five

A palm was stroking the length of her back when Penelope surfaced from sleep. Sprawled on her stomach, one knee bent and a fist curled near her face, she moaned as the strands of sleep fell away. She stretched in pleasure, arching her bottom into the caress. Keeping her eyes closed, she lay still, content to let him do what he wanted with her or give her direction.

The hand soothed from shoulder to hip, from bottom cheek to thigh, again and again, exploring her body and acclimating her to his touch. Finally, it reached around to cup her breast and squeeze her nipple. Her bottom squirmed side to side in response. Fingers traveled along her ribs, inadvertently tickling her and making her wriggle again. Smoothing around her hip, they dipped between her legs to pet her with alternating gentle taps and strokes.

She hitched her bent leg up farther, sliding a hand to grope behind her for him. Encountering his muscled thigh, her fingers gripped it once, then gentled. She liked the extra connection even in this act of one-sided pleasure. Her eyes remained closed as she floated on his touch on her and hers on him. She rubbed the coarse hair on his thigh, squeezing when he strummed an extra-sensitive spot.

He explored her folds, creeping closer to her

weeping center. After endless minutes, one finger caressed her opening and then dipped in to gather moisture. She wiggled eagerly, then stilled to see what he would do next. Smoothing its way up to her most sensitive nub, the finger circled, pressed, and circled again. She thrust her hips in rhythm with his finger, and her fingers pressed and released on his leg in time.

His hand left her abruptly.

She groaned, bereft. Then it landed on hers to guide it from his leg to his shaft.

Ooh… So that is how a cock feels. That ain't a cucumber! A tiny giggle escaped.

Before she could roll over to explore further, Michael's hand returned to her, gripping her bottom cheek.

He growled in mock outrage, "Are you laughing at my cock?"

"Oh gosh, no. I beg your pardon, my lord. It is so…hot." Her hand explored somewhat awkwardly. "And 'tis soft over hard, if that makes any sense."

"Hmm. Keep doing what you're doing, minx," he muttered as he wet his fingers in her again and returned to circle.

How does he find that tiny sensitive spot so expertly?

Her hips pushed back against him, bringing his cock in her fist up against her bottom. She squeezed and released as her bottom pushed and receded.

Pleasure roiled through her.

A wordless moan echoed in the room. Belatedly, she realized it had come from her.

Her nipples, tightly beaded, chafed against the sheet, sending sparks through her belly. Her position and his hand limited her movements, forcing her to wait and trust he would drive her up the peak. Fingers dipped again, then rubbed gently along the sides of her little pleasure point before giving it a light pinch.

Faster and faster, her grip kept time with his fingers as he repeated this cadence, clenching on him rhythmically, her hips moving in time.

"Oh yes, my—Michael." *I am supposed to be the professional, but gor, he knows his way around a woman's body. This is so much better than I ever expected.*

Fire coiled inside her, building ever higher, until she was on the cusp of the explosion she knew awaited. She froze, even holding her breath, to ensure his fingers stayed where she needed them.

Instead, Michael rolled, bringing her onto her back on top of him, his fingers still between their bodies, her hand forced to release him. His other hand reached around to pinch her nipple as his fingers stopped rubbing and squeezed her nub in tandem with her nipple.

The orgasm broke over her like a thunderstorm. Bolts of lightning shot through her, and the thunder of his satisfied moan rolled beneath her. Her head dropped back alongside his, and her feet pressed into the sheets outside his legs as her hips arched up, her whole body going taut as her core spasmed and contracted.

He returned to light, languorous rubs as her body lowered to lie on him, shuddering in release.

She sighed, sated. He shifted his hips below hers, pushing his cock to ride the crevice between her bottom cheeks. His cock had been leaking with eagerness since her hand first touched him. Now, it slid smoothly up to hit her lower back.

"Stay there," he growled and put his hands to her sides to hold her cheeks together. Thrusting up, he used her bottom for friction, setting a fast pace with short strokes.

Penelope hummed in renewed pleasure and rested her hands over his, pressing her hips into him to try to help.

"Ah, yes. Like that, love," he rumbled next to her ear, his hips moving even faster. After a few minutes, the thrusts became rougher, the strokes longer and uneven, and his hips lifted them both off the bed.

"Unh, unh." He panted, and his cock trembled and spurted up her back as he rode through the slickness to finish his orgasm.

Finally, he shuddered in turn, and his hands fell to the bed beside them. "Ah, gads, if only I could keep you forever. You are delicious."

Penelope had been enjoying the afterglow, but his comment doused the flickering flame of residual pleasure like a bucket of cold water. Reminded that this was a bought relationship and had a termination date, she rolled away. Her heart panged in pain before she silently scolded herself.

You have only known him a matter of days. Do not be ridiculous.

Trying to re-establish her equilibrium and the boundaries of her role, she pictured making one of her favorite pastries, gujiya, and recalled what she hoped to gain from their contract. While this was certainly fun as well as lucrative, she was *bloody well fine* with it being short-term. She mentally stuck her tongue out at him before schooling her features.

She grabbed her nightrail off the floor to clean her skin as best she could before offering it to him. "School did not teach us that position. Is it something you enjoy often, sir?" she asked politely, having reminded herself why she was doing this—money. To that end, she had to learn how to satisfy him.

"No, sweeting, that just came to me. I knew you'd likely be sore inside from last night and did not want to hurt you. In the beginning I was simply enjoying learning your body, but you are so responsive, I could not resist you." He grinned. "Now, you've made me hungry with all this sex. How long will that bread of yours need to bake, hmm?"

"Mrs. Thorpe has likely already put it in the oven."

He bounced out of bed and rushed to dress.

Unable to resist his good humor, despite a lingering melancholy over his comment about forever, she smiled and threw on a new nightrail and robe to lead him downstairs. Knowing his expectations was essential to keeping her mind focused on her end goal—a bakery of her own.

****

Over bread and jam, eaten at the dining room table for privacy from Mrs. Thorpe in the kitchen, Penelope invoked her training and asked about his routine. Understanding his habits and preferences was important and had to be established early in the relationship. She had recited the many responsibilities of courtesans so many times she had them memorized. Of particular importance was being available at her benefactor's behest.

"My lord, when shall I expect you?" she began.

Michael dipped his chin once in response to her

reopening the conversation of their first night. Setting his tea cup down, he replied, "First, as we discussed last night, 'tis Michael. Given the nature of our relationship, 'my lord' sounds a little priggish, don't you agree?" He smiled. "As Leah may have told you, this arose rather abruptly. I was not looking for a mistress. But then you misbehaved, and after getting that bottom under my hand and realizing you were, ahem…" He seemed to choose his words. "…offering yourself that evening, I had to have you."

She sipped her tea and nodded acquiescence. "Most people aside from my family call me Pen, if you prefer. Although sweeting was lovely, too." Her cheek dimpled in a half smile.

He grinned back. "Right, then. Pen it is. My schedule is only flexible for a short time. My parents stayed behind at Mansfield Manor. My father is ill and has better and worse days, so their arrival will depend on that. They will likely be here within a fortnight and expect me to participate in the regular rounds of balls and soirées to find a suitable wife. They would not approve of this." He gestured vaguely at the house, her, him. "In any event, their presence will make coming and going more complicated."

"I understand."

"Mayhap I am putting too fine a point on it, but 'tis more than not approving. My parents would be heartbroken. I—we—shall need to be more than discreet. I know some men attend the theatre and other entertainment with their mistresses. I cannot."

"Ah. Right, then. Thank you for explaining." She hastened to reassure him even as her heart sank at the possibility that their relationship might be very short.

Especially as he was not hard on the eyes and they seemed to be well-suited, at least in the bedroom. "Would it be easier to send a note mayhap when you plan to visit?"

"I can try, but I prefer not to be limited to a note. It smacks of permission, something I don't think I need here…" He sent her an expectant glance.

"Of course not, my lord." She continued with the formal form of address to reinforce that he was indeed in charge. "I simply meant that advance notice will enable us to have supper or…me ready," she added coquettishly with another one-sided smile, attempting to provide incentive.

"Hmm, I have not done this before, but to be clear, my expectation is that you shall *be* ready, whenever I arrive, frankly." He quirked a brow.

Penelope started to retort but considered her learnings again and the exorbitant amount he had paid. She bowed her head in acceptance.

Michael pondered for a moment. "I shall try to send word if I can join you for dinner. If not, and if there aren't leftovers, I shall make do with a cold plate of whatever is available, or I shall cook for myself. As I told you, it happens to be a hobby of mine as well. Please plan to be available during the latter part of the evening unless you send word ahead that you have a social engagement. And I expect there will not be too many of those."

He thought some more. "As for daytime, if I do not specify, the days are yours. I have opened an account with the modiste Leah recommended and a milliner and such. Most of my days are entangled in family and Parliamentary business, given my father's health."

He shifted in his chair and looked uncomfortable. "Er, Leah mentioned that you have ways to avoid a pregnancy?" At her blush and nod, his shoulders relaxed a bit. "Let me know if you need me to make arrangements with a physician." He made another vague arm gesture. "Any questions?"

Penelope bit her lip. The day-to-day details had been addressed, and she would practice with the contraceptive sponge. Was it too soon to ask about the longevity of the relationship?

He saw her indecision and dipped his head. "Go ahead and ask. All questions are allowed."

"Ah, well then, how soon do you expect to marry? And will you wish to continue our arrangement after marriage?" The idea was distasteful to her, as she could not fathom being unfaithful in a relationship. However, the Ton often approached things differently, and she was in no position to censure anyone's standards of morality, given her current situation.

"My mother has been pestering me to wed for years, and given my father's health, 'tis becoming more urgent. They have begged me to secure a betrothal this Season," he grumbled, his tone conveying his dissatisfaction with that plan. "And no, I will not disrespect my wife or besmirch her or my reputation by keeping a side piece."

She sighed, both with relief that his beliefs coincided with hers but also in disappointment. It appeared she'd have less than a year to enjoy this lovely house and a man who seemed very entertaining, provided excellent orgasms, and shared her love of the kitchen.

"Until your family arrives, would you care to join

me for dinner in the evenings?" she asked, wanting to know this complex man who obviously cared deeply for his parents.

"I cannot every night. Parliamentary duties include significant time at my club discussing bills with my father's peers and allies," he conceded. "But tonight, I should love to. I have cleared my schedule for a few days to get better acquainted,"—his last words were muttered under his breath—"and hopefully get you out of my system."

Penelope's lips curled in a slight smile. She hoped her classroom experience would translate to actions that enthralled him enough to settle a generous amount on her when he married.

****

Throughout the day, Penelope found herself humming under her breath. In the middle of a task—planting, making tea, sewing—her hands would still and drop to her lap, a portion of the night before and that morning replaying in her mind.

She had known the mechanics of sex. And students had been warned that intimacy too often blurred one's reason and invited emotion. However, the instructors added each time that girls should keep tight control of those emotions. Titled gentlemen did not marry women they bought. While they expected more than sex from their paid companions, including friendship and support, few arrangements lasted longer than a year. There was also no guarantee they'd settle gifts on their paramours at parting or assist them in finding their next benefactor.

Thus, she had gone into this hoping to enjoy a short-term affair, sharpen her skills, and earn as much as possible to pursue her dream. She had learned about a number of sexual interactions as well. Her morning interlude with Michael demonstrated an opportunity to mayhap learn a few more.

But the reality of being naked with a man she had only recently met, having him touch her most private places, was as different from those lessons as a meringue to an egg. Him entering her body with his fingers and his cock, spilling his seed in her and on her, were seven-layer cakes after expecting a tiny custard tartlet. She shivered in pleasure at the remembered sensations.

And now I am hungry as well as aroused.

She sighed. This was going to be harder than she had expected. If he had been older or uglier or the sex had been boring. *Wait, could sex be boring?* It seemed so…so physical that one could not lose interest. Although she suspected that was at least in part the man who had chosen her. Oh, and the spanking. Delicious.

Even his first discipline before the auction was titillating. To step in and take control and bend her to his will. She looked forward to seeing the evolution of his dominance as their relationship progressed.

But no emotions, Leah's and every instructor's voice echoed in her head. *No falling in love. Michael is not yours to keep.*

****

That evening, Penelope was taking dinner out of the oven when Michael arrived. Once she'd poured him a drink and carried everything into the dining room, they sat.

"How did you come to attend the School of Enlightenment?" he asked.

65

How could she summarize her reasons for this aristocrat who had likely never worried how to earn enough to live? The catalyst for her choice had been her mother's passing, so she began there.

"My mother died suddenly in February..." She described the emotions and the circumstances that led her to the school, hoping this rich, titled lord would understand.

On the day of the funeral, her stepfather, David Hunter, had sat with his head in one hand, elbow braced on the table in their one-bedroom cottage. "I still cannot believe she is gone." He sighed.

She dropped a hand to his shoulder in comfort. "Nor can I. I miss her so much. But I feel selfish saying that. I had her for eighteen years. You only had six with her."

He grabbed her hand and squeezed it. His hand, callused from his work as a blacksmith, was familiar, warming her heart as much as her skin.

"Don't say that. 'Tis not selfish to miss your mother, lass. 'Tis hard to lose a parent at any age, but you are still young. She didn't even get to see you married..." Tears gathered in his eyes for what seemed like the millionth time that sennight.

She dropped into a chair across from him. "So...we should consider what we do now."

"I don't know. The sewing you and your ma took in helped us, but with the costs of her illness and burial, we're behind, and I don't know how we'll catch up. Not to mention, there will be less with only one person sewing, right?" David asked.

They were both aware that his income from the forge in front of their cottage was not enough to feed the remaining three family members. At eighteen, it was time she made her own way in the world. If only she had determined what she wanted to do—or rather, what was practical for her to do.

"Yes." Her voice was glum. "And Mama was much faster than I am, so sewing earnings won't even be half now. I wish little Matthew could help." She flashed a sad smile at the kind man who had been part father, part adviser these past six years. "I wish, too, that I could learn enough to finish his schooling."

Her half-brother Matthew was three and a half.

****

Penelope approached the narrow blue house at the far end of town with unease. Her mother had always handled the sewing for these residents, and rumors around town said that the four women living there were retired courtesans. One might even be involved in a theatre. Penelope wasn't sure what a courtesan was, but it made for juicy gossip among the townsfolk. The women kept to themselves, so she was intrigued.

She tapped a timid knock on the front door. Hearing footsteps approach from the back of the house, she almost threw down the sewing she was delivering and ran, but her stepfather needed the money they'd receive for this delivery.

"Oh, hello dear. You must be Betsey's oldest." The woman who answered the door smiled widely. Tall and lithe with a few wrinkles that hinted at an age north of forty, she wore an unremarkable day dress in periwinkle and had her hair sloppily pinned up under a cap. "Come in. I have a pot of tea brewing. You've perfect timing," she said in one breath, holding her arm out for Penelope to precede her into the house.

Unsure how to react to this unexpected invitation, Penelope shrugged mentally and paced down the hall, trying to determine where the parlor was without peering into every room they passed.

As she passed the first doorway, the woman called out, "Go on in and sit. I'll grab the tea tray." She bustled down the hall past Penelope, who slipped into the room and perched on the edge of a settee, uncertain of what to do with the sewing still in her arms.

"'Tis lovely to meet you after all this time. I've heard so much about you from your darling mother. We were so sad when we learned of her illness. I am sorry for your loss, dear. Oh, let me take that." The woman set the tray on a nearby low table and held out her hands for the sewing. "Thank you so much for bringing it. We weren't expecting this quite yet, given the circumstances." She sped back in from the hall where she had taken the laundry, sat on a carved armchair across from Penelope, and poured the tea, doctoring it to Penelope's taste after asking.

"Ahh, thank you, uh, Mrs…"

"Oh, gracious! Silly me. The girls would never let me hear the end of that. I am Rachel, dear. Your mother and I often had tea when she picked up or delivered sewing, and we shared town gossip, life stories—she told me loads about you—and whatever else crossed our minds. I am sure you are busier than ever with her gone. I'm ever so grateful you had a minute for tea."

Penelope was not entirely sure she was needed for this conversation given Rachel's ramblings. But it was enlightening, and the tea was strong and hot and delicious, so she waited to see what would come next.

"Your mother was inordinately proud of you and

your brother. She wanted a great future for you both. And la, your stepfather, she loved him madly. How is he faring?" Rachel paused for breath.

"He has good days and bad days," Penelope replied. "For now, he's taking Matthew with him to the forge, but we're working to find other options for him to continue school or lessons for as long as possible. The James children are close to his age, so we're hoping to work something out with them."

"Ah yes, that makes sense. And what about you, dear? Your mama brought us some divine fig tea cakes and was telling us you hope to open a bakery one day. She mentioned you incorporated her grandmama's recipes carried over from East India? They were like naught I've ever tasted. What was that spice in them?"

"Cardamom. I am happy you enjoyed them, thank you. Yes, I combined family recipes with some traditional British pastries. When I've made enough to sell to the baker, they sold well. People liked them as a new twist on something familiar. But gor, the blunt needed to set up a bakery. I need to find a position that will earn a good wage, and teach me about business and the like."

"Ah. What are you thinking of?"

"We hadn't solved that yet when—" Penelope's throat closed around unshed tears.

Rachel leaned in and patted her hand. "I am so sorry, my dear. This has all been so sudden. I did not mean to push you. Mayhap you'll return to visit with me and my housemates when you've had a little more time to adjust?"

****

Her mother's absence was a gaping hole in

Penelope's heart. Eager to cultivate female friendships, she also hoped for guidance or at least suggestions for a path forward. These women were worldly, although they'd been here for much of the time she had. Surely they'd seen more of society and had ideas that could help her.

She returned to the blue house several times during the next few sennights.

She met Mary, a plump woman about her own height, a petite few inches over five feet. Fewer lines on her face than Rachel were countered by flashes of silver in her brown hair. Ann, an even shorter woman who was quite square, seemed terminally uncomfortable in her clothes and had very short dark hair that Penelope suspected she often forgot to brush.

On her third visit, she dared to ask about their rumored former profession.

She began, trying to frame her thoughts. "Mama and I were trying to think of roles that would afford me a path to independence and mayhap the funds needed to start a bakery. Mama believed becoming a governess would pay the most whilst providing opportunities to meet eligible men beyond Peterborough."

Mary snorted under her breath, drawing a look from Rachel.

Penelope frowned in confusion, but wanted to get out her question while she had the courage. "I wondered…are the opportunities better for an actress or—" She gulped. "—a courtesan?"

Rachel's gaze snapped to her, eyes wide.

"Shall we consider the upsides and downsides to those?" Ann jumped in. "It seems to me that the downsides are about the same whilst the upside for our profession was a much higher wage."

Penelope leaned forward. "'Tis similar to governessing but earns more?"

"Ah, no, that is not what I said. I only said the risks are about the same, if managed," Ann replied, not helping Penelope at all.

Rachel's gaze darted to Ann. "Ladies, that was not the career advice I intended for Penelope. Her mother would not desire that path for her, and I dread to think what would happen if her stepfather or townsfolk heard of us recommending such a thing to an innocent local girl."

The three women glanced at her, then each other. Ann shrugged. "We did not suggest it. She did. 'Tis her best chance at earning enough to own a bakery. You know that." She was very matter-of-fact.

Rachel shook her head. "No—"

Ann cut her off. "Leah returns from Town in less than a sennight. It might be best if she joins this conversation."

The three of them glared at one another, until Penelope finally asked, "Er, could you mayhap tell me a bit more about what a courtesan does?"

Mary snorted again, and Ann elbowed her.

Rachel, the most facile with words, took the initiative. "Some noblemen prefer to keep a woman on hand for their entertainment. Marriages are so often for political or financial reasons, rather than shared likes or tastes. Men sometimes look for the comfort of an easy relationship elsewhere, and are willing to pay for it. A courtesan is an exclusive paid companion for a wealthy man. They provide friendship, comfort, and intimate relations."

"Oh." Penelope mulled this over for a minute, scandalized yet intrigued. "And you're saying they earn more than governesses, even though they do not need to know Latin or Advanced Maths? That seems odd."

Ann muttered to Mary, loud enough that Penelope heard it, "There is *some* advanced knowledge they must know."

Mary shushed her with a pat on her arm.

Penelope's gaze darted between all the women.

Rachel sighed. "We could speak to Leah about sending her to the school…" The other women nodded vigorously. "At least that will give her the education and time to make her own choices. She could be a governess, actress, courtesan, or any number of occupations then."

A few days later, Penelope met Leah Godwin. Leah was a similar age to the other three, appearing closer to Penelope's mother's age than Penelope's. Her blonde hair was streaked with gray, and her faded blue eyes carried laugh lines around them.

Leah described the School of Enlightenment. "Girls from all backgrounds attend to learn a wide variety of skills. Young ladies of the Ton married or betrothed, girls training to be governesses or courtesans, and servants participate in an introductory course, although the groups do not intermingle. That first two-week program includes a broad range of subjects designed to fill educational gaps based on students' backgrounds. There are placement exams for reading, writing, and Maths, as well as classes to help manage relationships. In that vein, the course informs girls about their own bodies and sexual awareness."

"All the girls?" Penelope's eyes widened.

"Yes. We all have a right to happiness and independence, and self-knowledge is a part of that continuum. After that first program, each student meets with the headmistress and their sponsor to choose a career path. That choice will determine what advanced classes you take and how long you stay there."

"How costly is it?"

"The school offers a few scholarships. I am quite certain I can obtain one for you."

"Oh. Thank you, Leah." Penelope's shoulders dropped in relief as she heaved a sigh. Another question struck her. "And I'll live there?"

"Yes. Students stay in dormitories, separated by class."

"What do the advanced courses include?"

"That depends on the direction you choose after the introductory program. You might focus on learning different ways to please a man if you were considering becoming a courtesan, whereas you might take more Latin if you were pursuing a governess role. Does that make sense?"

"Yes. I still have time to choose my path."

So she had, which brought her to tonight with Michael. She looked up to see him nodding his understanding of her rather long-winded answer about how she came to be sitting there with him.

Chapter Six

Michael made an effort to arrive by supper most nights that week, wanting to learn more about Penelope before his parents arrived in the city. They quizzed each other in meal-sized chunks, and dinners became two- or three-hour affairs. He particularly enjoyed learning about Penelope's classes. The nights ended with long bouts in bed, where Penelope tested her teachings and he showed her what he liked most.

"How are you settling in?" he asked as she served him cod in a wine sauce, and he finished pouring their wine.

"Leah called on me for the standard post-auction cautionary check, and you passed." She teased him, but he had been very glad to hear about that practice when he hosted the auction. It offered girls in a new and strange situation a chance to ask questions.

"Do you like the house? Is there aught you need?"

"Oh gosh. The house is more than I need, thank you. And I appreciate the accounts you created. I suspect I shall venture out more soon enough. For now, I've shopped with Mrs. Thorpe when she's gone to the market, and I have planted some herbs and vegetables in the garden for later this summer."

"And the Thorpes?"

"They are lovely people..." Penelope fidgeted with her silverware on the tablecloth.

"I hear a *but* in that statement." He frowned, concerned. He'd thought they'd be a good fit for a young woman in this role. Their references had said they were supportive, unobtrusive, and discreet.

"No, no, they are truly lovely. 'Tis only that my mother was a housekeeper for a manor house in the north country before she married my stepfather." Penelope's gaze remained on her plate.

Why had she turned shy? Was she ashamed of her mother's work, or did she think he was shocked that she was from the working class?

"I did not realize." He ventured a guess, "Is it that you are simply not accustomed to servants of your own, mayhap?" He had not considered that dilemma, although her background made sense, given her current circumstances. Was her family supportive of her attending the school? What she had learned?

I'm not sure we have enough dinners before my family arrives. He hungered to know everything about her. He might never run out of questions.

"Exactly." She glanced at him as she seemed to search for words.

He kept his mouth soft, his expression open, to encourage her to continue. He wanted to learn more but realized the class difference might be a sensitive subject.

"Having servants feels…decadent. I mean, I knew what to expect if I participated in the auction, as it was, ah, a contract requirement, I believe?" She tilted her head toward him. At his nod, she continued, "Reality is simply more awkward than I anticipated."

He smiled. "I understand. I suppose you asked them to refer to you as Miss Penelope, then?"

She agreed with a dip of her chin.

"I chose the Thorpes over others I interviewed because they sounded easygoing and accepting. My theory was that could be important in circumstances such as ours. I hope you can become more comfortable with them, but if not, we can revisit."

"Thank you, my lor—ah, Michael. I am sure I shall," Penelope replied.

After a few bites, she asked, "I know your father is ill. I'm sorry to hear that. Are you close?"

"Yes, quite." He blinked at the subject change. He supposed she was as interested in learning about him as he was her. "He made me the man I am today. I only hope to be as well-liked as he is when I am earl."

"That's lovely. And your mother?"

"Eh. That is a conversation for another time. What do your parents think of all this then? Do they know about the auction? Would your mother rather you be a housekeeper?"

"My mother was a seamstress, and I helped her. She supported my dream of opening a bakery, and we were searching for a path to the savings I would need. She thought mayhap a governess would learn the ways of the Ton the quickest and pay well. Unfortunately, she caught a fever and passed this winter." Penelope folded and refolded her napkin, looking down at her lap.

At her sniffle, he reached across and stroked her arm once. "I am so sorry, sweeting." After she collected herself, he asked, "I am a little confused. Had you not said your mother was a housekeeper?"

She looked sharply at him, lips firmed.

Oh. It sounded as though he was questioning her

tale. He flipped a hand palm up, his mouth curling in a half-smile. "I think I missed a step?"

She mirrored his lopsided grin. "She was a housekeeper at the country estate when I was young. I had a very close friend there, too. The daughter of the caretaker of the estate, an earl's cousin." Penelope's smile grew full-blown. "But Mama met David, my stepfather, and we moved for his work. She became a seamstress for the townspeople in our new city."

"Ah, I see now. Thank you." He frowned. "Did your stepfather toss you out when your mother died?" He was outraged on her behalf, his hands fisting on his silverware.

"No, no. But I have a young half-brother, and it would have been difficult to feed the three of us without my mother's sewing money. Thankfully, the ladies I told you about—the retired courtesans—were some of Mama's and my best customers."

"You said Leah was one of them and spends part of the year in Peterborough? Tell me more about the others."

"Rachel is tall, talks faster than anyone I know, and wants to befriend everyone she meets." Penelope looked hesitant before she continued. "Mary was a governess once. She was assaulted by the master of the house more than once. She was thrown out by the man's wife and didn't have many options for work. She wasn't able to get over her fear of men, but she muddled along until she met Ann. I don't know how Ann became a courtesan, but she hated sex. Until she met Mary and realized she enjoyed sex with the right person. They had enough saved to get out of the business and be together. You can imagine how their experiences influenced my decision when I chose between a governess earning less, and this opportunity." As an afterthought, she added, "I had considered acting as well, but Leah assured me I could find ways to enjoy playacting in this role."

"Ha, yes, I enjoy a little role-play now and then. So you went to school determined to become a man's mistress?"

"No, I kept an open mind. Ultimately, school gave me a lot of information to help me decide, and I chose this path."

"Well, I for one am exceedingly glad you did. Now, let me see what I can add to this store of information." Grabbing her hand, he led her upstairs, ignoring his inner voice asking why he was so interested in her life when their affair would likely be short-lived.

****

The next night, Penelope sat down to dinner to find Michael looking thoughtful. She guessed he was going to ask more about his favorite subject—her schooling. Given the strict rules on what they were allowed to share, she sometimes prevaricated in the face of questions. When she did, his requests became more creative.

"What is on your mind, my lord?"

"A few things you shared with me about your past intrigued me. First, what do servants attend the school for?"

She nodded. She was learning her man. "I had the same question. It seems lords and ladies like yourself sponsor servants. For example, if you worried the Spanking Club was too risky given your parents' outlook, you might have a servant trained in your specific sexual tastes."

"Huh. And ladies of the Ton, too?"

"Same idea. Mayhap you will choose to send your wife there." Her lips twisted in frustration at that idea. *I am already trained. If only he did not need a wife.*

"So, these ladies told you about the program, and you decided it was your best path to your goals?"

"There were a few other factors." She described her friend Melody. She was Penelope's age, working in her da's pub, and regaled Pen with unsolicited details of various blokes' prowess in bed as she pointed them out. According to Melody, quite a few of them had no idea what to do, and she taught them.

"And then, last year, Mama sent me to Norwich to buy spices." Her mother had had occasional luck finding Indian spices there, transported from the port at Yarmouth. When Matthew was born and Penelope was old enough to go, Betsey began sending her with David when he needed supplies for the forge.

"On our return trip, we passed through Gressenhall, right by the workhouse that serves fifty parishes. A shift was finishing, and dozens of women were stumbling out after twelve hours of hard labor, some holding young children's hands. They were grimy from head to toe, exhausted, and had their hair shaved to avoid lice. Their clothes were threadbare." Their faces and posture had all looked older than her mother, even though many had the bodies of younger women.

"I refused to consider either path as a possibility for my future. Melody worked all day in the pub and entertained a multitude of men. These ladies were offering me an education, easier work, and a higher wage. Why wouldn't I choose to be paid to be one man's companion at a time for a few short years? I could save enough to achieve my dream and ensure I never ended up like those women in the workhouse."

"I never considered the scarce choices young women have, given their limited access to education." Michael hesitated, then asked his second question. "So you went to school, then the auction, as the quickest path to independence?"

She nodded, but before she could reply, he continued. "But...when you were at home in Peterborough, you had enough to eat, surely?"

"We did. There were leaner months sometimes, but Mama and David worked hard, and as I said, I've been helping for several years."

"And it sounds like you care for your stepfather?"

"Oh yes. He was wonderful to me and loved Mama to pieces. I know he'll take excellent care of Matthew. And I plan to send money home as soon as I can."

"Ah. Do you need my help with that? I can have my man of business send a draft."

She shook her head. *Nabobs. Everything was simple for them.*

"I doubt David could get to a bank to draw a draft, but thank you, and I am reluctant to send coins through the post. I shall take some funds when I visit next. At least once I know how much I can put aside for him and still have enough to support myself when needed."

"And how will you do that?" He cocked his head, narrowing his eyes.

"School prepared us to handle our own finances."

At that, he sat forward. "Really? What did you learn?"

"Very often courtesans' earnings are lumpy. I might receive a large sum of money from each new patron, then a more moderate allowance during that affair, and then have gaps of time with no income between benefactors."

Michael tensed at her statement.

She looked at him curiously.

Does he not like the idea of other benefactors? Even with the size of the settlement he offered for me at the auction, does he think I can retire? He can't understand what I need, when he's never had to think twice about money.

"Go on." His mouth was tight around the words, but his voice remained calm.

"Many girls would be overwhelmed at the amount settled on them in these relationships, and some might be tempted to spend it on frivolities. The instructors reminded us of what could happen if we did not save enough for a place to live and food on the table."

"I see." But he still frowned.

Penelope provided two quick examples, stepping him through them. "What happens to your future wife if you predecease her?"

"I arrange for such an eventuality. Every contract is different, negotiated with the girl's father. Some have clauses for settlements based on age or number of children or number of siblings the earl has." He tilted his head. "I suspect I might make choices similar to my friends who have married. The dower house at the estate, an allowance for the rest of her life. That sort of thing. Why?"

"And if one of you or your children becomes ill?"

"We would call a physician, of course."

"Which you'd be billed for later. Do you know how much a house call by a physician costs, either here in Town or at your estate?"

His lips twisted ruefully. "Not offhand, no."

"Because 'tis not a concern. For someone in my position, it is. I have the funds you settled on me through the auction. Before that, I needed my wages from the theatre to buy clothes for the auction and a few items to begin with here. Thankfully, I had been sponsored for a scholarship at the school. So at least I am not in debt, but I must save for health concerns. Likewise, when you grow old, your wife will still have a home, food, clothing, and much more. Even if I marry, I will likely not have those sources when I am older. Therefore, I must ensure I have enough to have a roof and food in old age, if naught else. The school encouraged us to be thrifty and to ask for what we want."

"I see." He smiled at her. "Is there mayhap something you wish to ask me for, Pen?"

"No!" she gasped. "My lord, I did not mean to suggest anything. I was only answering your questions, offering the reasons behind my choice and training."

"Oh, I know. I did not think you were prevaricating, my dear. You raised an excellent point, and now I am curious what you'd ask for first. I suppose I am interested in how thorough their education was," Michael said cheekily.

The deed to a house or a bakery. She wanted to shout it out, but she pressed her lips tight against the words. Housing had been the most expensive and concerning of expenses to her mother and then her stepfather. She'd worry about shelter until she held a deed in her hand, but to voice that request after only knowing him a fortnight felt very greedy. Yes, the school had decried modesty and encouraged boldness in asking for what one deserved, but they also recommended finesse in getting men to do one's bidding.

She settled on, "My lord, I would be thrilled to receive another small settlement when we part ways upon your betrothal. You have already been very generous. I do not need anything."

She expected him to nod and proceed with the evening, but he watched her with narrowed eyes. Cocking his head, he said, "I do not believe that is truly your first wish. Nor do I think the teachers would have recommended that answer."

Penelope kept her eyes wide and stared at him, mute.

After a brief staredown, he lifted one side of his mouth in a half-smile. "How much of your pin money have you spent?"

"My lord, I showed you all the lovely plants I bought."

"Mmm. Still not an answer. I shall assume you have saved most of it." He smiled fully now. "Which is excellent. I am very happy to hear that you have some insurance. I should not like to think of you worrying about food or a physician visit."

She shared a little of her barely-formed dream with him. "Actually, I do have another request, please, Michael. Do you know how much money I need to open a bakery?"

"Honestly? No. You mentioned that dream from your childhood. 'Tis something you are still interested in?"

She smiled. "Since I was old enough to reach the kitchen table, I have been experimenting with recipes from my great-grandmother, carried over from India. I have walked this neighborhood. There are three bakeries, all selling the same goods. I hope to interest people in other flavors, to add a little spice to their lives."

"That is excellent. I am happy to help. Let me see what I can find out."

"Thank you ever so much, Michael. That would be lovely."

"Now." He rose and offered his hand. "Shall we adjourn to your boudoir, mademoiselle?" he asked with a courtly bow.

****

Two nights later, Michael lounged in a kitchen chair while Penelope bustled around the kitchen putting the finishing touches on their dinner.

Hearing him sniff, then get up, she turned to see what he needed.

He reached for a jar she'd just used. "What is this?"

"'Tis a curry. I've used it in other dishes, but tonight, I mixed it into crushed tomatoes for a red paste on the roast."

He sniffed again, and his eyes widened.

"'Tis strong. I only use a little." She smirked at his surprise.

He returned to his seat, and she felt his eyes on her back as she moved back and forth. Feeling self-conscious, she asked, "How did an earl's heir learn to cook?"

"As a boy, I was mesmerized by the family chef's creativity. As the future earl, I was expected to focus on history, politics, and ledgers. There was not much time for creativity of any sort. While my sister Matilda played the pianoforte and sketched, I was practicing long division and reading treatises. But when my father broke for afternoon tea, I could escape. Given the vagaries of British weather, I often loitered by the back door evaluating whether I could get in a ride. Many days, I'd be distracted by the servants carrying bundles of vegetables and herbs in from the garden and transforming them into our dinner."

She smiled and passed him dishes to carry to the dining alcove in the front room.

"Even at boarding school, I hovered in the host family kitchen watching. During my final year before university, the host mother allowed me to help. After that—university, then home and London—I had much less time. But those first couple of years, when Parliament was not in session, and I was at Mansfield Manor, I had flexibility. Even an earldom moves at a country pace during the winter, and I apprenticed with the chef when I could sneak away."

"But you live in London most of the year now, do you not?"

"I do. When I moved from my parents' to my own townhouse, I stole one of the more senior kitchen staff and made her chef in my household. I try to give her at least one night a week off, as cooking absorbs and relaxes me. It requires enough concentration that I can't dither over the responsibilities waiting for me."

After they finished dinner, he raised his brows and added, "D'you know what else relaxes me? Spanking."

With a laugh, he flipped her over the settee to demonstrate.

Thus, Penelope was not surprised when she entered the kitchen one afternoon to find the housekeeper tidying. Mrs. Thorpe showed her the note from Michael asking that dinner be left to him and Penelope.

Kneading dough, Penelope looked up as a knock sounded and Mr. Thorpe's voice pointed Michael to the kitchen. He entered carrying a satchel with greenery poking out the top.

Mrs. Thorpe bustled around, wiping the counter top and putting a few last items away. When she glimpsed at him, she turned and bobbed a quick curtsy, murmuring, "My lord. I was just finishing here. Mr. Thorpe and I will enjoy our evening on the town, thank you." Speeding past him, she linked arms with her husband, and they strode forward to get their wraps.

Having only learned of his early arrival an hour before, Penelope worried that she wore a simple day dress. On the other hand, it seemed best suited for cooking.

"Good afternoon, my—Michael," she corrected, flattening the dough.

Smiling, he strolled forward and stole a pinch of dough before grabbing a cloth and swiping it down her cheek.

Ugh, flour. *Not very enticing.*

"Good afternoon. Mmm, pastry. Any particular plans for that?" he asked.

"We have some rhubarb from the garden I thought might work well in a pie," she replied. "I tend to add a hint of ginger, as 'tis my favorite spice."

He placed his satchel down, reached in, and drew

his hand out an inch at a time, gaze on her. "How about a treat?"

She watched as leafy greens appeared, but she did not have time to identify them before the succulent offering attached to them cleared the bag.

"Strawberries!" She squealed, flapping her hands once in pleasure.

"The first of the season. I stole them from a friend who has a chef with excellent connections. They are in from the countryside this morning. I do not know if there is enough for a whole pie, though." Michael considered them.

"That is fine. We can make strawberry-rhubarb pie then." She could not contain her excitement. Rushing over to him, she reached for the fruit, but he held it away with one long arm, snagging her around the waist with his other.

"Hmm, a proper greeting first, eh? And a thank you, mayhap?"

"Of course, my lord, I am sorry," Penelope said, aghast. *Gor, how could I have forgotten my training so easily?* Leaning up, she brought her lips to his in a gentle kiss. "Welcome, 'tis lovely to have you here with me."

"All is well, Pen. I was teasing you." He smiled. "But I would not be upset by you removing one article of clothing to thank me." He arched his brows in hope and took one step back, releasing her.

"Oh!" She considered, tilting her head. Then, with a small smile, she bent and removed a slipper.

"Will that do, my lord?" She slid him a sidelong look. Internally, she berated herself. *I should be thinking of these games. But I like that he created this one. I like playful Michael a lot, I shall do better in the future.*

He strolled over and fingered the bread peel, his lips pursed.

"At the very least, the pair is really one article of clothing as you always wear them together. Beyond that, I can see I will need to be more specific. Fair enough, young lady."

He chuckled, earning a smile in return as she slid out of her other slipper and placed them by the door.

She vowed to contemplate other diversions for them. In the meantime, she'd follow his lead. Would he continue this play as they cooked?

Chapter Seven

Michael's smile at her acquiescence to the play lingered as he turned to the kitchen table. He'd been distracted all day anticipating this evening, knowing he would not have these hours once his family arrived in Town. When he reached her house, he put his worries about responsibilities aside to enjoy the moment.

Then Pen had mentioned ginger, and he'd shivered with lust at the memory of her lips on the candy stick. He decided to play a game.

As he made his first request for a piece of clothing, he worried it might be too abrupt for their new relationship. As much as he wanted to trust her training, he also did not wish to scare a young woman only recently introduced to sexual play. He heaved a sigh of relief at her teasing response but disguised it by wandering to the bread peel.

"I shall unpack a few things as you finish rolling out the pie crust." He returned to the table and his sack. He had hung his coat and waistcoat on the apron pegs by the kitchen door to keep them clean and was in his shirtsleeves.

"Certainly, sir." Penelope made quick work of shaping the pie crust into the tin and cutting the top into strips to be woven. She put those aside and cleared the table to start the strawberry and rhubarb filling before turning to him.

After placing a small leg of lamb in a roasting pan, he chopped vegetables. He gestured for her to go ahead with the rhubarb.

Having planned where he'd take this game if she was amenable, he added, "Wait on the strawberries, please."

"Hmm. I believe a thank you for making dinner is in order as well," he mulled as he worked.

"Ah, right. And mayhap, in return, a show of gratitude for dessert is appropriate?" she dared to question.

Michael smirked. *This will be fun.*

"My lady, I will allow you to choose the item I remove if I may do the same for you?" he offered, with a quick bow and a grin.

She cataloged his apparel and pouted. His grin widened. He wore more articles of clothing than she did, as she had been home all day and wore only the dress, petticoat, chemise, and stockings.

"Sir, your shirt, please."

"Of course. I shall even offer the cravat with it, as I fear it would look rather silly without the shirt. For you, the dress, please."

She giggled at his imagery as she unfastened her dress and stepped out of it, then hung both their clothing on a hook next to his coat.

He tossed the chopped vegetables into the roasting pot around the meat, placed the pot on the hook over the fire, and made quick work of wiping down the table.

Penelope's eyebrows rose as though surprised at his efficiency and confidence.

Ignoring that, he focused on more pressing matters. Placing a few of the strawberries on the corner of the table, he gestured her closer and caught her around the waist to sit her on the table.

He hesitated, given her newness to intimacy. Then, based on her willingness to play the game thus far, he continued. He drew her chemise up with one hand, using the other to raise her arms over her head to whisk the garment off.

About to lay her flat, he could not resist her bare upper half. Placing one hand behind her head, he lowered his lips to hers and licked into the heat of her mouth as he slid his other hand to a breast. Cupping it, he flicked it with his thumb, and she arched, gasping into his mouth.

Ah, good. She is as eager as I am. He drew a few inches away. "Lay back."

"Like this?"

"Scoot up a few inches. Feet flat on the table." He shoved her knees apart to step between them.

Her petticoat flowed down her upper thighs to bunch at her waist.

Michael sucked in a breath. She was lovely. All rose and creamy caramel, with touches of a deeper blush—her lips, her nipples, and between her legs. His gaze rose to find her focused on him, a flush of red staining her chest and cheeks. He glanced down to where her nether lips darkened and swelled.

"We—" His voice was gravel, so much so that it surprised him. Clearing his throat, he adjusted the iron rod in his breeches as his erection strained against the placket. He grabbed the strawberries. Plucking one, he touched it to her lips.

He tried again. "We should test the sweetness of the berries before adding them to the pie."

Her gaze stayed on his as she bit, chewing, swallowing, her tongue darting out to lick at a drop of juice on her lower lip.

"Sweet," she whispered, nodding.

"I'd like to check as well," he commented, but he did not bring the half-eaten berry to his mouth. Instead, he rubbed it on each of her nipples. Gently at first, then harder, leaving bits of fruit behind.

Her back arched toward him, and he could hardly bear the wait. He wanted to end the play, drop the fruit, and thrust his cock into her, either between those shiny lips that surely tasted of strawberry or into her heated center.

Forcing patience, he bent and tasted the berry from her hardened tip, the color so dark it almost blended with the fruit. Juice ran down her breast, and he lapped it up before moving to the other one.

"Mmm. Yes, that piece is sweet," he murmured. "But what if the others are not?"

Holding a second red offering to her mouth, he waited while she bit into it. He had to remind himself that she was still new to all of this. She followed his lead so easily, was so accepting of whatever he wanted to do with her, to her.

He met her eyes, checking for nerves. She was watching him, her eyes glazed with desire. Her lips, shiny with berry juice, were parted to draw deep breaths, her chest rising and falling visibly.

Her aroma blended with that of the berry, and he took a deep breath. *No nerves, then.* He brought the fruit between her legs and traced her outer lips before smushing it against her hardened nub.

Tossing it aside, he lowered his mouth to her,

sucking and licking, biting then soothing, only to begin again. His eyes closed in ecstasy as he savored the blended taste of sweet and salty Pen and strawberry, his heart racing and his fingers flexing against her thighs.

Oh, the games we can play in this kitchen. How perfect that we both find this to be our favorite room in the house. Although, the bedroom—

"Ahh, my lord…Michael." She moaned, her hands gripping his hair as his tongue circled again.

He tugged her legs onto his shoulders, then seized her hips and dragged her toward him. As her hips tried to move up and down, smearing against his mouth to stroke the spot she wanted, he ground his face against her gently, giving her the pressure she needed.

Then he could stand it no longer. Straightening, he ripped his breeches open, grabbed his cock, and with one thrust of his hips, drove home.

Penelope yelped, and he paused.

"Did I hurt you?" he asked, even as her hips twisted to try to make him move.

Shaking her head, hair falling across her face, she cried, "No, no, my lord, please, more!"

"Hold onto the edge of the table." His hips pistoned, hard thrusts that threatened to push her up the length of the table.

She braced, enabling her hips to rise to meet his. Tracking his expression, she panted in time to his movements.

He grimaced in pleasure as his orgasm roiled up his back and through his groin. But he needed Penelope with him. He moved one hand from her hip to her stomach, his thumb reaching between them to her slick folds, finding the hard little bud, and rubbing it.

"Aaahhh, please, come with me," he muttered, realizing he'd said it aloud when she answered.

"Yes," she managed to gasp. "Yes, yes…"

Hearing her cry, he increased his speed.

As her nub hardened further, he pressed it with his thumb. It quivered beneath him, and her walls contracted over and over around him as her mouth opened in a soundless scream.

Her hips held high, frozen in the air.

He grabbed her thighs with both hands again, thrusting faster and harder for mere seconds before his hot seed gushed. His eyes slid closed in ecstasy and relief. Sagging over her, he held her legs so they would not dangle off the table and placed his head on her breastbone for a moment, gathering himself.

Her hands wove into his hair again, this time to stroke.

"Thank you, Michael. I fear I have only my petticoats and stockings to offer at this point."

Barking a laugh, he lifted his head with an effort to find her smiling, joy and gratitude swimming in her eyes. "I have never had quite so much fun cooking," he exclaimed before he stood and lowered her legs.

Retrieving a cloth from the shelf, he started to clean them both up, but she held her hand out for it. Eyebrows raised, he handed it over.

Leaning forward, she cleaned him first and then herself before straightening. "And the pie…?"

"By all means, Pen. I shan't ever eat a strawberry as sweet again, but the pie sounds delicious, sweeting." He stroked her hair away from her face.

Why must I marry? Why now? And why was my father able to marry someone unsuitable, but that very person insists I marry a pillar of decorum? His contented expression dimmed. *Blast it. No wife is ever going to be this fun.*

****

Michael's lips twisted when Penelope asked how he came to own a theatre, particularly the one used for the auction. *I hope this story does not raise her hopes, given Mama's obsession with "drabness."*

As usual, they talked over dinner.

"My mother was an actress."

His answer shocked Penelope into staring at him with mouth agape.

"My father was not yet the earl and loved the theatre." He grimaced at her expression of bafflement even as he explained. "He attended as many performances as he could. At first, it was purely love of the stories he had read in school being brought to life. But"—his lips curled in a small smile—"the way he tells it, one season there was a particular actress who stood out above all others. She breathed new life, different nuance into characters he thought he knew."

Sighing, he tossed his napkin by his empty plate. His parents' love story usually invigorated him, but with his father so sick, he worried their romance would turn into a tragedy. "Anyway, he so admired this actress's skills he decided he must meet her. He wooed her with flowers, gifts, offers of dinner in the finest restaurants. She declined them all, assuming he sought a mistress."

Michael hesitated, realizing that part of the story might sound disparaging about Penelope's choices. But she nodded, gesturing for him to continue.

"Mama did not wish to be anyone's mistress. She

adored acting and was quite happy continuing that career. He persisted, finagling his way backstage to wait for her after a performance. When he offered again, she agreed to meet him for coffee in a small sweet shop tucked away on a quiet street where they'd likely not be seen. So they met. Then continued to meet. My father became as fascinated with her as a person as he had with the actress and fell in love all over again."

He waved a hand, signifying that was the end of it.

Penelope scowled. "So, what, an"—she tilted her head—"earl's heir?"

He nodded, assuming she was questioning how to refer to his father's title at the time.

"—married an actress and lived happily ever after? And that still does not explain how you came to not only own a theatre but the exact one used for the auction."

"Oh, ah, right. Yes, he told his parents what he intended to do, and they threatened to disinherit him. Whether or not they could have is unclear, particularly as he was almost forty by the time all this happened, but he ignored them in any event. He and my mother ran off to Gretna Green and married, and he brought her home as his wife. She proceeded to charm the skirts off my grandmother and win her over. It helped that she became pregnant with me within a few months. Regardless, my mother is one of those calm, capable women who can do almost anything. She did not know how to run a large household, but she had handled her own for years in her career. Acting also helped her mimic mannerisms and even tones of the peerage. She appeared malleable but underneath had a spine of steel.

She still does."

He stood and stepped to the bar, returning with a bottle of port and pouring them each a glass.

"With his wife now on the actress's side and the new countess-to-be the soul of decorum at their estate, the earl—my grandfather—acceded. As for Mama, she was quite happy with a change of career, as long as it was a legitimate one. They are still madly in love to this day." He grimaced as he pictured the sadness and worry that lurked in his mother's eyes on his father's bad days.

Pen remained quiet, her eyes downcast.

Replaying what he'd said, he realized the implications of the word 'legitimate' against her choice and rushed to address the second part of Penelope's question.

"I bought the theatre in her honor. She was incensed." He raised his eyebrows in remembered shock. "I was astonished. She wanted me to sell it immediately, but my father was charmed with the idea. They have not attended performances very often these last few years due to my father's declining health, but it seems they shall this Season to help me shop for a wife."

"I am sorry your father is struggling. Especially as you've told me how close you are."

Michael had grown up at his father's knee, learning about the various estates, the tenant farmers' names, the key servants the earl trusted with estate management positions. He'd studied his father's approach to investing and how he managed risk to protect the family's standing. More than anything, he'd heard the compassion in the earl's voice when he spoke of the people in his charge and seen the care he took to teach Michael each aspect of the earldom in ways he could understand, even when he was young. He had a case of hero-worship for his father.

"Thank you." He cleared the emotion from his throat. "As for the auction and Leah, you have not yet met my friends, but we all belong to a particular club here. Not White's or Brooks, although we're members of White's as well. It is a flagellation club, or salon as Sarah, the owner, likes to call it. And Sarah helps run the auction, so she asked me about using the theatre."

Penelope sat wide-eyed.

Had she heard about such clubs? Most of them catered to men who wanted to be whipped, but a number offered alternatives—spank, be spanked, watch a show. But then again, most people could not imagine her training, either, so mayhap she'd take it in stride.

"Er, and this, ah, *club*." She clearly was not referring to White's. "It seems that you practice your, ah, *skills* there, then?"

He burst out laughing, both at her word choice and her expression when she realized what she had said. He appreciated that she viewed them as skills.

"Yes, yes, indeed. Although now I have you, my pretty." With a mock leer, he grabbed her hand and his port and, still laughing, rose to lead her to the stairs and bed. "I think I need more practice now."

****

Given his interest in the curry, Penelope had offered to make Michael one of her favorite dishes from her family recipes. The following night, he lounged at the kitchen table sipping wine and watching her as she added curry to the meat pie she was preparing.

"Where do you find the spices?"

Mrs. Thorpe knew of several less-popular markets and had taken her through one. There, Penelope had discovered food items from many cultures and procured several spices she had rarely found in Peterborough that suited her. "West London."

He speared her with a sharp look. "Did Mr. Thorpe accompany you?"

She nodded, warmth filling her at his obvious concern for her safety.

"I am not familiar with those flavors. Are they from your great grandmother?" he asked.

"Yes. She came here as an ayah—a nanny—to a British family returning home after being stationed in India. She wrote many traditional recipes down before she came here and packed some spices. Those recipes have been handed down through my mother's family." She gestured at a handwritten journal on the countertop. "I have yet to try all of them, as we rarely had access to those spices up north."

"I am happy to taste test anything you'd like me to." Michael grinned as he went to the dining room to set the table and pour more wine while she finished cooking.

They returned to his favorite subject over the deliciously flavored meat pie—her education. Of course, being a man, he was rather obsessed with the sex education aspect.

"Will you share more of what you learned?"

She had kept the conversation about school rather vague as they eased into the new relationship. More prepared after time together and his creative game the other night, she smiled and set out to entertain her patron.

"Certainly. After the first program of introductory courses, they offered us choices. By then, the instructors and headmistress knew each of us better and could point out advanced classes that might suit us."

"Did all the girls in your class participate in the auction then?"

"No. Some were not comfortable relying on others, even Prudence, Leah, and the other auctioneers, to vet a bidder to their satisfaction. Those girls preferred to interview men themselves and have several meetings. And not all were"—she shifted and looked away—"untouched."

"Ah. Right. What were the advanced course options, then?"

She glanced at his plate. They had both eaten most of their dinner. If they started discussing this, Michael would likely abandon the meal. On the other hand, superimposing his image on each activity she had learned made her quite amenable to that possibility.

"Hmm, did you want to hear about Latin or Applied Maths?" she teased him.

At his sardonic look, she snickered.

"There was costuming, creative thinking, acting, oral training, and corporal punishment." There were a few others, but she had given him enough food for thought for the time being. She needed to save a few to surprise him with another time.

"Wait, what oral training? Singing, reciting poetry, projecting your voice?"

"Ah, no." But she understood why he would jump to theatre-related skills.

"What, then, if I may ask?"

She smirked, glancing down at his lap, then up again.

"Oh!" Michael's eyes bulged. "Really? How did they train you in that? Wait, have you done that to a man then?" His brows creased.

"No, of course not." Although upon reflection, 'twas not such a strange question. When Michael married and she entered her next relationship, she could not be so indignant with the next man. She frowned at that thought before pushing the future away and closing a mental door on it.

"Well, then, how the dickens could you train for that?"

"We had, er, tools. Cucumbers and squash are remarkably useful, my lord."

He laughed, obviously delighted at the image. "Why those, aside from their shape?"

"Because teeth scraping along them left visible marks."

"Ah, I see." Now it was his turn to shift in his chair, dropping his hand to adjust his hardening length in his breeches. "And you were able to avoid teeth marks?" His eyebrows climbed.

She arched a brow, then jumped up, ran to the kitchen, and returned with an early squash. "Shall I demonstrate?"

Michael sat forward. "Please do."

She wetted the vegetable with her tongue to ensure it slid in smoothly.

He groaned under his breath.

Ah. Her pose resembled her auction walk with the ginger stick. He'd told her how much that had affected him. Her lips curled in a small smile.

Why have I not done this before?

His eyes were hot, his focus absolute. She wasn't sure if he was even breathing.

Hiding her teeth behind her lips and keeping her gaze on him through her upper lashes, she lazily glided her mouth forward until her lips met her hand holding the food. She pulled back, leaving wetness but no scrapes. Then slid forward again. Back.

He was definitely breathing now. It was audible, as well as visible. His mouth hung open, and his hands clenched on his thighs. He licked dry lips and leaned farther forward.

Half-afraid he'd fall off his chair, she stopped. With a pop, she pulled it free and held it out.

"Would you like to inspect it, as the instructors did?" She grinned.

He took the prop from her and rotated it, still agog.

"And to save the vegetables for dinners, we made do with other items. Sometimes, there was a column of leather filled with water, teaching us to hold it without biting or letting liquid squirt out. Other times, the tool was a long strip of rolled leather that we marked with how far we could take it into our throat."

He groaned again, his hand stroking his cock where it pushed against his breeches.

Penelope's gaze followed the motion, her tongue darting out along her lips.

His gaze flicked between her mouth and the vegetable.

"My lord? Mayhap I should practice on the real thing? Or would you prefer dessert?" She made a slight hand gesture.

"Mmph." He did not produce any understandable

words, though.

"I find myself craving dessert. Something to suck on…" Taking matters into her own hands, she pushed back her chair, dropping to her knees rather than rising.

Michael froze for a long moment, then sprang to life, shoving his chair around to face her. He reached for the placket of his breeches.

She smoothed her hands up his thighs, slipping them inward to grip his shaft as he pulled it free.

Licking her lips, she gawked at it for a moment. She'd held it in her hand and was accustomed to the heat and the silken feel of the rod, but she had not yet viewed it up close. It suddenly appeared huge, far larger than the squash sitting forgotten on the table.

She glanced up at his face, not realizing her fear showed on her face until he reacted.

Laying a hand on the side of her face, his fingers wrapped under her hair, and he brushed her dampened lips with his thumb. Though his face was taut with need, his touch and voice remained gentle. "Pen, whatever you do, I shall enjoy. Use your training. Try a few things. I shall direct you if needed."

She nodded against his hand, relieved.

Returning her gaze to the hard length in her grip, she gently levered it toward her mouth and licked it like a candy stick. It surged in her hand, which she had already learned meant he liked what she had done. Licking around the tip, she sucked just that head into her mouth.

He groaned, his hand tightening on her neck for a moment.

"Wet it all," he rasped, tilting his head back, only to drop it forward again to watch her with hot eyes.

She licked it, licked her hand, slid her hand up and down his length. His stomach contracted and expanded as his breathing sped up. His cock leaked in her mouth, and she tasted the thick, salty liquid and pulled back to swallow it.

Do I taste like that? Does it make his stomach flutter like his taste does for me? Her body flushed hot under her dress, blood pooling in her core, her folds dampening. *He hasn't even touched me, and I am ready for him.*

He groaned.

She looked up at him, realizing her power. He was at her mercy, even as she knelt before him. Was this how he felt when he spanked her? School had not taught the girls the connection created when they took a man's cock into their hand and mouth. It might be even more intimate than sex itself.

This could be addictive. No wonder he likes to control my pleasure. I can't believe it will be like this with another man.

Cutting that thought off, Penelope grew bolder, sucking his iron rod into her mouth until he hit the back of her throat. Remembering her lessons, she relaxed her throat and pushed harder against him. Her mouth tightened around him, resisting.

He groaned and muttered, "Swallow without pulling back, if you can. It might help."

She did, still on the edge of choking.

He moaned again, his hand tight in her hair.

Feeling his fingerhold, hearing his moan, kneeling before him flipped a switch in her. Her muscles relaxed—legs, shoulders…and throat.

He slid a tiny bit farther. Her eyes watered, but her

nipples strained against her chemise. Her pulse raced, and there was a rush of moisture between her legs.

She trusted that if she pulled against him, he'd release her, but she liked his hold. He'd taken control, and she loved it.

Shifting, she cupped a breast, finger and thumb squeezing her nipple.

Michael's hips moved back then forward again, then they snapped back, almost apologetically. "Pen?"

Rather than answer verbally, she nudged her head forward an inch.

He grunted, hips jerking back and forward again, then again. "Tell me if you need me to stop or sit back."

He was panting. His abdomen rippled against the edge of her hand where it gripped his base.

"Ah, Pen, so good. I cannot believe you have not done this. I might need to sponsor a scholarship."

If her mouth was not full, she might have giggled at his distracted babbling. As it was, she judged that he was ready for her to increase her speed.

So she did. She moved her mouth and hand in counterpoint to his thrusts. His cockhead banged into the back of her throat. She adjusted the angle to take him a little deeper.

His hand spasmed on her hair, and he threw his head back.

"Will you drink me? Otherwise, move your head, sweeting." He held her head still and thrust hard and fast but not as deep, considerate even now. Once, twice, thrice, and hot spurts of liquid erupted in her mouth.

Swallowing over and over, she managed to avoid drooling as he stilled, cock pulsing in her mouth.

Licking him clean, she wiped her hand on her

discarded serviette and sat back on her heels, dislodging his hand. She was panting as hard as he was and looked up at him, her pulse pounding in her ears, her nipples poking through her chemise and dress.

Was it acceptable for her to ask him for sex?

Chapter Eight

Uncaring of his open breeches, Michael leaned down to Penelope and reclaimed her head with his hand, drawing her to him for a kiss.

That *was her first time? Heaven help me after she's practiced more. I may never leave this house.*

She pulled away, putting her fingers to her lips as though concerned about the flavor of him lingering.

He yanked her hand away.

"I need to kiss you. That was quite possibly the most exciting sex I have ever had. Now I wish to revel in it." He tugged her head back to his and kissed her thoroughly.

She broke off the kiss, panted, still trying to catch her breath, then glanced down at his lap. "Er, Michael, my lord. If I may be so bold. Do you think we could mayhap, er"—she seemed to search for the right words, still new to all this—"engage in another act soon?"

He looked closer at her, relishing her obvious arousal. "You seem to have enjoyed that, sweeting."

"Yes, my lord. I should like to enjoy it a bit more, when you are ready, if I may." She peered at him through her lashes.

"There is no need to wait. Come up here." He offered his hand to help her rise, then gripped her hips to pull her sideways onto his lap to kiss her, one arm around her back for support. He tugged her bodice lower, and his hand swooped inside to pull her breast up and over the edge of her chemise and neckline. Leaning down, he licked at the hardened tip.

Penelope gripped his head with both hands, undulating on his lap.

Realizing she was already unbearably aroused, he sucked her nipple into his mouth. His tongue flicked it furiously as he swept his hand up under her bunched skirts. He opened her legs to press one against his hip and stretched the other to her abandoned chair.

Finding her center, he ran his fingers through the wetness. Spreading her lips and focusing on the hard tip there, he mimicked his tongue's action with his thumb.

Penelope's hips arched up of their own accord, her hands fisted in his hair.

"Oh! Yes, yes, that please, Michael," she begged.

"Shh, I have you," he promised. He eased a finger into her channel.

Penelope gasped and thrust against him.

A second finger.

She still pushed against him, her hips moving as his had earlier, grinding into his leg.

Recognizing her need for relief, he caught the tip of her breast in his mouth and his teeth closed around it gently. His arm around her back held her still. Pistoning his fingers in and out of her, he added his thumb to circle on her most sensitive spot and take her up to the pinnacle faster.

She arched against his arm and keened a moan through clenched teeth.

Michael sped his hand between her legs, faster but not harder, thumb circling feverishly.

Her inner muscles tightened, rigid around his

fingers before contracting and pulsing and drenching his hand in her essence.

Slowing his motions, he loosed his teeth from her breast to lick and nuzzle. His hand made only slow nudges to bring her down.

As her spine went lax against his arm, he raised his head. "Better?"

"Oh, thank you, Michael. So good."

"I am glad. One day soon, I will take you over with my mouth."

"I am not sure I could bear it. 'Twas so intense."

"That is because you were already aroused from sucking me." The corner of his mouth twitched as he grinned. "Mayhap we should always include that in foreplay."

She firmed her lips. "I was told men look for mistresses because they want variety." And then her laugh broke through her mock prim look.

He laughed with her.

Palming his cock, he was surprised how hard he was again in such a short time. He rose and led her upstairs to continue the evening.

****

Michael looked up from his desk when the butler knocked and entered, bearing a salver with the day's post. He had two last tasks to complete before he could go to Penelope's house for dinner. Hoping there was nothing urgent in this latest batch of letters, he rifled through them.

Seeing one with the Mansfield seal on it, he dropped the rest to read the next day and cracked it open warily. He'd been waiting to hear when his parents planned to travel to London, and a letter would only precede them by a matter of days, given the vagaries of the mail coaches.

Scanning it, he groaned.

No. Not yet, please.

He began at the top and re-read it more slowly. Sure enough, his father's health had improved once the spring rains had eased, and his parents were due to arrive in two days. That was almost a sennight earlier than they had originally estimated.

Blast. I needed every minute of that sennight for time with Penelope. He had expected to lose interest in her within a few weeks, as he might a new gadget. Then he could succumb to the marriage mart and the search for a wife. But the more time he spent with Penelope, the more he wanted—needed. He was not ready to succumb to marriage and "drabness."

She read his moods, knew when to distract him from his day versus when he needed to vent his frustrations, verbally or otherwise. He laughed at her teasing, mock-frowned at her deliberate disobedience, and spanked her for all of it. And he could not get enough of their dinner conversations when they shared family memories, opinions on politics, and everything between.

He enjoyed her company as much as he did Bags's and Robert's. But now much of his time would be wasted at balls and soirées, wooing some silly chit who was suitable. Then he'd have to skulk around to see Penelope in the dark of night, as he refused to give her up until he must.

'Twas not fair. Why could there not be marriageable ladies like Penelope, who society only saw as appropriate for fucking. The letter crumpled in his clenched hand.

He was very glad his father was having some better days and looked forward to seeing them. He wanted them to be proud of him and liked the idea of a wife and children to come home to each day. His subconscious made the connection. Each afternoon, he eagerly anticipated seeing Penelope.

He slammed a fist on the desk. The chair teetered as he shoved it back to stand and pace, his brain circling between respecting his parents' wishes and desiring Penelope. He did not see a resolution. There was no compromise. Earls married "drab" titled ladies, not working-class girls they'd won at auction. He growled in frustration, realizing keeping Penelope was a hopeless wish.

I knew this was temporary. Blast it. I had no place even bidding on her. I cannot let myself get any more entangled with her. She is my mistress, nothing more.

Frowning, he strode out of the library to call for his coat and horse, determined to cement her position in his brain.

He'd marry as he must. In the meantime, he'd enjoy the benefit he had purchased. *I shall simply keep reminding myself—she is mine, bought and paid for, to fuck. For now.*

****

Michael pounded on Penelope's front door even as he opened it. In this mood, he at least should warn her he was coming.

She emerged from the kitchen, brows knitted at the racket. "Michael?"

After banging the door shut behind him, he strode into the parlor and threw his coat, hat, and gloves onto the nearest chair. Turning to her, he clenched his teeth, trying for patience, despite knowing that his furrowed brow likely gave the appearance of anger.

"Penelope. Where are the Thorpes?" he gritted out.

"They have gone for the evening, as I was happy with a cold supper of leftover meat pie and cheese. Why?" Her voice was tentative.

He stomped to the sideboard and poured a double whisky, which he threw back.

"Good. I need you—now," he growled, pacing back to her with a second drink in hand.

"Now?" Her fingers gripped her skirt. "What of dinner?"

"'Tis that not what a good mistress is for? Whenever, wherever, at my behest?" He glowered as she flinched at his harsh words. His conscience twinged for hurting her, but he could not think, couldn't stop.

My mistress, nothing more. Mine to fuck, for now. The mantra thumped in his head.

"Certainly, my lord." She made a shallow curtsy. "How may I serve you?"

His brain stuttered on the specifics. He leaned against the back of a chair and glared from under lowered brows.

Penelope stepped forward, reaching for his drink. Taking a quick sip, she put it aside and nudged his waistcoat off his shoulders, loosening his cravat. Her hand trailed down his torso, firm with muscle and warm despite the cool evening air, and lingered on the waist of his trousers over his front placket. She glanced up at him through her lashes. "Shall I practice the skills you taught me the other evening, mayhap?"

His cock leaped to life under her hand as he

recalled his hand fisted in her hair, directing her through her first experiment with oral sex. He had already planned the next time. He'd talk her through where he most enjoyed her tongue, her mouth, her hands on him, the speed, the firmness, *the suction.* She had learned the basics of oral sex—*apparently with a cucumber*—but in one try, she had elevated it to an art form.

All those details disappeared in his frustration. He needed to vent that anger, to reassert his dominance, her submission. With a non-verbal growl, he nodded, shoving at her shoulders.

She grabbed a pillow off the chair and sank to her knees. Her hands made quick work of unfastening his trousers. As his cock jutted out, she reached for him with one hand to lick it as her other tugged his trousers down below his hips.

He growled again, holding her hands away. "Hands behind your back. I shall direct you. You are here to serve me, not play with me."

Penelope flinched again, and he swore, but with his cock at her hot wet lips, his brain had short-circuited to focus on his own pleasure—*no, needs.* He thrust into her mouth, holding the sides of her head with his hands. She could get out of his hold if she needed, but he expected compliance.

Keeping her still, his hips plunged in and out, making long, slow strokes, driving in as far as her throat allowed.

Without direction this time, she swallowed against him, making him surge forward another inch. Her eyes watered, but she remained still, hands linked at the base of her spine, gaze calm on his as he fucked her mouth.

Distracted by her lips distended around his glistening member, he eased back.

She sucked a breath in through her nose before his hips moved involuntarily, snapping forward again.

Another slow withdrawal, a gasp, and another shove forward.

He refocused on her face, and their gazes locked as he plundered, one hand gathering her hair into his fist to counter his thrusts. His other wiped tears away from one cheek, then the other before cupping her chin.

Damn me, she's beautiful. Dressed up, dressed down. Debating cooking techniques with that mouth or...this. I need more time. This fortnight has been the most fun I've had since my Grand Tour. 'Tis not the sex as much as the company, the sheer joy of being with her. Now, the clock is ticking down to the end of our time together, and there is naught I can do. And 'tis my life, blast it.

Then her tongue dragged along the underside of his cock, and his mind went blank.

"There, *yes*," he hissed.

Remorse tapped him on the metaphorical shoulder, taking the edge off his pleasure. His words and actions had been unduly harsh when Penelope had done nothing wrong.

"Dammit," he muttered. *I don't want to think right now. I want to enjoy every moment I have with this gorgeous creature who was made for me. But no, now I must woo some simpering miss who prefers discussing ribbons or the latest on-dit. My parents—much as I love them—had the chance to choose their mate regardless of rules. How can I be so powerless over my own future?*

The pendulum swung back to frustration.

Hauling her up, he kissed her hard before dragging her into the kitchen. Ignoring the sliced cheese on the counter, he bent her over the back of a straight chair that he dragged out from the table and placed her hands on the seat where he could see them. "Remain still."

Reaching behind him, he grabbed one of the long-handled spoons hanging next to the fireplace to stir soup pots. He drew it in front of him and saw it was metal, not the wooden one he had thought to use. He shrugged. In his current mental state, he did not much care. Flipping her dress and petticoat up, he ran his palm over her backside twice before planting his hand above it to hold her and her garments in place.

"My lord? Did I do it wrong?" Penelope whispered. "May I ask why I am being punished?"

"Because I can. You are mine to do with as I wish, are you not?" he roared.

She nodded mutely.

"I wish to spank you. Now hush and count the strokes for me." He completely ignored the fact that it was impossible to hush *and* count the strokes.

She subsided.

His arm swung up. At the last minute, he tempered his swing. He had not prepared her skin, and the implement he was using was metal. And she had done no wrong.

Smack!

"One, my lord."

Her bottom jiggled from the spoon's impact, and his blood surged as the red imprint formed on her skin. Aiming a smidgen below the mark on the same cheek, he set a pattern, a vertical line of spoon-shaped circles, before aiming for the other cheek. Then he moved to her thighs. Keeping the snap of his smacks fast, the fog in his brain cleared enough to check that she was not in pain or tightening up.

Vaguely, he heard her count reach eighteen, then nineteen, then twenty. He dropped the spoon, desperate to keep going but not wanting to scare her any further.

Ripping his trousers open again, he replaced his hand on her back when her face turned to him questioningly at the clatter of the dropped utensil. Seeing new tear tracks, he hesitated. His hand reached to cup her cheek, thumbing away her tears and sinking his thumb into the warmth of her mouth where his cock had been so recently.

He whispered, "Yes, cry for me, sweeting. Cry for us. I need to be inside you now."

He pulled his cock free as he shifted behind her and glanced around the kitchen for the cooking oil, assuming her body had not prepared for his.

Penelope widened her stance, opening for him in welcome.

Could she? Was she?

He brought a hand to her bottom cheek, rubbing the red marks and making her writhe and emit a low moan. His breath caught as his other hand dropped to slide his fingers through her folds.

Damn me, she's soaked. His cock surged, on the edge of erupting without so much as a touch.

"Good girl. You are ready for me, yes?"

He waited in wonderment as she nodded, still silent.

His anger sparked to life anew at the unfairness of his situation. *How can someone so perfect for me be so forbidden?*

Frustrated all over again, he palmed his shaft and sank home in one hard thrust. She grunted as his hips hit hers. The impact dragged the chair forward a few inches until he grabbed her hips to counter his movements. Wet slapping sounds filled the kitchen.

Her obvious arousal, despite so little effort and so much anger on his part, fed his ecstasy. Ah, he could love this woman given half a chance. But fate had put them in an impossible position.

He reached to tug her face around so he could check that he had not hurt her. Her lower lip was caught between her teeth, and he frowned again with concern.

"Pen? Are you hurting?" he groaned.

She shook her head. "I—"

At her negative gesture, he rammed home again, eliciting a gasp.

"—just did not—" Gasp. "—want to yell or moan and have you think you hurt me," she managed to get out, garnering a quick half-smile from him despite his dark mood.

Releasing her hair, he leaned over her, one hand braced on the chair to keep it from moving, his other hand slipping around to brush her nub of pleasure.

She shrieked and shoved her hips back against him, leaving no question that pleasure, not pain, had caused the yell.

"Be still. You will take it all."

The wet slapping sounds escalated as his speed increased, his finger flicking in time to his thrusts.

Every muscle in Penelope tightened for a long second before she cried out wordlessly, shuddering in bliss. A rush of moisture fell against his fingers as she quivered and convulsed around him.

Michael rode out his release through her contractions. After, he slumped over her, anger finally giving way to a strange happy-sadness at his remarkable…mistress.

****

After they cleaned up, they sat at the kitchen table to eat the cold fare with wine, watered down for her when Penelope demurred.

She had been more than a little concerned when he first arrived and even when he laid her over the kitchen chair. She had been warned she might not always enjoy the acts that a patron wished for, but if she maintained a calm and open mind, she could relax and endure without pain. This had appeared to be one such time for a moment in the kitchen, but then Michael seemed to pull his strike.

In the end, the spoon raised exactly the right amount of heat spreading through her, channeling her fear into a heightened sensitivity. So they had both enjoyed the interlude and his demeanor had calmed, even before the glass of wine.

Or mayhap that was due to the whisky he had gulped beforehand. Her lips curled in a small smile.

"My lord—Michael—may I ask what prompted your mood?"

"I received a letter from my parents. They are coming to Town earlier than planned. 'Tis good news for my father's health, but I dislike sneaking around. 'Tis why I never wanted to take a mistress. It was difficult enough stealing away to the club."

"Oh." *Oh.*

She wanted to cry even as she knew she should not

allow it. They would have much less time together starting very soon. No more long dinners, no more leisurely evenings in bed. She'd felt more like a friend than a paid companion, but that was likely to end now. And clearly he did not share her feelings of camaraderie. Hadn't he referenced that more than once when he'd arrived tonight?

All her instructors had warned her not to become complacent. She should have been wary of this all along, remembering that earls were not friends with working-class girls. They paid them for their time.

Do not fall in love. Leah had reminded her again when she brought her here.

"If even one word gets back to my mother, I shall be locked into a marriage contract and banished to the country at once."

"Could your parents do that?" she tilted her head.

"Mayhap. My father is an earl, after all, with all the requisite connections. I would not wish to test the theory in any event."

Despite wallowing in disappointment, Penelope forced herself to attend to business. "Our contract was for a year. I will be here as long as you want me, even if 'tis infrequent or at odd times. Unless…you would rather be safe and stop this?"

She offered fleeting mental thanks to Leah and the ladies that the agreement ensured her financial security for the year, even if he ended their association earlier.

"I cannot give you up." His eyes closed, and his head lolled back. A moment later, he righted his head and met her gaze. "Cooking was my way of relaxing when too many thoughts were circling my head, but without company or even an audience, 'twas lonely.

And I can't get enough of you. Sex with you is everything from fun to cathartic. How will I give you up to go to a marriage bed with some insipid miss?"

She flinched at the reference to her place in his life being temporary.

I must stop letting him hurt me. This was always going to be temporary.

However, she disliked being viewed as replaceable in any context. No longer hungry, she placed her fork on her plate.

Michael noticed. "God, I am sorry, sweeting. I am so frustrated, so angry at the situation. I simply meant…"

"I know," she whispered. She straightened her spine, recalling her role—to be accessible and amiable. She placed her hand over his on the table. "We've always had an end date. Let us try to enjoy whatever time we have, shall we?"

"You are right, but I did not think 'twould be this difficult. I should not have bought you, but gah, even now, the mere idea of you with someone else kills me," he gritted out. His hand clenched into a fist under hers, and his eyes flashed.

She remained silent, still smarting from the idea of him moving from her bed to a marriage bed. *He has no right to be angry at the idea of me in another relationship when he so casually references his intent to do the same. Unlike him, I do not have a choice.*

He rose to get another glass of wine.

Her throat worked against unshed tears. She had not expected to care this much, especially so soon. The more time they spent together, the more she valued hearing his thoughts. He had told her about Parliament and his concerns over the fairness of laws for the whole country, not limited to one area or one class of citizens. He had described what he loved about his childhood and his hopes for making his children's lives similarly happy. Hearing about the future of his personal life was distressing and depressing.

She had to use all her training to push aside her pain and follow him when he rose and held a hand out to lead her upstairs.

Chapter Nine

Given the new demands on his time, Michael informed her that his schedule of visits would change week by week, and it would rarely allow him to join her for dinner.

Within days, Penelope grew bored. Despite her frugal nature, she reviewed her finances and the accounts with the modiste and other shopkeepers and decided a few purchases were in order. First, fabric and lace so she could make a few pretty chemises for herself and to send back to the ladies in Peterborough to keep her hands and mind busy. Some books for self-entertainment. More spices from the shops in West London that she had not had in Peterborough. And last, because Michael had offered carte blanche, she splurged on a few fancier gowns and sexy undergarments for his visits.

A snide voice in her head whispered, *You'll want pretty things to attract your next benefactor, too.* She did her best to ignore it.

While shopping, she discovered the most precious find of all—a set of Nailsea hand-blown glass rolling pins from Bath. There were eight in all, from the narrow six-inch length for individual tarts to the largest at a three-inch diameter and over a foot long to roll pastry for multiple pies at once. Although she had always worked with one standard size, wooden rolling pin, these would elevate the appearance of her tarts and pies with their varied thicknesses and lengths.

She pined for them, until she asked the price of one. The cost would feed her stepfather and brother for a month. Having had lessons on financial management drilled into her, she could not part with that sum. With a sigh, she placed it back on the shelf.

Shopping completed, she sewed. She wrote letters and read. The first lace-edged chemise was finished for the ladies in her hometown who had helped her. She cooked, gardened, and wrote more letters. Alone in the house for so much of the time, she started to feel claustrophobic.

She had not yet bought a horse. Aside from the cost, she found that walking or hired hacks suited her fine, and Michael's horse was better hidden in the shared stable space. To get out of the house, she accompanied Mrs. Thorpe on outings to the market, chatting with her and the stall vendors for social interaction.

An idea occurred to her, and she sent a note 'round to Leah, asking her to visit.

When her friend arrived, Penelope ushered her in, almost bouncing in her excitement to have company. She had tea and pastries ready and quickly poured and passed.

After explaining her situation, she pouted. "I know this is a far easier life than I would have had in almost any other situation, but"—her voice rose to almost a wail—"I am bored!"

Leah laughed at her, shaking her head.

"I know, I know, I am whining. But I find it difficult to be a lady of leisure." Waving that subject aside, she asked, "So how have you been? And how are the theatre and the children's theatre group?"

"Now you sound like Rachel." Leah smiled. "Right, one at a time. I have been well—and busy. Following up with auctioned girls like you took some time, so now I am catching up with the theatre. The children are brilliant. We now have fourteen in the program, which is perfect for their productions. I am not sure any will ever be paid for their acting, but some of the behind-the-scenes skills they learn will be useful for them."

When Penelope had been debating attending the School of Enlightenment, she had asked the ladies if they regretted not marrying or having children. None of them did, and Leah informed her that there were many options to counsel children who needed it, should she wish to fill that void. Leah had set up a daytime theatre program with a few volunteer actors and actresses, for children who needed a warm place out of the cold. She considered them her family and maintained relationships with many of them long after their participation.

"Hmm. I suspect even rudimentary acting skills will be useful as well," Penelope commented, thinking of the night Michael had arrived angry. To both their pleasures, she had disguised her nerves and navigated through his anger until he calmed. She blushed when she caught Leah watching her.

"I hope you are not getting attached, Pen. You just finished explaining that Lord Slade is not coming to see you as often because he is looking for a wife," the older woman said bluntly, staring hard at her.

"I will be fine, thank you, Leah. I know the rules

and will abide by them." She managed not to wince but could not hold her mentor's gaze.

Penelope changed the subject, as the talk of the theatre had given her the opening she'd wanted. "Given all this free time, mayhap I could help you during the day at the theatre again, as I did before the auction? Mending and making costumes and the like?" *Please?*

"That is a lovely idea," Leah said. "However, you really ought to get Michael's approval. I know he's not involved in the details of management, but between him owning the theatre *and* being your benefactor, 'twould be prudent."

Penelope disagreed but nodded. "I shall discuss it with him tonight. Assuming all goes well, what time shall I be there tomorrow?"

Leah shook her head again, smiling at her friend's enthusiasm. "Let's say noon. Right, then. I am off now, so I can discuss with Pru what needs doing to ensure we can keep your seemingly-idle hands busy, young lady!"

The ladies exchanged cheek kisses in parting as Penelope saw her out.

****

I can't bloody well help it if Michael did not come by last night.

Penelope bustled out of the hired hack toward the side door of the theatre. *He would approve, surely? I am keeping busy, not to mention helping his business. Where's the harm? No one aside from the theatre manager will associate me with him, anyway.*

She had received a note from him that morning that said he could not visit again tonight as he had a social commitment. Pacing the house, waiting to ask his permission to ease Leah's sensibilities did not appeal.

Even the kitchen was less engaging when he was absent, which did not bode well for when he married and left her.

Knocking, she waited for someone to make their way to unlock the door. Once inside, she inquired about Prudence's or Leah's whereabouts and was directed to Pru's office.

"Good morning." Her voice betrayed her eagerness. "How can I help around here?"

"Ah, Penelope. Leah mentioned you'd be by. Gads, is it noon already?" Pru blew an errant lock of hair off her face with a huff as she dug through papers.

"I made a list somewhere. Dash it!" As she shuffled, she asked, "How have you been? Settling in? Arrangement going well?"

"Yes, thank you. Leah may have mentioned that Michael—Lord Slade—has many demands on his time, so I came to see if I could help you, as I enjoyed the work before. And of course, I can mayhap see a few theatre productions I might not otherwise."

"That sounds lovely, dear. Ah, never mind the list for now. See if they need costume repairs?" Pru threw up her hands at the mess on her desk.

Penelope nodded, thanked her, and withdrew. She skipped toward the costume room, ready to immerse herself in the roles represented by each outfit and prove useful with her needle.

Hours later, she had made progress on several costume repairs, caught up on gossip from the other crew members, mopped the stage and backstage floor, and helped the actors and actresses prepare their costume changes for the evening's show.

Pru bustled into the backstage area, looking

harried. "Who is back here?" she asked. "We are short two ticket-takers, dash it. One, we can live without, but down two, and the performance is liable to begin over an hour late." Frustrated, she huffed, blowing the same curl off her forehead for what was likely the hundredth time that day.

She ran her gaze over the room, scanning for crew who might help. Many of them were needed at the start of the production to ensure the show opened without a hitch. They could not afford to spend the hour beforehand out front.

Penelope stood from checking an actress's hem. "Mayhap I can help, Pru?" she ventured, unsure. "But I am not sure if that is acceptable to, er…"

Pru waved a hand, understanding her unfinished statement. She tilted her head. "Yes! Pen, 'tis time to put your acting skills to the test. Find a costume and wig, and no one will be the wiser." She hesitated. "You are sure you don't need to get home?"

She shook her head, wearing a rueful smile. "Not until later. It will be fine. I shall change right now and check in with the front manager to see where I am needed."

Finding a rather somber black gown that would do as a uniform, she pinned her hair and looked for a wig. The selection was slim on a show night, and in the end, she doctored her own hair with white powder mixed with ash, adding at least two decades to her appearance. Drawing in some fine lines on her face to match the hair, she nodded. She'd do. No one looked too closely at employees, and people tended to see what they wanted to see.

Especially nabobs.

Making her way to the lobby moments before the doors were set to open, she received her instructions. She found her position, grateful she had the gallery section for the patrons who had bought individual performance tickets rather than the boxes owned by the Ton or the season ticket holder seats in the orchestra. She was still more comfortable with people from similar backgrounds to hers, despite her training in the mannerisms and rules of the Ton.

She was checking tickets and pointing theatre-goers to seats when a familiar voice carried across the lobby. Her head jerked around.

"I hope you will enjoy this. 'Tis one of my favorite tales." Michael was with a short, curvaceous dishwater blonde who appeared to be about Penelope's age. Two older women and one man trailed behind them as they strolled toward the stairs to the boxes.

She stood, tickets in hand, frozen. After a long moment, the patron in front of her cleared his throat and tugged on the tickets for him and his wife. "Miss? May we go in?"

She looked down blindly, unable to see the tickets through tear-filled eyes. "Yes, yes, of course. Enjoy the show."

Grateful there was no one behind them, she abandoned her post. Signaling to the front manager that she was leaving, she lowered her head and slipped through a door to go backstage and change.

Slumping into a chair in the costume room, she sniffled. *Why did I think working at his theatre—any theatre—would be a good idea when, of course, attending a show would be one of his chosen ways to woo young misses to marriage? I'd give anything to be able to walk in on his arm for a performance, even as his mistress. But with his family's concerns, we cannot even do that.* After a long moment feeling sorry for herself, she sighed. *Now what? I am not sure I can sit in that house alone all day.*

She stood, stripping off the borrowed dress to return home. As she reached to hang it, her hand brushed a royal blue evening gown. A bag of accessories hung with it. An idea came to her. She assessed the risks. What would happen if she was caught? But no one in Town other than Michael and Leah and Pru knew her. She could not resist.

Mayhap if I see him courting these girls, I can better protect my heart. At the very least, I'll be forewarned when he accompanies the same one multiple times, so I can prepare for the end of our relationship. Her heart lurched.

An inner devil spoke up. *If he thinks to woo these girls then come to me every night, he can deal with a little teasing.*

She admonished herself. *He does not even know you are here. And besides, this is the nature of your role. You are the* mistress. *He needs a* wife. *Did you think he would marry you?*

Her hand crept forward to unhook the sapphire gown from the rack.

****

Michael paused on the last of the stairs leading to the boxes, admiring the crowd in the lobby gathered for refreshments during the intermission. He mentally cataloged the evening's profits before he remembered the young miss on his arm. She looked taken aback at the sea of patrons before them, straining back against his hold.

Milksop. He stifled a sigh and turned to her.

"Given the press, mayhap you and your mother would prefer to wait here for me? I can bring you lemonade, and then I'll return for my mother's." Patting her arm, he drew her to a less congested alcove.

"Oh my, yes, thank you, Lord Slade. I can't imagine how you will make your way through that throng," she answered in a high, breathy voice he had already begun to find annoying.

"I shall return in an inkling then." Turning, he tightened his shoulders and pressed forward, making slow but sure progress toward the refreshment bar. Catching the barkeeper's eye, he signaled for four drinks.

He ran into Robert on his way toward their favorite corner. His friend was there with a few of the other men from their club. They came to support Michael's theatre and avoid their mothers' ire by attending a performance before making their way to either White's or Sarah's.

With only a few feet between him and his drinks waiting, Michael relaxed his shoulders, then jolted in shock as an older woman in blue all but leapt in front of him.

Grabbing one of the lemonades, she tossed it back before snatching up the other one and turning. Given the width of her hips, her dress swept his legs as she turned, her overly painted eyes and rouged lips pursing as she focused on the second beverage. She surged forward, intent on the stolen drink. Then, realizing Michael was there, she stepped to the side to pass him as he sidestepped in the same direction. Almost slamming into him, she glanced up, then down again, leaving him looking at powdered gray hair.

His nose twitched, catching a scent he could not place.

"Excuse me, madame." He sketched a shallow bow. "I was, ahem, fetching some lemonades."

She reached out, clutching his sleeve, and moaned.

"Ah…" Swaying, she appeared on the verge of fainting, and he gallantly laid his other hand over hers.

"Do you need help back to your seat then, madame?" he asked, raising his head to search for a staff member.

Her gaze flashed up, but when he glanced around for someone to step in, she leaned more heavily against him.

"Mmm, no. Be all right in a moment," she semi-slurred in a low tone.

He grunted as her weight shifted onto him, although he was surprised she was not heavier, given her size.

Do I smell ginger? Or is it that Pen is always in the back of my mind?

He nodded to Robert to grab the fresh lemonades the bartender had put out for them and braced to support the strange woman until she gained her footing.

After a long moment, she drew upright. "Thank you, dear boy. Such a lovely young man. You'll make someone an excellent husband one day." She patted his arm and pulled away. "Now, where was I sitting?" she muttered, moving past him.

Sniffing surreptitiously one more time for the spice, he spun back to Robert. His buttock stung from a sharp pinch. Shocked, he gave a startled yelp, and his hips jolted forward.

Robert, turning back to pass him two lemonades, jerked his head back and frowned in confusion, arching a brow in question.

Whipping his head around, he started after the woman.

She was sailing serenely through the crowd with her filched lemonade, the hand that had pinched him hidden in her skirts.

He wasn't entirely sure what he would do if he caught her.

When Robert called to him, "What was that about?" he stopped. His gaze went past the strange woman to his guest. With a sigh, he turned back to his friend.

"She pinched me," he gritted in a whisper between his teeth.

"What? Who?" Robert asked. "You mean the old dame in blue? Seriously? That's rich, man!" Throwing his head back, he laughed long and loud.

Michael shook his head, delivered the lemonade to the ladies in his charge, and kept watch, searching the crowd for a glimpse of sapphire. He missed part of the second act as his gaze roamed the darkened theatre looking for bright blue. Unable to find the woman, he swore silently and refocused on the performance, pushing the strange lady out of his thoughts.

****

Michael's cronies reconvened at White's after Parliamentary sessions. While much of this was to review bills they wished to push through Commons and then Lords, he also used the time to catch up with Evan and Robert.

Like him, Robert was not directly involved in

Parliament. Evan, though, had inherited his title while on their Grand Tour and had to cut his trip short. The rest of Michael's and Robert's tour was decidedly less adventurous, albeit no less enjoyable.

Finding his friends in their favorite seating area, he slumped into a club chair and sighed. Robert sent him a sidelong glance before continuing his tale of the prior evening at the theatre to Evan.

"The woman turns, all but drooling in the second lemonade, and runs headlong into our friend here. We assumed she was drunk or overcome at the press of the crowd, but now I think she was faking."

"Why?" Bags frowned in confusion.

"She pinched his bum! I'll tell you. *All* the ladies flock to him."

"She did not. The devil you say." Bags laughed. "Excellent. Well done, chap. How old was she?"

"What, forty if she was a day, I'd say. Slade?" Robert turned to him.

"Dunno. Don't care, either." He glared at them both for a full second before he broke into a grin. "Never been so shocked in my life."

"Clearly, I did not provide enough of a variety of experiences on our Tour," Evan mock grumbled.

They all chuckled before Michael sighed again, dropping his head into his hand.

"Why so down? Not enough younger women pinching your bum?" Evan nudged Michael's leg with his knee.

"'Tis the same as always. The whole marriage mart pretense. The 'drab' young women." His friends had learned his mother's favorite term by the second quarter at university. Evan had suggested new adventures almost weekly. As quiet as Robert was, Michael had been surprised at how happy he was to follow Evan into mischief. When he joined Evan in cajoling Michael into a new foray, Michael capitulated. But he explained how heartbroken his parents would be if he was written up and made them go over their plans for each caper several times to ensure it was foolproof.

"There are some benefits to bearing the title, I suppose." Evan leaned back, lacing his hands behind his head. "As long as I keep providing for the extended family and servants, they leave me alone. Although one cousin is starting to lick his lips given my continued unmarried state." He lowered his arms and leaned forward, elbows on knees. "Not ready to be leg-shackled?"

Michael scowled. "Can you blame me? Between Sarah's place, your routs in the off-season, and now Penelope, why would I want to settle for some insipid miss?"

Robert chewed his lip, looking pensive. "You were always complacent about your wild days coming to an end at some point. Given that, I must ask, is it simply the timing, or is it Penelope?"

Evan cocked his head. "Ah, yes, the lovely Pen. I can still take her off your hands, you know, buy out your contract."

Michael growled, despite both his friends watching him closely.

"Penelope—"

"Oh dear, 'tis Penelope—"

Evan and Robert glanced at each other and spoke in unison, then looked back at him, grinning.

"You'll not have her. Even after I marry. I couldn't

bear it." He firmed his lips, shocked at his own words.

I've never been the jealous type before. Hell, I've shared a woman with Bags a time or two in our wild days. And how is it fair to declare her off-limits even as I talk of marrying someone else? But he could not see her with another man. Ever. 'Twas bad enough he could not keep her.

Evan shook his head. "You're in deep. You'd best be very careful. Mama Mansfield will not handle news of a mistress well."

Michael groaned long and low. "I know, I know. I wouldn't hurt my mother for the world, but Penelope is a tad addictive, I'm afraid. I need more time with her. It did not help that my parents arrived a sennight earlier than I had hoped." Knowing the issue was greater than that, he added, "She makes the 'drab' girls look even more drab." He sighed again.

"I say, you sound like a lovesick gel. Stop sighing, go fuck her for a couple more weeks and get over her, old chap." Evan shook his shoulder and grinned.

Michael sat up and schooled his features to hide his frustration at his situation. He could not afford to be perceived as lovesick, not with his parents in Town.

I can't be lovesick at all. I need to focus on a betrothal and, yes, get as much time with Penelope as possible whilst I can.

Chapter Ten

Penelope received a note that Michael planned to join her for midday Sunday dinner, and she planned an enticing menu with Mrs. Thorpe's help.

A letter from David had arrived the day before. Her family missed her, and she recalled her promise to be home for Matthew's birthday. It made her homesick, and when she needed a distraction, she baked or gardened. So she had run out to the market to see what fruit was available and spied hothouse cherries. While not as good as those she'd find next month, she could make do with added sugar as needed for cherry tarts.

After they finished preparing the meal, she dismissed the Thorpes to enjoy their own Sunday afternoon roast. She put the cherry tarts in the oven with the potatoes but waited on the fish, which she would serve with dark peppery greens, and wandered out to the garden.

Michael found her kneeling on a blanket to protect her dress, weeding. He tugged her up for a kiss.

"How have you been, my lord?"

"Busy. Too busy, dash it all. I missed you," he growled, holding her against him.

"And I missed you as well," she murmured, placing her lips on his in a fleeting kiss.

Groaning again, he gripped her tighter. "Gah, these girls my mother introduces me to, they prattle about the stupidest things. Who they saw at the ice shop, the latest on-dits, how paltry their pin money from their papa is…"

Bitterness rose in Penelope.

These young gels ain't even buying their own bloody hair ribbons, much less clothes and shoes and food. Yet they still manage to waste their parents' money on fripperies. And Michael comes to me to natter about them? How can he care about me and discuss girls he is wooing? 'Tain't fair.

Gathering her thoughts, she put her melancholy aside. Her lessons had taught her to relax her patron, make him forget his frustration at having to court a prospective wife. "Dinner will be ready soon. Would you like a drink?"

"I can come to the kitchen whilst you finish, even if I was unable to arrive early enough to help this time." He gestured for her to precede him inside.

He dragged a chair out from the center table and slouched in it.

She slid the pan with the fish onto a grate over the fire, checked the oven, then turned, maintaining a serene expression, as a courtesan should, even as she continued to seethe at the injustice. She hoped her silent swearing would dispel her frustration.

"Hmm, I can't say I ever had an allowance from my papa." She referenced his lament with a mock pout. "My only complaint with you is how little I see you."

His expression changed from even more irritated at "complaint" to happy as he digested her statement. His shoulders relaxed, as she'd intended. Shifting his arm to clutch her closer, he whispered into her hair, "'Tis *my* biggest gripe as well."

Penelope reflected on her foray into the world of acting. Had it left a lasting impression? "So, my lord— Michael. How was the theatre?" she asked with an impish smile, trailing a hand down his waistcoat.

"Excellent, as always. They are doing a remarkable job with this production. Scenery, costumes, not only the acting."

"Costumes, eh? Do you ever dress in costume to escape?" she asked, watching him closely.

"No." He shook his head, smiling. "Honestly, until recently, I had plenty of flexibility." His lips twisted as he seemed to consider it further. "One can hardly get more free than an earl's heir—all the benefits, none of the responsibility as yet."

While he was oversimplifying, he was right. He'd always have far more freedom than she would, aside from choosing who to marry.

And for that reason, despite her misgivings at spying on him, she decided to continue her little charades in costume. With so fewer choices, she must be prepared for the end of their relationship, and knowledge was power. Not only did she need to protect her heart, she needed to find a new home.

****

Barbara Slade, Countess of Mansfield, smiled at her son over dinner at the Mansfields' London home. "Michael, I am happy to see you are getting into the spirit of finding a wife."

He shuffled his hands over the silverware, then caught himself. Fidgeting was one of his tells. When he was prevaricating as a child, his mother had noted his restless hand movements. "Thank you, Mama. Now, can you help? Please?"

"Well, dear, you know you should not send anything more than flowers after only one dance at a ball and one evening at the theatre. 'Tis too soon."

"I know, Mama. But I wish to think ahead. And gifts beyond flowers take a little more time and effort."

"Right, then. An appropriate gift for a young lady." She tilted her head, finger to chin, ruminating.

"Jewelry?"

"Certainly not." Her tone was tart. "You buy jewelry for a wife. Or, well…" His mother firmed her lips and repeated, "For a wife."

"What, then?"

"The point is that it depends on the lady. What are her interests? Passions?"

Could he buy Penelope a new bread peel for the bedroom? But a gift was meant to be for the recipient. A paddle for the bedroom was for him as much as her.

Realizing his mother was waiting for a response, he could not say, "baking." Few if any members of the Ton baked as a pastime.

"What if I do not know?"

"Is there someone close to her that you can ask? A mutual friend? A sibling or parent?"

Ah, Mrs. Thorpe. Perfect.

"Yes, Mama. I shall do that. But only when I have settled more on a particular young lady. I shall be 'drab' at all times, I promise." Ignoring his mother's grimace at his term for her guidance, he rose, kissed her cheek, and excused himself to head to White's to meet Bags and Robert.

****

Penelope stared at another note from Michael indicating another theatre outing that evening. He

139

would visit the following night, barring any major mishaps. She shrugged. At least she had friends and work to keep her busy.

She headed to the theatre at midday to brush out costumes and check the props and curtains for needed repairs. The backstage crew worked as a team, and she had already made friends, so she chatted with people throughout the building. The day flew by.

Stepping out the side door for a breath of fresh air, a cup of tea in hand, she mulled her choices as she watched the sky darken. She could either snack from the cold buffet for the cast and crew as her dinner or head home.

Trying to ignore the fact that Michael would be arriving in less than two hours, she planned to depart. She had not asked the Thorpes to prepare anything for her dinner, but there were plenty of cold tidbits to snack on there.

She gulped the last of her tea and resolved to return the cup to the common room backstage and be on her way. After placing the cup in the bucket for used dishes, she wandered toward the front lobby to see if anyone had arrived yet. Mayhap she would even leave that way. Nonchalantly, she meandered toward the lobby door, nodding to the figures in black hovering to open the doors and start accepting tickets. She cracked the door to peek out. There were a few theatre-goers already milling about, the return guests chatting to Pru, the neophytes exclaiming over the artwork on the walls.

Michael had not yet arrived. She could dawdle for a short time without a confrontation. Strolling through the seating area and backstage again, she ended up in front of the costume closet. She ducked in before her conscience could censure her.

Her hands skimmed over the hanging costumes. There was the cerulean dress she had borrowed the other night and a few black dresses for the parts of widows that ticket takers and ushers also used as needed. Green, red, so many bold colors. A queen's costume, a fairy… Then she came to the rack of menswear.

She ran her gaze over the selection and could not resist when her gaze landed on a young gentleman's silver and gold brocade waistcoat.

Two hours later, after grazing at the buffet and biding her time, Penelope borrowed one of the actors' dressing rooms and makeup. She darkened her face, neck, and hands with a foundation, then used a makeup brush to dot ashes on her cheeks and around her mouth to create a five o'clock shadow. After she'd pinned up her hair, she donned a dark wig of Brummel-style curls, checked for wisps of her own hair, and skipped back to the costume closet.

Refusing to dwell on the ramifications if she was caught by Pru or Leah, or, worse, Michael, she dressed. She'd found a semi-clean white lawn shirt, gold breeches, platform shoes with gold buckles and heels designed to add height, and a rose velvet topcoat to go over the silver and gold brocade vest. She withdrew a ginger hard candy from a pocket of her discarded gown and tucked it in one side of her mouth before leaving the room.

Venturing out at intermission when the theatre had half-emptied into the lobby, she made her way up the aisle toward the back of the seat rows, surreptitiously eyeing the owner's box to see if it had been vacated.

Seeing only an older couple there, she hurried her pace, trying to take longer strides like a man. Swinging her arms higher, she got into character and marched into the lobby toward the bar. The crowd was almost a wall, but that never seemed to deter men, especially gentlemen of the Ton. She waded in, aiming for the same spot where she had run into Michael last time.

She shook her head as the crowd made way for her. *So annoyingly unfair.* She hoped her scowl aided her ruse. At the bar, she did a quick check of the patrons nearby, then leaned her forearm flat on the bar, poking her head forward to catch the barkeep's eye.

Snatching up the lemonade he set in front of her, she turned in place. She swept her gaze quickly down her front to ensure her bound breasts did not show. With the layers of brocade and velvet and frothy cravat, she was fine, albeit fancy for a man. But that was the idea.

Out of the corner of her eye, she caught Michael's tall form approaching, resplendent in a navy topcoat, a teal waistcoat peeking out. Shifting a few inches to her right, she ensured she was in his path as she pretended she was with the family group in the corner. He brushed past her, causing a shiver of awareness. As he waited for his lemonade, she turned toward him, unable to resist interacting with him.

Keeping her face at an angle to him and deepening her voice as much as possible, she said, "Bit of a crush, eh? Glad I nabbed mine early."

Michael glanced at her and sniffed as she raised her glass.

"Good job, that. But—" He gestured as two lemonades were placed in front of him. "—thankfully, I know the owner." Lifting one, he smiled, sniffing again.

"Hmm, lucky you." Penelope leaned closer, dropping her free hand to skim his hip, jostling her shoulders as though she had been pushed by someone in the crowd shifting.

Michael tried to jump back, but the bartop was right behind him.

She bowed, reaching down to pick up a handkerchief she had furtively dropped as she turned. As she bent straight-legged, she again fumbled as though bumped. Her hand with the handkerchief grabbed his boot before trailing up the inside of his leg. Straightening one vertebra at a time, she kept her gaze lowered, tugging on her rose velvet coat.

Michael sucked in a sharp breath.

"My pardon, my lord. I seem to have lost my balance." She leaned in with an arched brow and a small smile. "You're a very handsome man, my lord. I'll be in the alley there." She nodded toward a side door. "If you care to join me for a bit of…fresh air."

Shocked, Michael declined, his voice harsh. "You— I say, you are very much mistaken. Now please excuse me."

Rushing off to his party, he did not see Penelope's shoulders shake with suppressed laughter.

****

Michael alternated between outrage at the flamboyant youth's boldness, questioning if he'd imagined the whiff of ginger he'd smelled, and doubting the whole thing had actually happened. He missed the entire last act and simply hummed in agreement when his party exclaimed over the performance in the carriage.

He shook his head once to clear it. *What sort of clientele are theatre performances attracting these days? First, it was the older lady, now a young man. Are my patrons experiencing similar advances? I am not that attractive!*

He snorted at the conceited thought, earning a questioning look from his mother. Staring out the window, he sighed in relief to see they were almost to his guests' home.

After handing the ladies out and seeing them to their door, then doing the same for his mother at the family home, he paused on the carriage running board, calling up to the coachman. "Change of plans. Take me to Miss Wood's house, please."

After the strange man's touch, intermingled with the scent of ginger, he needed to bury himself in all that was Penelope. Her lovely ebony hair, her delicate smooth skin, and voluptuous breasts, her delicious scent that often had a slight overlay of flour with the spice, the warmth of her mouth and of her. He shifted on the seat, adjusting his cock as it hardened in anticipation.

The streets were dark in the residential neighborhoods as he traveled from Mayfair to Bloomsbury where Penelope's little house sat. Her house, too, was dark as they drew up. He told his coachman to return at dawn and strode to the door, key in hand.

While he planned to wake her, he'd rather it was not to the sound of footsteps on the stairs, which could alarm her. So after toeing off his evening shoes, he held them as he ran up the stairs and eased her bedroom door open.

Standing over her, he was content to watch her

sleep for a moment. In a sheer nightrail that was twisted around her hips, she lay on her stomach tilted away from him, left hand tucked under her pillow, left leg bent.

Delicious. And she's been amenable enough to provide easy access.

Tossing the bedclothes aside, he smoothed his hand up her right leg closest to him, bunching her nightrail in front of his hand as he went. When his hand slid over her bottom and hip, she shifted her head, moaned, then settled again as he held still.

Adding his left hand, he tugged the nightrail higher, reaching under for the side of her breast. He pressed kisses along her spine, ending at the dimples a little above her cheeks. As he spread more kisses over her bottom, he yanked off his cravat, undid his shirt, and unlaced his breeches. Seeing her eyelids flutter, he stood to hurriedly shuck his remaining clothes.

Edging onto the bed, he lay against her, his shaft nestled between her round cheeks. Leaning on his right side, his left hand slid in front of him and between her thighs to stroke lightly.

Penelope twitched, inching her left leg higher.

Ah, even in sleep, she trusts that she knows my touch. A rush of moisture slicked his fingers, allowing them to easily circle her hardened nub. His teeth grazed her shoulder as he leaned over her, pressing against every part of her he could reach.

As her hips pushed back, he glided his hand again to her breast peeking from under her arm and raised to his elbows, hips settling on hers. Nudging his cock against her, he couldn't wait. She was wet enough for entry, even if she was not quite awake.

Slipping in, he paused halfway inside, flexed his hips back an inch, then slid home in one smooth arch.

"Mmm, Michael?" Her voice was slurred with sleep.

"Ah, no. Were you expecting him?" he teased as he allowed her a moment to wake further.

Her eyes flashed to him with a grin before she relaxed back onto the pillow and sighed. "You'll do."

He rose up and slapped her once on the side of her thigh.

She yelped and blinked. More awake now, she moaned and levered against him. "Please, my lord, I didn't mean to interrupt. Pray continue." She shifted her hips from side to side, eliciting a gasp from him.

Shoving into her, he spread her legs with his thighs as he drew himself, then her, up on hands and knees. Leaning over her, he grabbed a breast and pinched her nipple as she favored, using his other hand on the bed to keep his weight off her.

Thrusting, thrusting, he wanted to touch her sensitive bundle of nerves but wasn't willing to release her delectable breast.

"Touch yourself," he whispered, lust filling his voice with gravel.

Her hand lifted off the bed to rub against his cock and gather moisture, causing his hips to flex in a sudden sharp arch. She shivered as her finger found the right spot to circle.

His hips pumped harder, smacking sounds loud in the stillness of the late night, faster. He ground out, "Come with me, Pen, please."

She arched, crying out, and swiveled her hips in a quick counter rhythm to his, pounding back into him equally hard and fast before she tightened and quivered and rippled around him. Unable to stand it any longer, he erupted in her with a growl that sounded suspiciously like, "Mine!"

She collapsed forward, bringing him with her.

He skimmed his hand down her side, then levered over her to the open side of the bed and gathered her close. "Thank you, sweeting. I apologize for the late hour."

"'Twas my pleasure," she purred, even as sleep took her back under.

****

Penelope yawned and rolled over. Looking around at the empty room, she vaguely recalled Michael rising in the dark to go to his family's Town residence. She hated the secrecy, but she could not regret his late-night visit, and she understood subterfuge was sometimes part of a courtesan's situation.

She would see him this evening anyway. Yawning, she made her way downstairs for a cup of tea and to start menu planning.

By midday, she had conferred with Mrs. Thorpe and was making lemon crème tarts for dessert when a knock sounded. As she wiped her hands, Mr. Thorpe entered the kitchen with a package.

"Delivery for you, Miss Penelope," he said, placing it carefully on the table. "They said it was fragile."

"Did they say who it was from?" she asked as she examined the gift, contemplating how to open it without breaking whatever was inside. It was wrapped tight in a pretty basket inside the satchel.

"No, Miss."

"Oh, there's a card." She drew it out from where it

was folded along the side of the oval basket.

Dear Pen,

I didn't know which size was most useful, so I bought the set. I hope you like them. Mayhap you will make me something wickedly delicious with them.

Yours, Michael

"Well, that is mysterious." She selected the longest, thickest of the items. All were cylindrical, with the biggest over a foot long and thick, stepping down in size to about six inches long and narrower. They were each wrapped in layers of soft cloth.

Laying the first item on the table, she untucked the ends of the cloth and slowly rolled the baton shape out. As it cleared the cloth, she gasped. "Oh my gosh! He—but—all eight? Oh my, the cost! Oh, 'tis lovely, but—eight? I…"

She wrung her hands in a horrified mix of excitement at the items and agony at the cost. A Nailsea glass rolling pin from Bath was beyond expensive. She had mentioned them to Mrs. Thorpe when she returned from her shopping excursion, complaining the one she admired was too dear. And he had bought the *set*?

Mrs. Thorpe sidled over, her hand hovering over the rolling pin approximately the same size as the wooden one Penelope used most. "May I, Miss?"

"Oh, yes, of course."

"This is beautiful. Hand blown, with the different colored decorative bits in it. Is this the one you saw the other day in the shop? And 'tis a whole set here, you say?"

"Yes, well, for individual tarts, 'tis so much easier with the smaller pin. And then depending on the thickness of the pastry…" Penelope wrung her hands again.

"Miss, if you don't mind me saying…" Mrs. Thorpe hesitated as she handed the kitchen utensil back.

Penelope nodded, unable to tear her gaze from the gorgeous glass rod she held.

"A piece of jewelry would likely cost more than this set, would it not?" the housekeeper asked, tilting her head.

"Er, I do not actually know. Either way, 'tis a ridiculous sum of money."

"You let his lordship worry about that, Miss. He obviously thought you would like this better than jewelry." The housekeeper cocked her head at Penelope, her brows raised. "Do you?"

"Gor, yes." Her working-class vernacular slipped out in her excitement. "I read about these a year or so back when I was working at the theatre. I scoured London on my mornings off to merely look at one or touch one in a shop. When I did, I almost could not put it down, but 'twas more of a dream than something I expected to own." She shook her head.

"Well, if you like the pins better than jewelry," Mrs. Thorpe retorted, ignoring the last of her response, "and he wished to buy you something nice and chose such a suitable gift, you should accept it gracefully and say thank you."

Reward good behavior, so it happens again. Was the gift to reward her for her companionship when she'd been torturing him at the theatre intermissions? She might need to rethink how she amused herself in her spare time.

With shock, she counted the days. She'd only known Michael for a few sennights. Yet despite his schedule and their limited time together, he was rapidly becoming the center of her world. Her days were spent waiting to see him, no matter what she did to pass the time. And the nights he visited were spent learning what she could about him and reveling in his attention. It seemed he had also listened to her to find such a thoughtful gift.

How am I supposed to keep my distance when he is so bloody perfect? He is kind and caring and downright masterful in bed—and in the kitchen and— She snickered before sobering. *He is* not *perfect. He spends many evenings searching for another woman to be his wife.*

Whatever the reason for his gift, she, too, needed to reward good behavior.

Chapter Eleven

When Michael arrived, Penelope had their evening meal ready and the little dining room table set. She poured drinks and brought out dinner. Sitting, she raised her glass with a huge smile. "Thank you for the beautiful rolling pins, Michael. They are lovely, beyond anything I could imagine owning. I hope you will enjoy the dessert I made with them."

"Ah, they are helpful, then? I hoped they would be." He smiled, clearly happy he'd succeeded in pleasing her.

"My lord, you've given me more than enough. I do not need fancy objects. But I admit they are helpful and brighten up the kitchen with color. They are absolutely gorgeous."

"I look forward to dessert." He leered at her.

She chuckled before changing the subject. "If I may ask, what prompted your late-night visit?"

"Eh. The theatre crowd has grown a tad wild. In contrast, the young lady I attended with last night was another empty-headed chit. I lost patience with waiting to see you." He shrugged one shoulder up.

"Wild, my lord?" She couldn't resist asking, pleased with his response. She had managed to discomfit him with her costume. More importantly, his banal dismissal of his escort offered her hope that their time together would not be over too soon.

"It seems like a more varied group? I can't say exactly." He flipped one hand on the table.

She wondered if he realized he was rubbing his thigh where the strange young man had touched and permitted herself a small smile. She'd also noticed that he twiddled his fingers when he was uncomfortable. Having decided not to tease Michael further, she felt no need to confess her previous disguises, but she realized she had not told him about her daytime hours at the theatre.

"My lord, er, Michael. As you are busier these days, I asked Leah if the theatre needed assistance. I liked working there, and I cannot shop or bake every day. I've been spending afternoons there helping when you have other plans. I hope that is acceptable?"

"Do you need money for something?" He frowned, looking confused.

She understood why he'd ask, given their conversation early on about saving. And 'twas not as though she wore a different frock every time he visited.

"No. I mean, Leah insisted on paying me, but 'tis more for the company and the…well, the theatrics of it. I have friends in the cast and crew. Actors are some of the most honest, open-minded people I have met in London. And it does give me more to send home to my stepfather and half-brother whilst still saving for my own future."

He nodded. "Ah, I understand. And thank you. The theatre can always use an extra pair of loving hands. I suppose I know where to find you if I have a free hour or two. I'll even be sure to wear dirty boots in the hope of having a reason to spank you." He winked.

"Ha! As though you need a reason," she said,

wrinkling her nose at him.

"Oh? Excellent," he retorted, reaching for her.

"Now? Oh no, Michael, the dessert— I so want to show you what I made for you." Penelope leaned away, trying to evade him.

He mock-glared at her. "You dare tell me no? Later, then, but it will be a higher count, especially after the no."

"Yes, my lord," she replied with a sassy pout. "If it pleases you. Later." She couldn't stop her grin though, not minding the idea of a longer spanking at all. "If you'll pardon me for a moment, I will run and get us dessert. I had the Thorpes retire after serving the main course." She braced her hands on the table, tacitly requesting permission to excuse herself. "You may desire sherry to go with the dessert, as 'tis sweet."

At his nod, she rose and gestured to the liquor cabinet as she exited.

Returning a moment later with two lemon crème tartlets, she saw he'd cleared the plates and poured only one sherry. He took a sip before reaching for the plates and moving them to the sideboard.

Handing her the glass, he gestured for her to sip as he backed her up to the table.

As she swallowed, he reclaimed the glass and placed it blindly behind him on the cabinet, then turned her. After unlacing her dress, he shoved it off her shoulders. Clad only in a chemise and a single petticoat, she shivered in response as his hands skimmed her skin.

His hands at her waist turned her back around. He drew the chemise up and off and helped her onto the table. Pressing a palm between her breasts, he urged, "Lay back."

Penelope felt the cool wood against her back, pebbling her nipples as her hair fanned around her. She watched him, torn between wondering where he'd take their play next and wanting the heat of his body against hers, his cock in her.

He stood over her, plate and fork in hand. Cutting into the tart, he hummed in pleasure as he chewed the morsel. "This is delicious. Excellent pastry, sweeting, and beautiful artistry along the edge. However, it will taste even better on you."

He set the plate on the table next to her, dipped a finger into the lemon crème, and spread it across her smile.

"Ah! No stealing my dessert," he exclaimed when her tongue darted out.

Mmm, that turned out well. I hope he's going to share.

Scooping more, he slathered it on one nipple, then repeated the process with her other breast and surveyed her.

Well, then. She could live without a tart if he'd eat both off her. She smiled.

"A tasty-looking morsel, to be sure." He untied her petticoat, skimmed it down her legs, and tossed it aside. Another fingerful and he hovered it over her body.

Eager to be decorated with the velvety concoction as a guide for his tongue to follow, she inched her legs apart.

Michael's knee wedged between hers, propping her thighs open even farther.

"Hmm, where will this taste best? What can I lick and lick?"

Her skin heated, and her own cream pooled in her

nether lips. She shivered again, the fine hairs on her skin rising at the vision of his tongue passing over her sensitive flesh. She recalled the strawberries he'd brought on one of his first visits. Her nipples poked through the lemon crème, hard points calling for his attention.

His clean hand reached to part her folds. A fingerful of lemony sweetness followed and was dabbed on her raised bundle of nerves.

She jerked with the coldness of the crème against her hot flesh, the silkiness of it, and the firmness of his finger behind that softness. 'Twas quite different than the texture of the berries. Where they'd been solid bits that his tongue and even teeth had had to ferret out, this was smooth and buttery, easing his path. Her hips rose, trying to follow his finger as it withdrew to be inserted into his mouth. They both moaned, then she moaned a second time as the digit emerged wet and shiny.

Finally, he leaned over her and licked the sweet sticky custard off her, swirling his tongue on her lips, then nipples. He circled and circled to ensure he had cleaned off every bit before dropping to his knees. His hands spanned her hips, and his thumbs held her nether lips open. He dove his face into her.

Her back arched as she cried out wordlessly.

His tongue teased, and she craved more pressure. Then, when his nose and lips and tongue all pressed against her, the sensations were almost too much. Yet still, she wanted more. Every lick and rub against her sensitive flesh tortured her and took her higher. Her inner walls contracted, wanting his cock. Sparks ran over her flesh like oil spatters out of a hot pan, so intense they felt like pinpricks.

Lifting her hands to his hair, Penelope attempted coherence. "Michael, please!"

"Please what? I am enjoying this delicious dessert you were proud of. I could eat this every night." His breath fanned the flames of her desire as he spoke against her hot wet flesh.

"Please, enough. I need you." She'd had enough teasing. She needed him to fill her—her body, her mind, her—

No. She refused to finish that thought. She tugged at him again.

"Oh, no. See? Two can play that game. You refused me earlier. Now 'tis my turn to tell you no." His tongue pushed into her nub, flicking around it to capture the last of the lemony dessert.

She panted, clutching fistfuls of his hair. *Oh yes, there.* Her body tightened, on the edge of ecstasy, and she pushed her hips against his face. The sparks burst into flame, her fingers and toes burning with the heat pulsing out from her center.

Untangling his mane from her hands, he shot upright.

She whined at his withdrawal. Appalled at hearing her own high-pitched cry, she shook her head to clear it, licked her lips, and waited for him to unbutton his breeches to take her.

Instead, he sat down in his chair, retrieved his remaining bit of tart, and finished it. "Up and over my knees. You are due a spanking, if I recall."

What? No, not when I am so close.

"But—but, oh my." She bit her lip, her hand creeping toward her mons. She only needed a flick.

"Don't you dare. Get over here. You may not touch

yourself."

Rising, she struggled off the table and over his knees, realizing he was still fully clothed and this had been his game all along. Despite her frustration, she was suddenly intrigued as to where he'd take the game. His choices had always resulted in more pleasure than she could have imagined. She sighed, deciding to trust him and play along.

"I am sorry, my lord," she said, hoping to lighten her punishment.

"For what?" Michael replied, his voice calm. He ran his hand over her bottom, sparking her nerve endings.

"Er…" She needed a minute. It was an effort to think through the throbbing of blood in all the places he had licked. "For…for being flippant about the spanking," she managed as his hand came down hard for the first slap.

"And?" he prompted.

"And, eeee!" She flinched as the second strike hit. "And telling you no. I'm sorry!" she squeaked out, even as the third smack burned.

"Good, my girl. Now sit still for a few more, and no more squealing."

Thwack! Thwack! Thwack!

Penelope panted through the stings. Her bottom smarted, and three in rapid succession gave her no time to process them. But he was an expert at pacing these for her to ride that edge.

A hand smoothed over her flesh, and she sagged a bit, only to have more smacks rain down on her thighs and the crease of her bottom. Spreading her legs, she sank into the hot stinging slaps, letting the heat course through her and center in the hot throbbing button between her legs. Arching, she drove her bottom toward him, begging for more attention, preferring fingers rather than spanks.

Michael's hand returned to soothe her fiery flesh, and she sighed in delight. Fingers probed, gathering wetness and then circling her pleasure point, over and over, building her to the edge before stopping abruptly. Again.

She gritted her teeth, mentally alternating between chastising him then herself to patience. Her world tilted, and she grabbed him to anchor herself. He leaned back in the dining chair and sat her astride him.

"Unlace me," he said, his tone guttural with lust. His hands kept a firm hold on her so she could have space to reach the fall of his breeches.

She wrenched them open and drew out his cock. Stroking it, she sucked in air, shifting in urgency.

He dragged her up, her toes scraping the rug in an effort to brace herself, and gripped his shaft to center the tip on her opening. As soon as her wetness touched him, he glided it through and up, thrusting into her as he yanked her down roughly.

She nearly went over just from the one thrust. Her inner muscles clamped around him as though not wanting to let him pull out. She clenched her teeth and closed her eyes, her hunger for his mastery overriding her wish for an orgasm.

His hands returned to her hips, and he braced against the chair, driving them both in counterpoint, setting a fast and hard rhythm.

She clutched his cloth-covered shoulders, hanging on for the ride. At this angle, each thrust bottomed out inside her and caused her hardened nub to hit his pubic bone. Little flashes of light sparked behind her eyelids and again in her fingertips and toes. Every muscle between those extremities pulled taut, never having come down from the last near-pinnacle. She keened through her teeth. Writhing on him, unable to stand it any longer, she threw her hips forward and her head back and cried his name as she convulsed over and around him.

He increased the pace and force of his thrusts. "Damn me, Penelope, you feel so good. I want to keep you. Keep y—"

He hunched forward in his own release, his hands sliding from her hips around her back to clutch her close.

****

As he had so many evening engagements, Michael asked if he could bring work to Penelope's house some afternoons. Despite his parents' presence in Town, he was loathe to lose time with her. His father's tendency to meet in the morning, when he had the most energy, and divide work between Michael and himself, provided Michael more flexibility in where he worked after lunch.

He fell into a new routine with Penelope. He'd set up at the dining room table, even when she wasn't home. She'd come in from tending the garden or from the market with Mrs. Thorpe and find him with papers spread before him, elbow on the table, head propped in his hand, frowning at a document. As she walked by the room, she sometimes darted in to kiss his hair or shoulder without interrupting him.

He'd trail his hand over her hip and bottom as she

continued past, enjoying the illusion of a wedded couple, content to conduct their day-to-day chores but also enjoy the mere presence of one another. At least until he left for his evening social events with eligible young ladies.

He'd heard her ask Mr. Thorpe to send a note round to the theatre if Michael came to the house when she was working there. More often than not, on the nights they spent together, she dropped her plans for the coming days into casual conversation, so he'd know when she would be home. And she listened to his schedule and planned her activities accordingly.

If he finished his work and did not have a social engagement, they cooked supper together, relieving the Thorpes from duties for the night. Or if the menu was simple, he'd pour a brandy or a glass of wine and sip and watch her, asking about the spices she used or venting about whatever negotiations he was in regarding a particular bill he and his father wanted passed.

Once dinner was served, Penelope regaled him with stories about her childhood or asked about his youth. The breadth of subjects fascinated him, even beyond the sexual ones.

He confided one night, "I have written to Helen Montague to see about sponsoring a student."

"Really? I thought that was simply the heat of the moment."

He angled his head, thinking. Then he laughed. "Oh!" The first time she had sucked him to completion, he had muttered something about the idea in awe. "Well, mayhap then it was, but as we discussed the school more, I became serious. People like your family and friends at home have such limited choices, and even those depend on how good the local schoolteacher is, or even how close, and what children are needed for at home. And as you've pointed out to me, girls have even fewer choices than boys do."

He could not fathom not having meat on the table with more in the kitchen or being unable to buy new boots when he wished. To worry how he was going to buy food or clothes for the rest of his life was incomprehensible. Even the responsibilities drilled into him as the future earl, protecting tenant farmers and servants who depended on him for funds to buy food and clothing, had been abstract before meeting Penelope. His new awareness made him wonder about his mother's childhood and how she came to act, a subject his parents declined to discuss.

Penelope had not raised the subject again, but he had not forgotten that he had promised to help her evaluate what she'd need to start a bakery. While he could have made a stab at doing that, Bags had an almost unending memory for facts and figures and was a financial wizard, so Michael had asked him to help. He enjoyed puzzling out new opportunities and investment considerations. In fact, Michael imagined he had done his friend a favor by giving him a new type of business to evaluate. He grinned at that, amused at his justification for handing off the work but confident she'd benefit more from Evan's guidance.

In addition, he was considering buying this house and giving it to Penelope as a parting gift when he entered a betrothal contract.

His conscience continued to prickle him about that. *You can't put terms on a gift. You may be giving her the house to try to prevent the need for future relationships like ours, but you cannot control what she decides. Besides, you'll be married to someone else, so don't be a hypocrite. If she does not engage a new benefactor, she may marry. You have no say in the matter, house or not.*

No. He shut that train of thought down each time it reared its jealous head. He was doing it altruistically.

In the meantime, he would help her with the business plan. "I should like you to meet Bags and Robert. You've heard enough about them. Could we mayhap invite them to dinner soon?"

"Certainly, Michael. I should enjoy meeting your friends. Send me a note when you know which night is best."

****

Michael wasted no time in coordinating an evening, taking care to warn his friends to arrive in secrecy, and Penelope began planning her menu.

She asked him about his friendship with both men. The relationships reminded her of Sophia, her childhood friend before moving when her mother married David, and she missed Sophia anew. She wished she had lifelong friends like his.

"We met at boarding school, then attended university together. Bags—Evan—is the wildest of us. He usually devised the schemes and led us into trouble. He still does. Sometimes I am happy to go along with his outrageous ideas, and sometimes I swear he's daft. And Robert is the quietest."

"Ah, a bookworm, mayhap?"

"No, that was Evan, too, come to think of it, which was useful. He could always think on his feet when needed."

"When you were caught, you mean?" She smiled.

"Yes, or when the scheme did not turn out as expected. We will always be friends. Boarding school alone creates a lifelong bond."

"Why?"

"A group of boys on the cusp of manhood, emotions and sexual urges going wild, with a single housemistress or housemaster to supervise as many as ten, results in chaos at least some of the time. Pranks, you name it. That alone will cement a friendship. Then add in the fact that the person in charge of the house often administered corporal punishment. As you know now, that has a sexual element to it for some, and boom! 'Tis a powder keg set to explode."

"Hmm, if 'tis only boys at the school with all those sexual urges, did you experiment with each other?" She was curious. She had learned there were many options for sexual partners and pleasure.

Michael stared at her, surprised she'd asked, then his expression turned sheepish. "There were maidservants and laundresses and the like, but yes, some boys experimented with one another."

"And?"

"That was, er, one of the escapades Evan initiated, if you must know. Upperclassmen had cornered us and birched us, and he did not take kindly to being birched. Then the older boys tried to have us, ah, attend to them. We escaped, and as the houses were separated by year, they could not bother us once we were back to our residence. A fortnight later, we snuck out, stole the birch from its place in the main hall, and broke into their lounge on the top floor of their house. Their housemaster drank a few pints most evenings and slept heavily. We surprised them, and there were more of us, and we had the birch." His fingers fidgeted in his lap.

"Yes?"

"Evan's goal was to have them service us. We did not really want to put it to them, but a good suck would go a long way for an underclassman. So we offered them the choice of the birch or attending to us." He flushed and looked away, rubbing the back of his neck.

"That was a terrible choice. Do you not feel badly?" She frowned.

"At least we offered a choice. They hadn't. But yes, I regretted it. Years later, when I met up with one of the upperclassmen in White's, I took him aside and apologized. You'll never guess his reaction. He laughed. He said they had been lording it over the younger boys for two years, and it was their turn. The chap was not at all put out. Which was a relief."

"Oh, that is good." She regretted questioning him. How would she survive him ending this when he kept proving what a good man he was, even in how he handled his mistakes?

Chapter Twelve

Penelope deferred dinner preparation to Mrs. Thorpe after baking a mixed fruit tart for dessert, including a touch of ginger and cardamom to test a recipe she liked.

The men arrived together, their plan to head to White's from her house for the strange mix of socializing and political jockeying the club hosted.

Watching the three men interact, Penelope wished for a close friend nearby. They were so comfortable with one another, each bringing a different facet to the friendship. She thought of them as Michael referred to them—by first name. Robert was the shortest but appeared to be the strongest with his broad shoulders and thick chest. His height and dark blond hair allowed him to remain as a quiet backdrop to the tallest man, Evan. Golden of hair and eyes, he was long and lean, every gesture conveying his ease with the world. She wondered if anything disturbed his carefree outlook. Michael was between them in height, build, and personality.

After being introduced, the Earl of Cheltenham—Penelope could not fathom calling him Bags even in her thoughts—bowed low over her hand, murmuring, "I do not believe the best man won you. You are exquisite." Michael's elbow hit his ribs with a sharp jab as he straightened, and he grinned, unrepentant. "Oh, and I do hope you have candy sticks for dessert, hmm?"

Lord Orford—*Robert, or Ford*, as Michael and Evan referred to him—rolled his eyes and forcibly replaced Evan's hand with his, bowing to her.

"Mademoiselle, you are very gracious to host us on such short notice."

"My lords, thank you for coming." She addressed them both but directed her smile to Robert, more comfortable with the reserved man already. "Please, may I offer you a drink?" she asked, gesturing them into the parlor.

Michael waved her off. "I will pour, Pen."

She perched on a chair, the men lounging on the settee. "I understand you all attended school together?"

"Ah yes, the good old days." Cheltenham shook his head as Michael grunted. "I jest. School was a necessity for us to be properly formed for our all-important lordships."

She frowned, taken aback at how flippant he sounded.

"So is an earldom not to your liking, then, my lord?" She was not able to keep the sneer out of her voice.

Cheltenham guffawed at her.

"Ignore him, Miss Wood," Orford spoke. "He lacks manners."

"I say! I shall have you know I can be polished when I want."

"Ah, so 'tis simply that I do not warrant it, then?" She stiffened, smarting at his insinuation.

He snapped his posture upright, seeming to realize his gaffes. "My apologies, Miss Wood. I meant no disrespect. I, ah, felt so comfortable here, among friends…"

Michael snickered and offered his friends their preferred drinks. "Quit whilst you are behind, Bags, or she may decline to feed you."

"Please forgive me, madame. 'Tis jealousy that Michael outbid me when he knew I was interested."

Her eyes widened at that information. She knew the men had been at the auction, even before his candy stick comment, but had not realized Cheltenham had also considered her contract. "Ah…" She blushed. "I cannot offer apologies, my lord, as 'tis *my* belief that the best man did win."

Robert and Michael laughed, and after a moment, Evan joined in. "Touché, Miss Wood." He nodded. "Slade tells me you are a baker at heart. Tell me about your plan for a pastry shop?"

"'Tis not so much a plan as it is a dream, sir. I know very little about opening a business or marketing it. Thankfully, I at least know a bit about the bookkeeping and negotiating with suppliers." She glanced at Michael, confused by Lord Cheltenham's interest. She wasn't prepared, as he hadn't had time to help her formulate a plan to date.

He jumped in, correctly interpreting her confusion. "Bags is far better at finances than I am. I told him what you are looking for, and invited him here to help you. I wished to surprise you."

Stunned, Penelope stared at him for a moment.

He asked a bloody earl for help? For me?

She had wondered if he remembered her request for help. He had followed through and even brought her someone with more expertise out of respect for her dream. Still dazed, she offered Michael a dazzling smile, then turned back to Evan. "Well, then, my lord. Mayhap I *can* apologize."

Cheltenham clutched his stomach and hooted a laugh. "I see how this works. Nay, madame, too little, too late. But lucky for you, I cannot resist a challenge. And call me Cheltie. Most do, except these two loons. I have already reviewed several aspects of bakery business needs. Shall we discuss my findings after dinner? Your apology lacks food right now."

She grinned, already fond of Michael's friends. Like Michael, they were good men with a devilish streak. Did the other two enjoy spanking, too? Not that she wanted to know firsthand, but it fit with the rakish gleam in their eyes.

"Let me run up and fetch the notes I've made from visiting nearby bakeries, as well as what I remember from the one in Peterborough. Dinner is due out of the oven in five minutes, gentlemen."

As she returned, she heard Cheltenham say, "She is from Peterborough, eh? That might be an interesting connection."

"Why?" Michael asked.

"Charles's widow, Lady Charlotte, Dowager Countess of Peterborough, is an investment partner with me on several ventures. The woman is a bloody genius with money—"

She rounded the corner to see the other two men look at each other with raised eyebrows.

"—and she prefers to invest in women's businesses when possible. No surprise there." He rolled his eyes and grinned, but she suspected he was teasing. Why else would he have come tonight?

They sat to eat, the men exclaiming over her tart.

After dinner, she summarized her notes for Evan.

He dove in. By the end of the evening, Penelope's head was spinning with facts and figures. He'd asked dozens of questions, many of which she could not answer. Then he had sketched out additional details for her to consider. There were estimates of square footage needed, costs per square foot in the parts of London she was targeting, rough projections for equipment and supply costs, and even a few marketing ideas.

The man had so much knowledge in his head, she wondered how he then absorbed Parliamentary bills, but Michael had once told her Cheltenham could remember those almost word for word as well. He was frighteningly intelligent, if somewhat contemptuous for the rigidity and rules of society and his position in it.

Regardless, he had given her a taste of freedom, and she was both excited and daunted by the possibility, and beyond grateful to Michael for arranging the consult. She suspected the earl did not have the patience to help many people like this, despite his stated love of a new challenge. Yet Michael had requested time for her. She envied their friendship. Like the ladies back in Peterborough, these men understood one another and were willing to help each other, and even a newcomer.

She wondered again where Sophia was now. Mayhap she'd write to her old address when she was in Peterborough next, as it was not too far a trip.

What was clear by the end of the evening was that her settlement from the auction would not cover what she needed to start the business. She'd need another patron or else someone to invest in the bakery, which seemed unlikely given how few people she knew in London.

Penelope tried to hide her distress. *If only Michael could delay marrying until next year. With more pin money and the right ending settlement, I could avoid being a high flyer to another cove.* Her heart lurched, countering her common sense. *I knew one patron would not be enough, even before tonight's lesson. Gor, at least now I have the knowledge I need. One more year or so, and I shall be free to do what I want, not some man's bidding.*

The trouble was that she rather liked doing Michael's bidding. The bakery was her dream, but running it without him by her side would not be as much fun.

Tonight had taken her vision to a new level. He had arranged for an earl to help her plan a path she loved, not one chosen out of financial necessity. No other man was going to support her dreams like he did, make love to her like he did, cook with her like he did. Moreover, he was considering sponsoring another student, being kind to a stranger, out of care for his mother and—*dare she hope?*—her.

Oh dear, Leah is going to be cross with me. I have fallen in love with him!

****

The theatre was again short-staffed.

Penelope had received word from Michael indicating he had another social commitment. So she had come in to work and be with friends. He had not specified his plans, and she did not want to be tempted to tease him further, so she was determined to leave before the performance began.

Then Prudence found her and asked if she could help with ushering again.

She revised her plan. If she covered one of the side doors rather than the main entrance, she might avoid Michael even if he arrived with a debutante in tow, as the owner's box was centrally located over the orchestra section.

She handled the inflow of ticket holders and lingered inside the doors as she adored this particular production of *A Midsummer Night's Dream*. Finding an empty seat on the end of a row, she slipped into it to watch. Prudence offered all the employees the option to use vacant seats to enjoy performances as their responsibilities allowed.

Entranced, she jolted in surprise when another dark-clad usher squatted next to her and whispered, "Maeve was serving the fancy boxes but started clutching her stomach with collywobbles. Pru sent her home and bade me come look for someone ta help. Please, Pen?"

Resigned, she nodded, hoping Michael was not in attendance.

She rose a few minutes before the end of the first act and made her way up to the box level, hovering near the stairs. The other three ushers had decided that two would monitor the stairs while she and the fourth served anyone who remained on that level for intermission. Often the occupants visited with their peers in other boxes rather than descending to where the general public from the pit also gathered.

She made her way to the west wing of boxes as the curtain fell on the first act. Waiting for the exodus of patrons, she popped into each box to ask if anyone wished for libations and ran down the back stairs to the bar for them as needed.

She dawdled but did not dare skip the owner's box for fear of Prudence hearing a complaint about staffing. Finally, unable to wait any longer, she poked her head through the curtains.

Drat! There he was with another beautiful, perfectly-dressed girl close to her age and an older woman she guessed was the girl's mother.

Clearing her throat, she stepped through the curtain. "My lord, ladies, can I offer you any refreshments from the bar?"

Michael's head shot up from conversing with the young lady. Staring at Penelope, he frowned.

"My lord? Mayhap lemonade? Or"—the girl leaned closer, away from her mother, making Penelope grind her teeth—"champagne?"

Penelope wanted to smack her.

That is our *drink.*

Tears threatened. She bit the inside of her cheek and reminded herself that there was no *our*. If there were, she would not be serving this Lord drinks as he entertained another woman with expectations of marriage.

This is what you agreed to. You have no right to be angry with him.

She raised her eyebrows. "My lord?"

"Mmm, champagne for Lady Grace, please." He fidgeted with his cravat pin, then shot his cuffs.

Seeing him fidget somehow calmed her. She was not the only person uncomfortable in the room. She dallied, asking, "And for you, sir?"

He sighed as though resigned. "Champagne will be fine, and for Lady Lud, please. Three glasses and the bottle." He nodded to the older woman as he said her name.

"Yes, sir."

She flew down the stairs, grabbing a bottle from one shelf and three glasses from another before she flew back up. Her mind was in chaos. The same devil that had caused her to wear costumes twice before raised its head again.

Shake the bottle. Just enough it doesn't scare the ladies.

No, she swore she would not upset him. The situation was awkward enough for both of them, and she preferred their more lighthearted spankings to a punishment in which she might not gain pleasure from him.

She slipped through the curtains to set the bottle and glasses down on a small table beside his chair. Picking up the bottle again, she took hold of the cork. Pulling and twisting, she fought with it for a moment before it popped free, and—

Golden fizzy liquid bubbled up and out. Apparently, no shaking had been required, or her run up the stairs had done the job.

She inadvertently turned a few degrees, as her focus had half been on him the whole time, just as his gaze had remained on her, so most of the spill landed on his trouser legs.

He gasped in shock at the surge of wetness on his thigh.

The spillover stopped almost immediately, but the damage was done. She started to stammer an apology as she leaned forward to try to mop up the spill with the cloth from around the bottle. "My lord, I am—"

"Argh," he cried, as the bottle leaned with her and

more spilled, farther up his lap, right on his groin.

And I hadn't even been trying! She stifled a manic giggle.

"Oh, my lord, let me—" She swiped at his pants with the cloth, following the path of the spill up his thigh. Then lingered, her naughty side at work again as she carved the towel around his manhood, caressing as much as blotting before trailing it down his trouser leg.

His hand gripped her wrist in warning. His eyes flashed.

She widened her eyes in innocence, offering him the cloth. "Here, ah, mayhap you'd prefer…"

He gritted his teeth and shook his head infinitesimally.

Uh oh, punishment.

They remembered the other box occupants and glanced around to see if they'd been observed. The young lady had sprung out of her seat at the first spill, and she and her mother were in the corner making a fuss and dabbing at her dress, although Penelope was quite sure it had not been marred.

"Expect me later. You shall be home and waiting docilely." Michael's words came through clenched teeth. He released her wrist, saying louder, "Thank you, anyway. I shall pour."

He plucked the bottle from her hands, dismissing her.

****

Michael entered the small row house quietly and removed his dress shoes before climbing the stairs. He was curious to see what Penelope was doing and wearing or if she was even awake, as it was quite late.

Frustrated by this situation of his own making, he'd

removed Penelope from temptation as quickly as possible. It was all he could do not to follow her. He craved the feel of her bottom under his hand, their shared hilarity about the episode.

Despite his discomfort in being damp—and hard, anticipating his late night activities—the entire time, he had assured the women that he could remain for the last acts. Then he had taken them home in his coach and stopped at his home to change clothes before coming here. He deliberately chose not to rush, trying to build Penelope's anticipation and anxiety, wondering if she'd fall asleep.

An opportunity to punish her further would not be amiss.

Throughout the second act, he had waffled between anger, frustration, and laughter at the memory of the champagne. The play was not a comedy, however, so he had to be careful not to let his amusement show. Instead, he remained calm by contemplating suitable retribution.

Despite his entertainment, Penelope's discomfort had to outweigh his own by a wide margin. He was still considering what approach to take as he attained the upstairs hall.

Seeing light spilling from under her bedroom door sped his pace. Opening the door, he found her on the bed. On top, not in, as she lay on the gold coverlet, her burgundy wrapper open around her, her nude beauty stealing his breath.

She had a bottle of champagne and a half-empty glass in hand. With her head propped on pillows, she dipped a finger in the shallow champagne glass and touched it to her skin, right between her breasts.

Trailing it down, she reached her navel and returned for more liquid, which she dropped into that indentation to circle the wet finger. The damp trail on her skin glistened in the flickering candlelight.

Damn me, she is unparalleled. Lady Grace would never take the initiative to do this. In fact, any other woman would have been furious or at least sulking.

His thoughts distracted him for a second before her finger rose again and regained his full attention.

Her next fingerful went between her legs, touching the spot that delivered the most pleasure, nudging the nub back and forth. Raising her finger to her mouth, she sucked on it and moaned. Her voice roughened with desire, she said, "Hello, my lord. How was your champagne? Mine is delicious."

Ripping his coat and cravat off, he struggled to unbutton his trousers over the erection tenting them.

"Do not presume to think this little act will spare you a punishment, young lady," he growled.

"As you wish, my lord." She rolled over, propping herself on her elbows to sip more champagne before putting the glass on the bedside table. Her hand snaked under her torso, and her fingers appeared between her legs, her bottom raising an inch as her hips jogged up from the stimulation. Sliding a finger into her channel, she moaned again.

Punishment now? Or pleasure? She was deliberately distracting him, the minx.

"Right, you've delayed it," he muttered, shedding the rest of his clothes as he hopped and staggered across to the bed.

He received a husky laugh in reply as she rolled back over and sought his mouth with hers. This champagne tasted far better than that in the theatre. Refusing to further compare his earlier companion to Penelope's greeting, to contemplate how right this felt, more than any other part of his day, he sank into her caresses.

****

Penelope woke to find Michael gone. But her relief was short-lived. Had she avoided a punishment or simply delayed it? Her mind returned to Michael's theatre companions.

Gor, the girl was pretty. And wore a flash dress. And spoke like a lady.

Because she was a lady. She had her own title, even without marrying Michael. The perfect earl's wife.

She sighed. *'Tisn't a competition. I am not even eligible for the contest.*

She was torturing herself working at the theatre at times when she'd see him accompanying his candidates for marriage. But the work there also kept her sane and added to her bank account.

As the days grew longer, Michael's schedule remained busy. He had regular social events centered around the marriage mart which required his presence. His days were spent carrying much of the weight of estate management and even preliminary reading of bills for the House of Lords. His father did not allow his age and poor health to preclude him from attending most sessions, but it did slow his efforts to manage all the reading and correspondence, so Michael helped.

He rarely escaped early anymore or came to work. More often, he visited late at night after he had paid his dues to society's expectations.

She never knew when he would visit or what to

177

expect when he arrived. Some nights, he lit candles and woke her if she was asleep, then demanded a small show of her disrobing before dragging her under him. Other nights, he caught her at her toilette and brushed her hair. He ran the brush lightly over her skin to heighten her sensitivity, then licked and sucked every inch of her. Still other times, he did not bother with lights, tugging their clothes aside, spitting into his hand, pushing into her even as he woke her with a hand in her hair, and riding her hard.

She dared not ask the names of his companions at the theatre and other social functions.

However, reality was bound to intrude as the theatre remained shorthanded. Over the course of a fortnight, she spied him with the same young lady twice more. Task forgotten, Penelope watched as he and his companions ascended to the owner's box. Her shoulders sagged, and a hollow feeling settled in her chest. She slipped through the crowd to the back of the theater. Changing back into her own clothes, she made her way home, her movements desultory.

Her half-brother's birthday was in a fortnight. She had promised him she would return to Peterborough for it. Now, the timing seemed serendipitous. She needed some time away from Michael and London. Hopefully, he would not oppose a few days away for a trip home, given how busy he was.

She straightened, certain she could gain his permission. The school had given her all the tools she needed.

Chapter Thirteen

Despite wanting to tackle the subject of Peterborough as soon as he arrived the next evening, Penelope needed a strategic approach. She arranged candles in the bedroom, lit the fire, carried two snifters of brandy up, and changed into her favorite dressing gown.

A fine lawn with scalloped lace edges from shoulders to toes, it met in a deep vee between her breasts and fastened with three togs, remaining loose from her upper thighs to the ground. Designed to be worn over a more modest nightrail or to cover underthings whilst having her hair dressed, Penelope chose to forego anything beneath it for this particular evening.

She wanted Michael to see what he would be missing when he married, even if only by firelight. Leaving her hair down, she sucked on a ginger candy to freshen her breath.

Drowsing in a chair by the fire, she straightened and stretched when Michael's footsteps tapped up the stairs. She gripped the brandies and turned, stepping toward the door as his frame filled the opening. She smiled as his gaze dropped to her bare leg visible through the opening, the gown swishing around her as she came to him, snifter outstretched.

Without moving his gaze, Michael took the brandy

and raised it to his lips. "'Tis late. I expected you to be asleep. This is a lovely surprise."

She drew his gaze where she wanted it by closing the gap in the lower part of the gown and trailing her hand leisurely up her middle to rest between her breasts. Her nipples peaked as she suspected they always would under his warm regard, despite any impending betrothal. Arching her back, she dipped a finger in her snifter and painted her lips with it. Dipping again, she drew a line of fragrant dampness from the hollow of her throat to the vee of her gown.

"Mayhap you'd care for more brandy, sir?" she asked huskily.

"Right." Voice hoarse, he reached out blindly, finding her dresser by luck with his snifter before he stepped into her. First licking at her lips, then sucking on them, he speared his tongue into her when she opened to him.

She melted against him in pleasure. The brandy, his scent, and his taste swirled through her senses, making her dizzy.

His arm wrapped around her, under her arms, to arch her backward as his mouth traced her neck to find the brandy trail she had left. His other hand found the top tog and unfastened it as his lips and tongue soaked up the liquor and wound their way to meet his hand. The second closure opened, then the third. Straightening, he nudged the gown off her shoulders.

She shivered in arousal and from the cool air against the damp line he'd traced. Her nipples pointed at him, begging for his touch.

As the gown fell away from her arms, she raised them to shove his jacket off as well, moving to unbutton his waistcoat. She wanted to caress his skin as much as she wanted his hands on hers.

Michael weighed her breasts in his hands, thumbing her nipples.

She struggled to focus on undressing him as tendrils of pleasure snaked from her breasts to between her legs. Finally, two layers were off, and his cravat pin undone. After tossing that next to his snifter, she made swift work of divesting him of the cravat and tugging his shirt free of his trousers.

Eager to taste him, she dropped to her knees and swallowed the saliva pooling in her mouth.

Michael drew in an appreciative breath. He held still, watching her as if to see whether she would remove his shoes, socks, and pants.

She did not bother. Reaching up to his waist, level with the top of her head, she unfastened the fall of the trousers and peeled them down to his hips.

She licked her lips, and he moaned.

His cock sprang free, and her hand was waiting for it. Using a firm grip, she circled the base with her fingers and slid up his length. Her thumb rubbed past the sensitive underside of the crown, then caught a drop of the fluid leaking from the tip and smoothed back down. Her tongue darted out to lick around the head.

Michael's hands shot to her hair, fisting in the loose locks.

She hummed, enjoying his scent, then opened her mouth wider and swallowed his length until her lips met her fist. She stilled there as his fingers tightened on her scalp in enjoyment.

Her goal of seducing him was forgotten. Usually, she felt powerful on her knees for him, knowing that she controlled his pleasure. Now, she desired only to please him, to suck him inside of her and keep him with her forever.

I want to relieve his weariness from the responsibilities weighing on him. His frustration at the strictures of his parents' expectations. Even his yearning for me. I can draw it all out with my lips and teeth and tongue, because I know him, I care for him, I am his.

She withdrew slowly, keeping her tongue flat against the underside of the hot hard stalk until she flicked it against his cockhead at the last minute. Then she sank down his length again, mashing her lips against her hand, her nose brushing the coarse hairs surrounding the base.

Michael groaned and began to participate more. Then retreated with a frown.

"Unh. It tingles…" He tilted his head, brow still furrowed as he gazed down at her.

"Tingles?" Penelope's brow furrowed in thought. "Oh, it must be the ginger candy I ate. Does it bother you?"

"No. It unnerved me a bit, but it, uh, adds a twist."

"Well, then." Her eyes lit up, and she licked him from base to tip before engulfing his length with her mouth again.

Her beaded nipples begged for attention. If only she could kneel close enough to rub them against his furred legs for friction. Her core wept, and she wanted to grind on his booted foot for relief. But this was for him. And, if she was honest, for her to gain some distance and hopefully perspective.

His hands returned to her hair and tugged her back,

then pressed her forward, his hips moving in counterpoint.

She placed her hands on his thighs for balance and embraced his lead. Keeping her teeth sheathed behind her lips, she sucked when she could, breathed when she could, and trusted Michael not to gag her.

Each time he held her impaled, he flexed his hips another inch, nudging against her to get as deep as he could.

Her eyes teared, and drool ran from the corner of her mouth as she was not given time to swallow. Then, as she became accustomed to the rhythm—slide out, slide in, hold—she started swallowing during the pause.

Michael nearly came apart when her throat convulsed against his length, grunting and pushing harder into her mouth. He drove so deep he blocked her air for a moment before tugging her back then thrusting again.

She squeezed her throat around him again, and his pace sped up. With no pauses, she focused on breathing on the withdrawal and wrapped her hands around his thighs to hold on for the ride.

Only a few plunges later, he cried out and pistoned his hips one last time, not going quite as deep. His cock grew even harder as he made shallow pushes in her mouth, her lips tight below the mushroomed head. Arching his spine, he shot spurt after spurt of hot salty liquid into her throat.

Gulping, she swallowed it all as his thrusts slowed, allowing her to lick and suck him clean before sitting back.

"Blast, I am not sure I can make it to the bed," he panted. Despite his words, he grasped her above her elbow to help her stand, and they both stumbled the few steps to her bed.

Realizing that both their brandies sat on the dresser, he stripped off his lower garments and solicitously brought the drinks over, only then collapsing beside her.

She sipped the brandy, hoping she'd have her turn at pleasure.

Once his breathing slowed, he leaned up on an elbow and traced one finger around her closest nipple. "That was magnificent. I think we might need to change the rules, Pen. Can I get my choice of that or spanking you for punishments?" He grinned.

She lay on her back, still wildly aroused. "You shall need to convince me why I should agree to that, my lord." She lowered her gaze to his finger circling her pointed tip and arched it toward him.

"Mmm, I may be able to think of something." His head lowered to replace his finger on her nipple, and he licked his finger before lowering it to the curls between her legs. He needn't have licked it. There was plenty of moisture waiting for him.

She moaned and raised her hips as his finger made similar circles around her swollen nub like it had on her breast. Sucking his cock had stirred her so much she could hear his fingers as he ran his fingers and thumb through her wetness, coating them.

Turning his hand sideways, he thrust his first two fingers into her, pressing his thumb on her most sensitive button. A finger slipped against her and slid toward her bottom. Thinking it was just due to the amount of moisture, she was unprepared for the digit to enter her bottom hole.

Her hips jerked off the bed, and both her hands came to grip his wrist. *Oh my.*

Something inside her *there* felt wrong—no, strange. She had learned a little about such play, that it was not only for men who liked men. However, she had not considered that it might be pleasant, assuming the act was more for the man's pleasure.

Michael released her nipple with a quiet pop and looked her in the eye. "Did I hurt you?"

No. His insertion had not hurt. But the surprise and strangeness had taken her breath. She felt invaded. Unable to form words, she simply shook her head, hair tangling on the pillow.

"Then let go." His hand moved against her, retracting then driving his finger into her tightest entrance again.

Nerve endings she hadn't known she possessed lit, an onslaught of new physical responses drawing her focus to that solitary finger in her rear passage. But the more she concentrated on that movement, the higher her sensual pleasure swirled.

"Unh." Still wordless, she loosened her hands, intrigued as to where this would lead. Shock morphed into blossoming ecstasy as his fingers glided in and out of both her channels. His thumb pressed and released her hard little nub, and his lips returned to sucking at her breast.

Penelope held her breath when he added the fourth touch, her excitement spiraling. She could not process all the sensations.

Gor. This is definitely not only for the man's pleasure. 'Tis delicious.

Tingles of passion streaked through her even as

they centered at his fingertips. Her focus was intent on every movement of his hand and mouth. Her stomach tightened, an orgasm brewing faster than ever before. Then, when the sensations normally would have crested, they built higher. She wasn't sure whether to fear the pending explosion or welcome it.

Knowing Michael would keep her safe, she embraced it. Her hips lifted off the bed, feet planted to hold her core to his hand, driving against him in counterpoint to his plunges. Her hands returned to his wrist, but to hold them to her and to ensure she was countering his pace.

Quicker and quicker, her hips made shallow mid-air thrusts, and she gasped in time to them. Her nub hardened further, her internal muscles clamped down on him, and a high thin scream split the air.

The strangeness of being filled in two places and the intensity of those sensations rolled together and sluiced through her like a bucket of hot water, the scalding heat surging into a more intense explosion of ecstasy than she'd ever experienced. Her head thrashed, the room disappearing in a dark haze of rapture, and blood rushed in her ears. She belatedly realized that the scream she heard had been hers. Her inner muscles and the button under his thumb continued to spasm and spasm, and she clutched his hand to keep it still now as she shot into hyper-sensitivity.

When the convulsions faded, they cleaned up and returned to the bed to sip their drinks. She stared at him in dazed wonder. "Michael…" She still did not have words. After a long sigh she strung a few together. "That was the most intense sensation of my life."

"Excellent. It was the least I could do after you

greeted me so prettily."

Her smile was tinged with awareness that their games would likely not continue much longer.

She took a breath, foregoing the post-coital cuddling she sought most nights. "My lord, it appears you are actively wooing the young lady with you last night."

Even living outside of "polite society," she understood the expectations set by his behavior.

Michael appeared surprised she had recognized the girl. Or mayhap it was the stark contrast of the subject after intimacy.

She did not wait for a response. "As it seems your social calendar will be even more active in the coming weeks, would you mind if I made a visit home, please? My brother turns four in a fortnight."

He frowned. "But—I need you here."

She gritted her teeth.

Does he even understand what the bloody word means? Spoiled heir wishes to have his cake and eat it, too. Does he even care if he hurts me?

Schooling her expression, she remained calm and proceeded cautiously. After all, Michael did not realize her heart was engaged. Nor was it his business.

****

Penelope's brows drew down at Michael's bald statement.

All right, I do not need *her. But blast it, I have paid for her company, and I desire her here. More, I care for her and I look forward to this part of my day more than any other.*

Michael frowned at his own statement. *'Tis selfish.* He knew it. He simply did not want to admit it. Family was important. Keeping her from her stepdad and brother was not fair.

Her face smoothed to a calm mask. "If I may ask, why?"

Knowing he was fighting a losing battle, he responded anyway. "I spend my whole life obeying society's rules. Working with my father and our allies in Parliament to convince more members to vote with us. Handling tenants' conflicts when I sometimes want to scream at them to work together. Succumbing to my parents' wishes to choose a wife and playing nice with debutantes. Here, with you, is the only place I can be myself. I can put all of that aside for a few hours and relax. Beyond that, I very much enjoy your intellect. You have opinions on the theatre and society and even some of the laws I review. You listen to me. You cook for me and with me."

"Right. But won't this young lady do that for you as well, the more time you spend with her?"

"Gah. All these girls—and yes, I know they are about the same age as you, but they seem so immature. I suspect they do not notice anything outside their library and sewing and music rooms. Even the theatre is 'nice.' They give no thought whatsoever to how a stage production comes together to provide that entertainment for them. They natter about their narrow little lives, buying ribbons, or who said what about whom. I ended up with Lady Grace because she is quiet. She at least listens to me, even if she has no opinions on my world."

Penelope stared at him.

He tensed as he saw what might be pity. He knew how ridiculous and whiny he sounded. The poor heir, such terrible choices, when he had a lovely home, family support, and money in the bank. He could never even fathom living as she did, knowing their contract would end within the year and she must start again. All their conversations about her path to this point, her dreams for the future, played in his head.

She is so much stronger than I am. The perception threw him, but he returned to the battle of the moment.

He stood to pace. "Pen, please. I do need you here."

"Michael. Think about it. How long until you're betrothed? Then married? You've said that I shan't be in your life after you are wed. This will be a mere sennight. Then, if you can keep the betrothal at bay for another few sennights, we shall have our last bit of the Season, and you'll have the opportunity to get to know—" She swallowed. "—Lady Grace. To know more what to expect when you marry." She straightened, her voice firm when she added, "As you know, my family's financial struggles are what led me to choose this path. I would like to take them some money."

His arguments crumbled. He declined to admit it, but her desire to get money to her stepfather and brother overrode her reference to their final nights together.

"Blast it. Of course you must go. You should enjoy your brother's birthday. I know as well as anyone how important time with family is." Grimacing, he considered again his father's health and all the reasons he was giving in to a betrothal this year. "Come. Let us sleep, and tomorrow night I shall help you make arrangements."

****

Several days later, Penelope had packed a few

things, withdrawn the funds she wanted to carry with her, and hidden it in small amounts throughout her bags and in a pocket she'd sewn into her petticoat. Michael and she had argued about her taking the mail coach. It was her least expensive option but took an extra day for all the stops and had her sleeping in—or on—the carriage. He was not fond of the safety or the time wasted in travel, but she pointed out gently that waste was a matter of perspective. If one did not have a carriage and matched set of horses or the funds for a room at an inn, one made do.

He understood and grumbled that he would pay for her travel. He simply did not want her gone too long, but she refused. Her thrifty childhood did not allow her to waste anyone's money when the mail coach worked perfectly well.

Michael strode through the door as she descended the stairs to hire a hack to transport her and her luggage to the nearest post.

"Michael? 'Tis lovely to see you, of course, but what are you doing here?"

He planted his feet and crossed his arms. "Going with you."

"Pardon me?"

"I am joining you. My carriage is around the corner for secrecy. I've cleared my calendar for six days. That is all I can manage. We can get there and back in less time this way, though, so that should be enough for you to visit with your family?"

"Of course. I only planned the three days there anyway, given my commitment to you." She tried not to think about the fact that he was the one who would soon end that commitment.

"I am acquainted with the Earl of Peterborough, so I've sent a letter saying I shall be in the area and may drop by. I presume there is a reputable inn where we can stay?"

"Ahh…" She had planned to stay with her family, but with Michael, that would not be possible. Nor was it appropriate for them to stay together at an inn. "I am certain there is. I shall think on it in the carriage, my lord." She hesitated as it all began to sink in. "Are you truly able to join me for six days?" Her voice rose in excitement at the end. "It will be like a true holiday."

This was the closest she would get to a holiday with him and likely with anyone for many years. She could not bear to think about that, not wishing to tarnish these six days with worries about the future.

She frowned at a sudden thought. "Ah, I shan't be meeting the earl, shall I? I did not pack clothes for that. We never saw him when I lived there, although my friends have written that he married recently and his wife helps with herbs and medicines for the parish when the physician is not available."

"Oh." A crease appeared between his brows. "I don't know. I hope to meet with him."

"Michael, if he is married, you cannot very well introduce your light-of-love to an earl and his countess!" She was shocked he'd even think there was a possibility.

"You would be surprised what some earls and viscounts do, given what we discuss at the club." Michael laughed, then considered. "But I agree, a meeting is unlikely."

Which club was he referring to? He'd mentioned both White's and Mrs. Potter's Spanking Club on occasion. Meeting this earl could prove interesting.

"Would you mind if I ran and selected one more dress in case?" she asked, hand already on the banister.

One dress became two, with matching slippers and bonnets, but Penelope and Mrs. Thorpe hurried, and her trunk was downstairs and ready in no time. The coachman and Mr. Thorpe hauled it up to the top of the carriage, and Michael handed her in.

The carriage was luxurious but did not bear the family crest, so it must be one of several. She bounced on the seat in excitement. She had never before been in Michael's carriage.

Nor will I again after this sennight. And he did not use the marked carriage because I am his dirty secret. Her mouth twisted, but she again shoved that out of her mind. She was too happy about seeing her family and having Michael with her to allow their circumstances to mar her mood.

"Right, then." Michael sat back against the squabs of the forward-facing seat across from her. "However shall we pass the time?"

She was at once amused and a little aroused. "My lord? Mayhap I should thank you properly for coming with me and for these luxurious accommodations." She made a slight hand gesture to his lap.

"Hmm, that sounds delightful. But no, I was teasing you, Pen."

I can always try again later when we're out of London. She pursed her lips in regret as she glanced down but relegated herself to conversation. "Will you miss much in the House of Lords this sennight, then?"

"Not terribly. I was able to read several bills ahead, as the infernal discussions on each take so long. I met with my father the past two days and talked through them all and left summaries. He shall work with our associates to get the outcomes we prefer to the extent possible. I hope I did not wear him out. He appeared strong for our meetings, at least."

By now, she knew that his father's illness came and went. Some days and weeks, he had more strength than others. It was not seasonal, and the physicians could not pinpoint treatments that helped or hurt. They suspected it was a weak heart, so he took one day at a time.

"If you do not mind me asking, what did you tell your parents about this sennight?"

"Given my father's health, they need to know where I am, so I said I was checking in with Peterborough, as he's been an ally in the House several times. He runs a horse training business at his estate, so he splits his time between that and London during the Season."

"Interesting. I do not recall hearing of any Peers running a business. Is that not a bit unusual?"

"You are correct, as usual. He was the second son. His brother Charles was the earl. He was about ten years older but quite fit. Although he was married for seven years, they did not have any children, and he died suddenly a few months ago. Edward has been learning the tasks of an earldom and, somehow, also managed to find a wife and marry within a few fortnights. Which did not help my parents' pestering me to find my own."

"How long have you known him then? And how did you meet?"

"A few years. When we all descended on London for our first Season of our majority, we were rather wild. We had finished university, although he and another friend went to Cambridge whilst I attended Oxford with Bags and Robert. Then our Grand Tour, and then home. We had whatever monies and titles vested at our majority and the Town at our disposal. There is a whole different London for young men like us—no balls or stuffy soirees, no musicales or museums. Clubs of all sorts, theatres, women of the demi-monde. We met at White's with Bags and Robert, and as we were headed to Mrs. Potter's, Evan invited Suffolk and Peterborough to join us. Our friendship went from there."

Ah, both clubs. This may indeed be another unusual earl. And that answers my questions about Michael's friends.

"More recently, he has asked for my support on a few bills, and I offered help on a few other aspects of managing multiple estates. He and Nicholas, the Earl of Suffolk, are close, so when Edward married and bundled his bride off to Peterborough, I coordinated with Nick. However, it does no harm to check in with Edward. It might help me to see how he is settling into marriage, as well."

As soon as he said that, her mood plummeted. She could not very well avoid thoughts of the future if Michael referenced it. Her expression must have shown her feelings.

"Ah, sorry, sweeting. I hate thinking about it, too." Michael reached out a hand to pat hers.

She could not respond past the lump in her throat.

"Here." Michael slid over and patted the seat beside him. "Come over and let me hold you. I want to enjoy this closeness and privacy since we have it."

She awkwardly shifted around to sit beside him and leaned her head on his shoulder as his arm came around her. She stared out at the drizzling rain and welcomed his warmth. The month of June had been colder than normal. The coachman sat above them, hunched under a coat and a brimmed hat. How would the trip have been in the mail coach? The rain and Michael's warmth lulled her to sleep.

Chapter Fourteen

After Penelope fell asleep, Michael had pulled out some paperwork and waded through it, sorting it on the seat opposite as he worked. He did not want to fall too far behind.

They stopped for the night at a lovely inn that Penelope would never have chosen for the cost. He borrowed the Thorpes' names and checked them in as a married couple so they could share a room. He had chosen the carriage without the family crest to better avoid being set upon by brigands, important given that Penelope was carrying cash. It also helped avoid questions from the innkeeper.

The proprietor, therefore, did not offer the usual private dining room he would to aristocracy, and Michael enjoyed watching the other patrons as they ate in a quiet corner of the public room.

They were only a few hours from Peterborough by that point, and he spent the morning carriage ride asking Penelope about the townspeople they were likely to run into. She described the Cathedral Square, the pubs, and businesses of her childhood. The city contained higher-end shops as well, given that it was a county seat for the earl, but she had not had occasion to venture into them.

Given her story of the four women in the house at the edge of town and having worked with Leah at the theatre, he looked forward to meeting the others. One aspect of being two days' ride north of London that made this trip more relaxed for him was the leniency of societal rules. Here he could blithely consider meeting retired courtesans, having dinner with a blacksmith, and visiting an earl and his new bride with no one caring much and no threat of gossip among the Ton. Which meant word would not get back to his parents.

Penelope had sent word ahead to her friends and family, including a second one to Leah at the theatre, as she frequently traveled back and forth. His own note to Edward annotated his travel dates and stated that he'd enjoy a brief visit if Edward's time allowed. As his decision had been so close to the trip, he was not sure Edward would receive the note in time or would be free. If he was, he'd know to find Michael at the nicest inn in the town.

They gained Peterborough at lunchtime, and Penelope paced impatiently as he checked them into adjacent rooms at the inn. She had argued that she could stay with her family, but he desired her near, and she acquiesced. He suspected the size of her family's home and the fact that her two very male family members had been living there alone for months might have had something to do with it. When he'd paid and received their room assignments, he directed the coachman to take the trunks up and they made their way to a nearby pub where she predicted her stepfather would be eating his lunch.

****

Penelope spotted David at the bar, chatting to the barkeep as he ate. The lunch crowd was light, and she sped around the tables to reach him, calling his name.

Michael followed behind as she and her stepfather hugged and laughed with joy. The barkeep leaned over to plant a kiss on her cheek as well, welcoming her back. As Michael reached her side, she introduced him as they had planned.

"David, this is Lord Michael Slade. He is a friend of Leah's who I met in London and owns the theatre where I worked, so I see him often. He is here to visit Lord Peterborough and offered me a ride."

David gestured to a table. "Lord Slade. Would you like to join us?"

She looked to Michael in question.

"Why do you not join your father and talk, and I shall head back to the inn to finish some paperwork?"

"Oh!" A bubble of happiness pulled her lips into a smile. "Do you mind? Thank you, Mich—my lord."

"Sir, I look forward to meeting your son. I invite you all to dine with me, mayhap for your son's birthday?" Ignoring her verbal stumble, Michael nodded to her and David.

David's eyes widened in surprise at this generous offer from a titled lord. "Oh, ta, your lordship. We'd be ever so honored by your company."

"We shall plan on seven, then, so as not to be too late for the boy. I will leave you both to lunch. Penelope, please come find me at the inn when you are ready, and we can walk over to Leah's."

"Certainly, my lord." She cast her gaze down with a small curtsy in an attempt at decorum.

****

Penelope sank into a chair, unable to contain her questions long enough for her companion to even draw breath to answer them. "Oh, David, 'tis lovely to see

198

you. And you look to be doing well. How is Matthew?"

He smiled and patted her hand affectionately. "Rick," he called over to the barkeep, "bring Pen here a sausage pie, will ya?"

"Already put the order in." Rick laughed as her inordinate fondness for that lunch was well known.

"Penelope, 'tis lovely to see you, too," David said. "Thank you for your letters. You know I do not have the same way with words, so I hope you'll forgive us gents for the less frequent replies. London sounds…well, interesting to say the least. And you are enjoying it so far?"

"Yes, so much, ta."

"And you have nice friends there, then? Do you still see Leah often? And the couple you mentioned, the Thorpes? They look out for you?"

"Yes, yes, you needn't worry about me. I am fine." She tilted her head with a grin.

"Well, your ma would come back and haunt me if I did not worry a bit, so please bear with me." His smile showed his affection, and invoking her mother was only an excuse for voicing his concern.

"Where is Matthew? How soon can I see him?"

"He's with Mrs. James, doing schoolwork, as he should be. We received your letter but were not certain when you'd arrive. Are you truly able to stay for his birthday in two days?"

"Yes. 'Tis why I timed it thus."

They dawdled over lunch as a few townsfolk who came in for their own lunches stopped by to greet Penelope. Eventually, David had to return to the forge, and she made her way back to the inn to collect Michael for a visit to the ladies.

****

Not seeing Michael downstairs or in the stables, Penelope made her way to their rooms. He was at the desk writing correspondence.

He looked up when she skipped into the room. "You seem to have enjoyed lunch."

"Oh, yes, thank you so much for giving us that time. You're invited to accompany me to the cottage later, as I couldn't wait until tomorrow to see Matthew. Did you get any lunch?"

"Yes, thanks. I had a cold plate sent up, and they've already returned to remove it. I am ready to have a stroll after all the sitting if you are ready?"

"Let me fetch the gifts I packed." She had more embroidered lacy things for the women in the house at the end of town. She would need to warn them that the packages should be opened later, or they might give Michael an eyeful.

On the street, he took the satchel from her and offered his arm. As they made their way up Eastfield Road, she introduced him to a few shopkeepers and pointed out other businesses she'd described to him. The forge and her family's small cottage was behind them, the other direction from the inn. At the end of downtown, they turned right at an angle up a hill and arrived at the last house.

Knocking, she bounced in excitement. Who would answer the door? Was Leah in town? Had they received her letter?

Then the door was thrown wide and Rachel was charging out and hugging her, bouncing with her. "Penelope! Love, come in, come in. We have missed you so! But all those lovely letters. Thank you so much.

And that chemise—oh la la! So how was the trip? And you must tell me more about your house and your garden, and of course, your beau—" Her gaze shifted over Penelope's shoulder.

Ah ha! So there is at least one thing that can pause Rachel's word flow. She chuckled a bit at the expression on her friend's face as Michael stepped into view. He had been off to her right as the door opened but redistributed his weight as Rachel attempted to drag her into the house bodily, bringing him closer.

"Good afternoon." He offered a courtly bow. "Mayhap I can help with the last bit?" He smirked at Rachel.

"Oh, fiddlesticks, you must be Michael—er, Lord Slade. You may, good sir. You come on in as well. Nothing like hearing it from the horse's mouth," Rachel said and chortled at her own joke.

They stepped into the entryway, Pen automatically turning left into the parlor as voices carried from the kitchen.

Not waiting, Rachel bellowed, "Pen has arrived! And you'll never guess who is with her!"

Mary and Ann came into view from the kitchen and rushed forward, each hugging Penelope in turn before stepping back. Rachel preempted her with the introductions for Michael, finishing with, "and I am Rachel, in case there was any doubt."

He bowed to them all again. "Michael, Lord Slade, at your service, ladies. It is my great pleasure to meet all of you. Thank you for having me in your beautiful home."

Rachel fanned her face with a handkerchief, falling theatrically against Penelope.

She should have gone on stage.

"Well! Leah said…but I did not believe…"

Penelope's smile was smug, pleased at her friend's reaction and at Michael's deference to women who were considered beneath him by society's standards.

"Rachel." Mary's tone carried a warning to her housemate before she herded the guests into the parlor. "Come. Let us all sit, and we can visit." When Penelope claimed her usual spot on the settee, Michael took Rachel's place next to her.

"Is Leah here?" she asked.

"She was due today, but she has yet to arrive."

"Ah. Well, I do see her at least once a fortnight when she's in London, so I dare say we'll make do either way. I know Michael sees her there as well, am I right?" She turned to him to try to ensure he participated in the conversation.

"I see her sometimes, as she joins meetings with Prudence, the theatre manager," he added to the ladies, in case they were not familiar. They nodded. He handed Penelope the bag he had carried for her.

"Oh, right! I brought you a few things." She pulled wrapped parcels from the bag. "Mary, a lace chemise with a bit of extra stitching to help with—er, support. Ann, some garters that I know you, or at least your friend, will like." A smaller one, this one purchased rather than made, "And Rachel, ivory that the maker said was strong enough even for your hair."

"Excellent."

"Thank you so much."

"Yes, thanks."

Sitting back, she stopped them as they tugged at the string. "Ah, mayhap you should open those later, and we can visit now?"

They looked up, and she tilted her head toward Michael.

"I shan't mind if you do it now." Michael's cheek hollowed where he'd caught it between his teeth to stop from laughing.

Arching a brow at him, she drawled, "Please ignore his lordship, ladies. He is teasing me, or you, or all of us. He has seen what sort of gifts I make, as I wore one for him a few nights ago."

Michael's eyes narrowed as he shifted in discomfort from the memory of the lacy confection that Penelope's nipples had poked through, begging to be sucked.

"Minx," he muttered under his breath as she turned back to the women with a smug smile.

Mary's mouth was agape at her audacity with her employer. Rachel was snickering as she eyed Michael's lap, and Ann laughed and took Mary's package, putting both of theirs to the side. She leaned over and whispered to Mary, just loud enough for the room to hear, "I'd rather try them on in private anyway, love."

Mary's face went up in flames, and she buried it in her hands, making the rest of the ladies giggle again.

"How long are you able to stay, Pen?" Rachel asked.

"Three days. We are visiting for Matthew's birthday, but Michael needs to return to London for business."

"You'll be able to visit again whilst you are here?" Rachel's gaze flicked between her and Michael.

Pen laughed under her breath. The ladies wished to hear about her well-being without him present.

"Oh yes. I hope to visit every day. Now, each of you tell me what you have been doing, and only then will we allow Rachel to interrogate Michael."

They all laughed before settling in for a chat.

****

Back at the inn, Penelope collapsed on the bed, arms flung out. "I am eager to see Matt, but gor, I need a quick laydown and a cup of tea before I'm good for much of anything. I never realized how tiring talking can be."

They were in his room. "Right, then. You just lie back and think of England. I need to see if you are wearing that delicious lace camisole you made for yourself."

She was too tired to even giggle. He rolled her to her side, her limp body sprawling when he flipped it. Unlacing her dress and stays, he pulled one side down, then rolled her back to tug on the other side enough to expose her chemise and the top of her stays. He shoved the straps of her chemise down until her breasts popped free of the neckline. Leaving the undergarment where it caught on the loosened stays, he leaned over and sucked a hard tip into his mouth hungrily.

She arched, the strong draw skirting the line between pleasure and pain. She grabbed his head, unsure if she desired to pull him back and catch her breath or press him closer. In the end, she merely held him as he moved to her other breast, palming it with one hand as his arm braced his upper body next to her head.

His tongue swiped back and forth, harder than he had in the past. Her other nipple, damp from his ministrations, tightened further when the air hit it.

She stopped trying to decide if she liked what he was doing or not and simply gave herself over to him. He would do what he wished. She was his to play with, and she always ended up enjoying his ministrations.

Bolts of pleasure shot through her, and her hips jerked, jolting the bed and his leg. She loved hovering on that edge.

Levering to stand, he shoved his jacket and waistcoat off and dragged up her skirts.

Stealing a decorative pillow off the chair behind him, he sank to his knees by the bed to hook his hand behind her legs and draw her toward him.

Her skirts caught under her, so he grasped the front of them and flipped them over her waist.

Watching him lazily, she idly wished he'd remove his shirt, but she was too tired to ask.

Smoothing his hand up her inner thigh, he wetted two fingers and feathered them across the lips of her sex. Tugging each, he encouraged her sensitive flesh to swell and emerge.

She moaned under her breath, throwing an arm over her eyes and tilting her hips for him. Fatigue was forgotten. Tingles of pleasure ran along her skin. Her fingers itched to grab his hair and drag him up, but she knew he wouldn't allow it. He'd rise when he was ready and not before. Her stomach clenched. She liked his control.

Sighing, she sank into his advice. She'd lie back and relax and enjoy.

And enjoy she did. He blew on her swollen outer lips, making her hips twitch. Tapping the protruding nub, he then glided one finger down, opening her inner petals. His finger made a shallow dip inside and returned to slide around her most sensitive spot, making it harden more. Then he licked his first two fingers thoroughly, pressed his tongue to the sensitive knot of nerves, and drove both fingers into her core, withdrew, and speared in again.

Her breath caught, her body trying to process this intrusion that toed the line of being too rough. But this was Michael, and she trusted him. Relaxing her inner muscles that had clenched, she focused on his mouth first, then his fingers, as her body accommodated them better. Every bump of knuckle rubbed her walls in a different way than his cock but aroused her just as much.

His tongue wiggled side to side, his fingers plunged again, and a flood of wetness rushed within her to coat them. He curled the digits forward, pressing on some magical spot inside her, making tiny movements in and out now and tonguing her swollen nub back and forth.

Oh. Oh. Another new sensation. What did he do with his fingers? Better than any cup of tea, the build to orgasm energized her. Heat built within her, her limbs became lighter, and her heart raced. *Yes, I want this. I want you.*

Her breasts jiggled with his movements, the tips hard little points of sensation. Awake now, she wanted more even as she held her breath, hoping he would not stop what he was doing. Her stomach muscles tightened, her sheath became ridged around him, and her button hardened even further. She held still, anticipating that delicious explosion he excelled at coaxing from her.

Gor, so close.

He drew away for a moment, and her eyes popped open, her mouth opening to beg. Looking at him past her perked nipples and ruched skirts, she watched him rip open his breeches and extract his cock.

"Yes, please." It was a whisper of sound, but his quick grin showed he heard as he shoved into her.

Gasping, she clutched his arms as he leaned forward and braced his weight with one hand, pinching a nipple with the other. Holding her breath on a sharp inhale, she arched up, caught on an erotic edge of stinging pain. She circled her bottom, rubbed her nub against him, and moaned.

"Michael," was all she could manage.

His hips pistoned, snapping back, then forward hard enough to shake the bed.

Less than half a dozen thrusts, and she was coming, throwing her head back and keening, still gripping his arms as her core clenched around him, milking him, and sensation rippled through her from head to toe.

He groaned and straightened, grabbing her hips to make two final quick jerks before shuddering over her. "Ahh, Pen."

She opened her eyes to see him stumble back to half-fall into the chair to recover, breeches still undone, his cock still wet with her juices.

Reaching beside him, he grabbed a cloth, dipped it into the ewer of water, and cleaned himself before redoing his clothes. Then he wrung out the cloth and rewet it to clean her as she lay supine, unmoving where he had left her.

"Pen, you awake there?" His voice held a smile.

"No." Her languor had returned full force.

"Right then. Shall I go alone to introduce myself to

your brother?"

"No. I'm getting up," she grumbled.

"Tea first, I promise." He held his hand and helped her lace up before leading her downstairs.

****

They visited with her family at the little house behind the forge. When Matthew convinced Michael to play a game of shuttlecock with him in the stable yard, Penelope withdrew the sack of coins she had brought for her stepfather.

"David, I have been doing very well, and I even have some savings in a bank in London." She set the cloth bag on his desk in the corner. "There has been no need to sell any of Mama's jewelry. I cannot thank you enough for helping me get started on this path."

"Now, Pen, I don't need your money…" he began, frowning.

As he reached for the bag to give it back to her, she stepped in front of him.

"I know you do not. But I find myself with plenty, and I wish to share it with those I love. You offered me a home for years and provided my food, clothing, and education. I want Matthew to have every opportunity he desires, so please, let me do this, David. 'Tis not repayment. You did all that because you are such a good man, and you loved my mother and me. I want to help you and Matthew like you helped me."

"Ah, my girl." David grabbed her into a bear hug as he always had, and she pretended not to notice him wipe his eyes, even as he ignored her swipe at her own.

Chapter Fifteen

Michael received a message from the earl inviting him to the estate, so he borrowed a horse to ride out there while Penelope walked the ladies' house for a second visit. He desired to see more of the horse training Edward had described and hoped to meet the new countess.

Having been shown to the library while Edward was fetched from the stable yard, Michael strolled around the office. Drawn to the wax seal collection on the shelf behind the desk, he picked one up to admire it. His experienced eye noted the shape of it, and his imagination flared.

Most of them are inordinately smooth, albeit different sizes. Interesting.

The current trend was to have much more ornate, often faceted crystal seals. The more detail the better. This was a deliberate choice or taste. He traced one that was longer than most, a gently curved column with a rounded tip, set on a narrow gold neck that held the wider stamp below it.

'Tis like a cock, albeit on the small side. With a flange so it could be used in any orifice.

Given his host's history at the Spanking Club, he guessed this shape was not coincidental.

He heard booted footsteps approaching in the hall and quickly replaced the seal, then moved back toward the settee and chairs near the fireplace. Folding his hands in front of his own *column* with a snort, he composed his expression.

The tall, dark-haired earl entered, his face weathered and his boots muddy from the stableyard. "Slade. Lovely to see you. Tea? Coffee? Brandy? Whisky?"

Michael sketched a bow. "Peterborough, thank you for having me. Tea would be most welcome."

"Call me Edward, please. A man after my own heart. I can never understand the lords who drink brandy at all times of the day and night. No wonder White's is so often raucous."

"To be sure." He hesitated, not wishing to intrude but not wanting to offend either. "I understand you married recently. May I offer my felicitations?" He bowed again.

"Why, thank you. Yes, I did. And I've never been happier, my friend, in case that last was a question. I hope Sophia will join us if she is about. She often rides around this time."

"Ah. I look forward to meeting her. I am in town for a few days, so there may also be other opportunities."

"What brings you up this way?"

"Well, I was, ah, interested in your horse training business, but the reason to be here rather than in London is...well." Michael frowned, frustrated he hadn't anticipated this question. He hoped Edward's days at the Spanking Club were not too distant and was belatedly glad that the earl's new bride was not present. "If you may recall, last year my theatre hosted an—er, event?"

"The auction? Yes, I saw the handbill posted at Mrs. Potter's but was not in Town for it. I was here working with the horses. I don't know much about it beyond the obvious."

"We had a second one this year. Come to think of it, 'twas around the time of your wedding." He'd seen the announcement.

"Ah, well, that explains why I did not hear of it. I was preoccupied with my bride." Edward's voice was happy, his eyes lighting up as he spoke of his new wife.

"I too must marry soon," Michael muttered, distracted from his tale by the look on his host's face.

"Oh?"

"My father's health is in decline. He and my mother insist that I get settled and start focusing on the earldom in preparation."

"I am very sorry to hear it. Are you close to your family?"

"Very much. My parents allowed my sister and I free rein out of the limelight of London society so we could enjoy our childhoods. Even learning my responsibilities as heir was fun with my father. And my sister is one of my closest friends, although we see each other less now she's married. We wrote regularly when I was away at school and still do."

"Ah, good. May I ask the specifics about your father's health?"

"The physicians say his heart is weak, which leads him to shortness of breath and an inclination toward pneumonia. The past two winters have been a struggle for him, and this cold, wet summer is not giving him a chance to recoup."

"I am very sorry. It does sound like he needs your

help."

"Thank you. Yes, 'tis difficult to see him struggle, although, of course, I never mind helping him and participating in Lords."

Edward snorted. "You're a better man than I am, then. Dash it, the paperwork alone could bury a man, never mind the endless tedium of speeches."

"Ha. You are right. Those are not the entertaining bits. But I do enjoy the strategizing to ensure our country progresses in the right direction."

"Apologies, though, you mentioned the auction? Is that why you are here? To recruit for next year's crop or some such?"

Edward, as the presiding Peer, would be aware of the house at the end of town. As the earl, he set the tone for the city and its inhabitants. Given what Penelope had told Michael about the ladies' stay here, Peterborough's tone was one of tolerance.

"No, I, ah…" Michael was unsure how to frame his circumstances. It was one thing when they were both carefree, untitled youths fresh out of university, playing in the spanking club, gaming hells, and any other after-dark pursuit London offered away from the marriage mart of balls. But now Edward was an earl and married to boot. Michael was unsure if the gentleman's perspective might have changed as a family man.

Flexing his shoulders, he gave a mental shrug. He remembered Edward as forthright and fair. He doubted the earl would condemn others for a lifestyle he might forego now but had participated in for years.

"Well, I somehow found myself with a mistress from the auction." He sighed. Wording it that way was bound to prompt all sorts of questions.

"Really?" Edward drawled. Michael detected a note of sarcasm when he continued. "As in, she plopped onto your lap and adopted you?"

"Well, no, not exactly."

The dark-haired man chuckled. "Right, we shall leave that for now. Mayhap I shall ply you with whisky later and dig the tale from you. Would you be so kind as to explain how you now somehow find yourself here in the north'?"

Michael smiled, resigned. He could not fault the earl's humor at his expense. He deserved it. "She is from here. Her father—well, stepfather—is the blacksmith. It seems he works with your stablemaster?"

"Oh! She is Hunter's daughter? I met her years ago when she and her mother first moved here. She was about thirteen, I think, and they had just had Matthew. How did she end up in the auction? Ah, the ladies, of course. So I was not too far off. She was recruited here, but not by you."

Michael nodded. Like he and his father kept an eye on the villagers near their estate, it appeared Edward did as well.

"She was. I knew Leah Godwin through the theatre." He left it at that, as everyone with knowledge of the School of Enlightenment was sworn to secrecy. It was not up to him to judge whether Edward could be trusted with that information. Only a select few had that authority, and they were all women. He did not even know if Leah had permission to share facts with newcomers. "Anyway, 'tis Matthew's birthday in two days, so Pen asked me to come back with her."

"Pen? Is that her name? I couldn't recall."

"Yes. Well, Penelope."

Edward stared. "Penelope. Right. And she and her mother came here to marry Hunter around five or six years ago." He seemed to be looking through Michael, not seeing him. His voice was flat, staccato.

"Are you quite all right, my lord?" He reverted to formality as he voiced his concern.

"Yes, yes." Edward blinked, seeming to put his upset aside for the moment. "Sorry. How long are you here for then? I should like you both to meet Sophia."

It was Michael's turn to stare. "Bring Penelope?"

The earl wanted him to bring his mistress to meet his countess? Society rules were lax in the country, but as Penelope had noted, that was beyond the pale. Would the new countess not be concerned? Worse, what if she snubbed Pen?

"Yes. I should enjoy seeing her now she is grown. And Sophia loves everyone. She is a country girl from a neighboring shire. London and all its rules were never her thing." His host appeared to understand his concern.

"Well, then. Thank you. Let us know when is convenient. Other than tomorrow evening for Matthew's birthday, our schedule is open." He stood, giving Edward a brief bow before making his exit.

****

David and Matthew arrived promptly at seven o'clock, and the innkeeper showed them to the private dining room Michael had arranged.

"My lord, you needn't have gone to all this trouble for us." David stared around the room, making Michael wonder if he'd ever entered it, despite living only steps away for years.

Matthew ran to Penelope, calling her "Penlappy," which made Michael grin. The boy began regaling her with everything he had done since he had seen her the night before, almost as though she had never been away. Both Hunter men had wet hair, and their clothes were pressed. David had a reasonably white shirt and cravat and a coat that was shiny with use but did not exhibit fraying. Matthew was in a skeleton suit—a pair of overalls that had become the rage for young boys—that Michael bet Pen had made for him.

Penelope had hidden her birthday gift for Matthew so it did not preempt dinner, and the innkeeper served their first course soon after they arrived, per Michael's request. He had kept it to two courses before dessert, not wishing to make the Hunters uncomfortable. And after checking with Pen about Matthew's favorite dessert, he had arranged for marzipan treats in the shape of horses for dessert.

After dinner, Matt was awarded his gift, an impressive selection of toy soldiers that his sister had searched high and low for in London. There were both infantry and cavalry in two different uniforms, so he could stage battles as he wished. He put her into service as the opposing general, leaving Michael and David to sip port at the dinner table.

"My lord, if I may ask, you seem to know Penelope rather well. How long ago did you meet her?"

He was wary but saw no reason to lie about this. "Soon after she came to London."

"Hmm. So you know the family she is positioned with?"

Michael knew that David presumed she was a governess, as that was the training she had told her stepfather about. But she had been very careful never to name her role when she wrote to him, quoting, "I have an excellent position and am well-compensated and happy," as she had told Michael.

"Er, yes." He supposed that was true. She was employed by him and positioned with the Thorpes.

"And she's happy?" That seemed to be David's biggest concern.

"She says she is. I believe her."

"And she is safe?"

"Most definitely."

"Good, good. I worry about a young girl in London on her own. All the—pardon me for saying so—entitled nabobs, and she is beautiful like her mother. I want her to have time to find a good husband, someone she loves. Like her ma and I did. She deserves that."

Michael gulped. Unable to find the right words, he nodded.

"And what of you, your lordship? 'Tis odd for you to be traveling together, even if London doesn't catch wind of it, and for her to be staying at the inn with you?" David's brow was furrowed as he threw the gauntlet, bringing the awkward situation into full light.

"I am not sure what you mean." He hardened his voice, aiming for stern and aristocratic, trying to ward off any further probing. "I believe she thought it best to stay there, as you and Matthew were likely accustomed to being without a woman in your midst."

"Word from Larry—"

Ugh. David knew the innkeeper. Michael mentally rolled his eyes.

"—is that you paid for both rooms."

"I offered as a gentleman, and she accepted. She had planned to stay with the ladies if not you, but that did not seem like the best idea." He must remember to tell Penelope of the bluff.

"Hmph."

And that was that, thankfully, as it was close enough to Matt's bedtime that the Hunter family said their goodbyes.

****

The next morning, Edward sent word around to the inn that he was stopping in the town and would enjoy Michael's company for a pint in the afternoon if he was free. Michael lounged downstairs at a table until Edward arrived, and the two men made their way to the pub in the center of town.

On the way, Edward explained that he liked to eat or drink where the locals chose to, rather than in the inn with travelers. He hoped Peterborough residents would then be more comfortable calling on him should they need him. The men chose a table in a corner of the front room. A good compromise, it enabled them to speak without being overheard while the earl still showed his support to townsfolk.

"'Tis not the best, but it is the local brew, and I always have one." Edward nudged a full pint glass across the table.

Michael cast about for a subject to preempt questions about Penelope. "Tell me more about your transition to earl and how you met your wife so quickly."

"Sophia is Nick's cousin. You remember that Suffolk and I are close from school, and then later, the, ah, Sarah's club?"

"Right, of course. Suffolk has been married a few years now, has he not? I do not recall him having a cousin, though. Was she still in the schoolroom then?"

"She grew up near here. As I mentioned, she is from this area. Her father was the caretaker for one of Nicholas's estates to the west. When he passed, Nick called her to London to give her a Season."

Michael had watched with interest as his fellow members of the Spanking Club married and often bet with Robert and Evan who would keep their membership and who would leave. Both Nicholas and Edward had withdrawn. But mayhap they could benefit from the School of Enlightenment. Penelope had mentioned a program for young ladies of the Ton, for before or after marriage. He might need to have a word with Leah, but in the meantime, he dared to venture a question. "Do you miss Sarah's at all, then?"

Edward barked a laugh. "Not even a little."

"Huh. You were one of the regulars. I confess I am surprised."

Edward simply grinned.

"Well, married life certainly agrees with you. You look happy, old chap. I am very glad for you." Michael drained his glass and watched as the earl finished off his pint. He arched a brow. "Ah, Scotch, mayhap?"

The earl gestured to the barkeep. "Two glasses and a bottle of my favorite Scotch, please."

They spoke of a recent bill up for review by the House of Lords and Edward's business. Before long, the bottle was a third empty.

Edward pounced. "Explain to me how you somehow had a mistress fall into your lap."

Michael snorted, envisioning draping her over his lap to spank her the very first time he met her. But he was not quite ready to share all the details. He did not know Edward well enough. And besides, the man outranked him. He must maintain some circumspection. He took a moment to consider his response, one hand fidgeting next to his glass on the table. In the end, he simply said, "I had to have her."

Edward nodded, silently urging him to expound.

"My mother—" He stopped. If Edward was not aware that his mother had been an actress, there was no reason to share that detail. "Suffice it to say that she is very focused on me finding a suitable, decorous wife. She is…scandal-averse." He suppressed a laugh at his wording and recognized the effects of the whisky. "It was easier to visit the club rather than risk my parents hearing about me keeping a mistress. And this year, with my father's illness progressing, 'tis time for me to find a wife in readiness for assuming the earldom." He tipped his glass at Edward, knowing the new earl would understand. "I want my father to know I am settled and to meet my wife, mayhap even see a grandchild or two."

"Hmm. But you needed to attend the auction as the host, and then…Penelope."

"That sums it up nicely."

"Have your parents discovered her existence yet?"

"No, thankfully. I am spending a few evenings a week courting suitable young women from the Ton. My family's priorities are that and my help with Lords."

"So, ah, may I ask what you shall do when you marry?" Edward asked, his tone neutral.

Michael could not read his opinion on the fact that many Ton marriages did not interfere with maintaining mistresses.

"I shall end the relationship with Penelope." He struggled to say the words aloud. "I will honor my marriage vows, however unfashionable that may be."

Edward smiled and sighed a breath of relief. "Well, consider Nicholas and me unfashionable with you, then. But we married women we fell in love with."

"I still hope that might be possible." He could not picture being in love with a wife.

What does it say that I can picture being with Pen forever? I cannot love her. Or at least, I cannot have her. It might be too late to avoid the first.

He sighed.

"And..." Edward leaned in. "What of your, ah, preferences that the club caters to?"

He contemplated the school. Mayhap as Pen had suggested, he could send his wife there, at least for a few days, and see if she'd be willing to learn? After all, he had considered it for Edward's wife. Of course, he had no idea how he'd raise that subject with a young debutante. Even with the school, he doubted anyone could compare to how well Penelope fit him in all ways.

His only reply to Edward was, "I suppose that will depend on my wife to some extent."

The earl sat back and considered him with narrowed eyes, swallowing the last of his whisky.

****

Penelope had told her stepfather she would get Matthew from the James's home after tea with her friends. She strolled the length of Eastfield Road to their cottage, set a few houses off the main avenue, and knocked.

The door opened to reveal a woman in a butter yellow dress worthy of Hyde Park that almost exactly matched her hair.

"Hello, is Matthew…" She tilted her head, staring at the woman even as the lady stood frozen, staring at her.

"Pen?" the lady breathed.

"Soph?" She reached out one hand, not even sure what she was reaching for. She'd have known that face and hair anywhere.

"Criminy, is it really you?" the woman bounced once and then leaped at Penelope.

"Sophia, Sophia! My word, I have missed you! You must tell me everything!"

From behind Sophia came a voice, "My lady? Do you know each other?"

Penelope drew back sharply.

My lady? Oh no. While the people here in Peterborough did not know her profession, if Sophia spent any time in London, it would quickly become apparent. An association between them was beyond unseemly.

"We seem to have quite a bit to catch up on, *my lady*," she quipped, arching a brow.

"Bah, stop that. You are Pen, and I am Soph, always." The petite blonde nodded her head once in emphasis.

Fast footsteps sounded, and Matthew came barreling toward Penelope, throwing his arms around her legs. "Penlappy! Time to go home? Today I learned—"

"Uh—" Sophia gestured toward Matthew with her chin, her focus still on Penelope. "Something you'd mayhap like to share with me, as well?"

"Matthew is my half-brother. Mama married David Hunter, the blacksmith here in town."

"No! Have you been here this whole time? I only arrived a couple of months ago, but I would hate to think that I had not discovered you when you were so close."

"No, I am visiting from London, as 'twas this little imp's birthday yesterday."

Sophia knelt. "You had a birthday yesterday, and you did not inform me?" She put a hand to her chest in mock outrage.

Matthew, even at four, seemed to know Sophia well enough to recognize teasing. "My apologies, my lady."

He bowed, and Penelope had a moment's pause from her awe of finding her childhood best friend to be impressed with his manners.

"Mayhap a birthday trip to your stables?" he asked hopefully, with a cheeky grin.

Sophia threw her head back and laughed.

"We shall see." Standing, she did not even bother brushing off her skirts. "Pen, please. How long are you here? I must see you. Can you come out to our home tomorrow? Please?" She bounced again, clasping her hands to her chest in fervor.

"Er, I take it from your title that you are the Countess of Peterborough, then?"

"Yes. Yes! So much to tell you and to ask."

"Right. We are scheduled to visit tomorrow then, as Michael and his lordship know each other."

Bloody hell! More questions would arise from that statement.

"Oh. Are you married as well, then?"

"No." Her mouth was a flat line, and she glanced at her brother pulling on his coat. While she refused to be embarrassed by her profession and would share it privately with Sophia, it was not something she wished to discuss in front of the Jameses or Matthew.

"Right then." Sophia took the hint. "We shall cover all of that tomorrow. I hope you plan to come for lunch, so we have plenty of time."

Pen curtsied. "Thank you, my lady. I look forward to seeing you tomorrow then."

"Stop that!" Sophia retorted, frowning. "I mean it."

She nodded and took Matt's hand to walk him home for dinner. Time enough tomorrow for her friend to learn that a renewed friendship was not to be.

Chapter Sixteen

Michael handed Penelope out of the carriage in front of the Peterborough estate. She had alternated between elation over seeing Sophia again and hopelessness at navigating a friendship given the directions life had taken them. Given her waffling, she had not told Michael about recognizing her childhood companion.

Sophia flew out of the front door, nearly knocking over the butler who had opened it. Skimming down the steps, she again threw herself at Penelope. "I kept worrying that it had been a dream!"

Pen clutched at her for a moment before her brain seesawed to the difficulties of their circumstances. Taking a half-step back, she almost curtsied before catching her friend's warning expression.

"My lady, Sophia, may I introduce Lord Slade?" Gesturing to Michael with her right hand, she nodded to Sophia.

Sophia's smile was no less warm for Michael as he took her ungloved hand and bowed over it.

"My lady, a pleasure."

Edward hovered in the doorway, calling to his wife, "Sophia, mayhap you could allow them into the house?"

She laughed up at him and scampered back up the stairs, gesturing to their guests.

"Yes, please. We shall have tea in the music room."

The earl shook his head at his wife, even as he smiled. She leaned in and spoke low as she passed him.

Penelope could swear she heard, "I am sorry again for spoiling your surprise, my lord. I cannot help that we rediscovered each other in town. But you may punish me later if you like."

She schooled her expression as Edward glanced toward her and Michael to gesture them toward the music room.

I must have heard wrong.

The women reclined on the settee together. Once Sophia poured tea, the men adjourned to hover near a window that looked out over the stables and yard where Edward's horse training business centered.

"Tell me everything." Sophia leaned in. "Wait. First, I must ask, did you not get my letter? I sent one about a month after you left."

Pen shook her head. "No. Never, I am sorry to say. Gosh, where to start? 'Tis hard to believe six years have passed."

"How long have you been in Peterborough?"

"We came straight here from Stamford when Mama married David. But what of you? When did that happen?" She angled her head toward Edward.

"A little over two months ago."

"Are you happy, Soph?"

"Oh yes. Edward is…everything. But we were discussing you. How do you come to be here with Lord Slade?"

"Mama wanted me to be a governess, but I needed more schooling. Then…she caught an inflammation of the lungs and died this past winter."

"Oh no." Tears sprang to Sophia's eyes. As she lifted a trembling hand to her mouth, Edward's head turned to check on his wife. She waved him off. "Pen, I am so sorry. I loved your mother, too, and have many fond memories of her teaching us to bake in Father's kitchen. You were so good at that, unlike me. But you are a governess now? For Lord Slade's children?"

"Er, no. He does not have children." Penelope shifted on the settee, setting down her cup, and changed the subject. "Tell me how you've been? How did you come to marry Lord Peterborough? And how is your dear father?"

Sophia pursed her lips. "Father died last year. It was sudden—his heart—on his way home from tending a sick animal in the village." Sophia's father had been a veterinarian in addition to acting as caretaker for the Earl of Suffolk's northern estate.

Penelope clutched her friend's hands, one still holding her teacup and saucer. "Soph. I don't know what to say. I am sorry for your loss."

Disentangling her hand to place her cup down next to Penelope's, Sophia returned to holding her friend. "As I am for yours. We have both had terrible losses. But—you seem happy? I know I am, although I miss Father every time I pick up a newspaper or mix a salve."

"I am glad. So how did you meet Lord Peterborough?" Penelope again evaded further questions about her current circumstances, still not certain of how to navigate that conversation with her now-a-countess friend.

"Ahh, Edward." Sophia's smile stretched across

her face. "He is best friends with Father's cousin who holds the estate back in Stamford. Nicholas—Lord Suffolk—offered me a Season. But once I met Edward, I did not need the balls and such. He is everything I ever wanted and some—" She snickered. "—I did not even know I desired."

"Hmm, that sounds interesting. I will echo your sentiment. Tell me everything." Pen laughed at her friend, unable to contain her happiness in the moment, no matter how it might unravel later.

Sophia glanced across the room at her husband and leaned in. "Nicholas had asked him to help introduce me to society and navigate all the rules and whatnot. And Edward loves horses mayhap even more than I do, so he took me on morning rides in Hyde Park."

"So that is how you met. But I am guessing you are not leaning in to tell me that in secrecy," Penelope mock-whispered back. *Gor, 'tis as though we were not separated for six years.*

"Well, no. I, uh, snuck out with some of the stable hands to a horse auction at Vauxhall. Edward ended up needing to rescue me." Sophia smiled dreamily.

Penelope sensed there was more. "Oh gosh, I am surprised your cousin did not disallow you riding privileges after that." Her brows arched in question.

"Uh—" Sophia snuck a peek at the men's distance again. "I confess I begged him not to tell Nicholas, so *Edward* punished me." She sat back, lips tight together in a flat line as though she realized she had overshared and was loathe to say more.

"Soph. Come now, you cannot leave it there. How on earth could an unrelated gentleman punish you? Not ride with you? Not call on you?"

"He, er, spanked me." Her friend's lips hardly moved, less a whisper and more of a wisp of sound escaping.

"Soph!" Penelope leaned in, understanding without it needing to be said that their friendship would always mean secrets remained between them and went no further. "And did you enjoy it?"

Sophia's eyes opened wide in shock. "And why would you ask that? How do you even know about things like that?"

Penelope sat back. There it was. She'd known it would come to this sooner or later.

"Sophia." She took her friend's hands again. "I am not a governess. After school, I—with the help of a friend—became a courtesan." She released Sophia's hands in case her friend wanted to withdraw from Penelope's presence.

"Pen. What? How? Ah, by choice? Are you happy? Or do you need anything?" Sophia's hands fluttered before returning to grip Penelope's.

Pen smiled, relieved. Of course her friend's generous spirit prompted that first reaction. And while they could not continue their friendship in London, at least she would have Sophia here to visit with away from Town.

"Yes, by choice. I am happy enough. Michael is my first—er…" She stalled. After all, she was in an earl's home whom she did not know. One did not discuss these subjects.

"Ooohhh." Sophia looked around at the men, her gaze scrolling up and down Michael's form as he chatted with Edward. "Hmph. He is not the worst you could do." She slid a side glance at Penelope, quirking her lips to try not to laugh.

Penelope batted at her arm. "No, he is not. Although…" It was Penelope's turn to lean in now. "He, too, is prone to punishments."

Sophia turned back to her. "Start from the beginning. How did you meet?"

****

After tea, Edward offered his guest a quick tour of the grounds before lunch.

At his request, Michael had shared the name of the young lady he'd been wooing, along with a few other recent names, and Edward provided whatever he knew of their families. By all reports, the Luds were respectable, making Lady Grace eminently suitable for Michael and his parents' expectations.

Now as they walked, the earl pointed out some of the training operations. He also inquired about several Parliamentary Acts being reviewed in Lords and impressed Michael with his ability to retain details. Michael vowed to discuss—or correspond—more with Edward in the future. It seemed the man spent as much time here as possible, as both he and Sophia preferred the estate over London, even during the Season. But he had told Michael they planned to tour his other holdings and come into London to help push the Poor Law reforms along.

"I am sure we will see each other again soon, especially if you work with Nick on the Poor Laws revision. Mayhap by then, you shall be betrothed or even married. Regardless, Sophia will wish to see Penelope again."

Michael's emotions splintered at that. Would he be married that soon? It appeared likely. Which meant that

Pen might be with a new benefactor. He ached at the idea.

When he glanced up, Edward was staring at him rather hard. Accompanying his mistress to visit her family was out of the ordinary, but what was on the earl's mind?

"Tell me more about your family."

"What do you mean?" Michael prevaricated.

"How did your parents meet?"

He studied his host. Did he know? Or was he fishing? Either way, he was not ashamed of his mother. She was a wonderful mother to this day and had made an excellent countess throughout his life. "My father was an avid theatre-goer. He met my mother there."

Edward nodded. "I thought I remembered something along those lines. I heard a lot of gossip in my younger, irresponsible days in London. Your mother acted, correct?"

He nodded.

"And yet, you do not believe you can marry Penelope?"

He stopped, turning to the dark-haired man. "How can you ask that? Even before this"—he gestured to the estate—"you knew enough of the rules to know 'tis impossible. My mother and father did everything they could to protect my sister and me from gossip. They were very selective about their friends and social events they attended all my life. Now my father is gravely ill, and they desire to see me settled. More, they want to ensure that I shall not be put through what they experienced."

Edward folded his arms and gentled his voice, asking, "Have you ever asked them if they'd do it differently if they could?"

He cocked his head. "I am not at all sure I wish to know the answer to that, as I would not be here today if they had." He smiled, but the earl did not.

"Mayhap you should ask. Would your father have married for duty and left your mother if his parents did not approve? For that matter, I cannot believe they did approve."

"Are you saying I should marry Penelope?"

"Not at all." Edward turned and restarted their stroll to the stables. He tossed a casual statement over his shoulder. "I never wanted to marry. I was certain I would not find a woman who fit my life."

How did the man end up married to Sophia within a few sennights then? What was so different with her than other ladies? He daren't ask, given the newness of their friendship.

"When I did marry, I did because I could not imagine being with anyone else for one night, much less the rest of my life. Call me a hopeless romantic—"

Michael snickered, and Edward flashed him a grin.

"—but I wish that for everyone. I hope you will marry for love, whoever you choose."

Michael was silent.

"How is Cheltenham these days?" Edward said, changing the subject. "And Orford? Are you three still close?"

"They are doing well, and yes. I forgot you know them."

"Back in my wild days, I looked forward to Cheltie's parties. Sophia even attended one of his tamer ones at the start of the Season. Now she wants to try one of the wilder ones." He shook his head, chuckling.

He was shocked at the earl's ease with that idea. He supposed there were benefits to not having a close relationship with one's parents.

He and Penelope took their leave a short time later, the ladies having said their goodbyes, promising to write often.

In the carriage, he asked, "What did you and the Countess talk about? And why did she greet you like that?"

"Oh. I met her yesterday briefly when getting Matthew from his caretaker. D'you remember me talking about moving to Peterborough and losing my closest friend?"

He nodded.

"'Twas Sophia. We were both so shocked. She seems to want to take up where we left off six years ago. She was not bothered in the least by the nature of my relationship with you. She was only concerned I had not had a choice in the matter." Her surprise was evident in her tone. "I mean, of course we cannot promenade through Hyde Park together or attend the same teas, but still. It shall be lovely to have her friendship again, in letters and here at home when I can visit."

He nodded. He understood all the reasons even a simple tea was a bad idea, even if Edward refused to see it.

****

Michael was quiet in the carriage on their return trip to London. He could not stop reviewing Edward's reaction. He had expected the earl to slap him on the back and encourage him to keep Penelope on the side. If not after marriage, at least during the engagement, as many Peers did. He could have understood even a referral back to the Spanking Club.

Instead, the man had poked at his allegiance to his parents' wishes and encouraged him to follow his heart.

After hours of mental circling, he could stand it no longer. He needed a distraction. After their lunch stop, he dragged Pen across to him and unfastened the top of her gown.

This. This will get my mind off marriage.

He unlaced her bodice, tugged it and her chemise below her breasts, and cupped them to sup with pursed lips. She slid her hands into his hair as he liked, yanking when he sucked harder, petting when he licked and soothed.

However, the distraction did not work as intended. His brain waffled. He imagined never seeing these beautiful breasts again, never smelling Pen's unique scent of ginger, lemons and sometimes flour. Then he pictured the disappointment in his parents' faces if he told them how he'd met her and that he was marrying her.

After a few minutes, she pulled his hair harder, tilting his head back, and leaned down to kiss him. "Michael, you are obviously preoccupied. Do you wish to discuss it?"

He shook his head and buried his face in her breasts for comfort now. She wrapped her arms around his skull and held him to her, offering succor however he allowed.

They stopped for a quick supper and a change of horses at an inn in Hertfordshire but had tacitly agreed to push on to London. They nodded in the dark carriage until it slowed. When the carriage stopped, Pen woke with a shiver in the icy darkness and saw her street.

Michael alighted first and handed her down. He walked her to the door and ensured she got inside but declined to come in with her. Dropping a quick peck on her lips, he thanked her for her company and departed, pensive again. He needed to be home, in the family's London house, to remind himself of his obligations as the next Earl of Mansfield.

****

Michael's abrupt departure and continued silence of the following days did not surprise Penelope. She was preoccupied as well. The dichotomy of surprised joy at finding Sophia was offset by a spiral of sadness at not being able to pursue their friendship. Even without her chosen profession, Sophia's new station in life precluded a public relationship between them.

Until Michael's mood became obvious in the carriage, she hadn't considered what the men had discussed while she and Sophia visited. But something was troubling him. Mayhap the amount of time they had spent together was too much.

Was he tired of her already? Put off by her humble origins now he had seen them?

She did not believe that was the case, as they had talked about their childhoods enough before the trip, but aristocrats' reactions were unpredictable when faced with the reality of daily life for the working class.

The lease on the house was until Michaelmas, well past the Season, and Michael had promised her she could stay throughout, no matter when or if he became betrothed.

However, the Season was also her best opportunity to find her next suitor. She had a month before

Parliament adjourned and the Season was declared over. She had to evaluate her options.

As she went about her gardening, food shopping at the market with Mrs. Thorpe, and helping with dinners, her thoughts circled. She was working up to going back to the theatre to help out but kept putting off sending a note 'round. Missing Michael was further compounded with now missing Sophia and thinking of details they hadn't yet had time to share, questions she wanted to ask. Having fallen into a state of despondency, she had yet to find her way out.

Finally, Leah came to call. She was the perfect audience for Penelope's heartache. She had been there from the start. She knew Penelope's background and more recent events that had led her to this, except for her childhood friendship with Sophia.

She poured her story out to Leah over cups of tea, the pot refilled twice before she finished.

Her friend's reaction was not what she had hoped for. Leah set her cup and saucer down, firmed her lips, and lowered her chin, looking at Pen from under her brows. "What was the most important rule we taught you?"

"What?" Penelope was confused. Was Leah asking her if she knew how to win Michael back? She'd need him to at least come visit her to even try.

"Do *not*, under any circumstances, fall in love with your client. This is a job. It can be a very successful career, but not if you fall in love." Leah sighed in frustration.

Oh, that. Her gaze dropped to her lap. The instructors' direction had been clear, warning the girls of the pitfalls, particularly during their early years. As young, beautiful mistresses, they'd get showered with attention and gifts, and it could go to their heads.

She had tried to keep that lesson in the forefront of her mind. Michael had been clear that they had an end date. She knew better, but she had fallen in love anyway.

"Were you aware that Lord Slade has offered to sponsor another student?" Leah asked.

"He told me he had written to Mrs. Montague, yes."

"What if he is looking for his next mistress? You preferred not to be with a married man when we placed you, but not all girls have the same sensibilities."

"He did that because of a conversation we had about working-class girls' choices. His mother... Well, never mind, but I know he is not looking for a mistress. If he was, I might reconsider my 'sensibilities.'"

Leah shook her head, obviously frustrated that her warnings had fallen on deaf ears.

"Leah, I know that Michael needs to marry. I know that Sophia is a countess. I am a realist. I always was, long before the school. This shall pass, and I shall get back to working toward my bakery," she vowed as much to herself as her friend and mentor.

Leah nodded once. "Right, then. You can take another day to wallow, then back to your routine. I shall expect you at the theatre tomorrow, dear." She set her teacup down.

Penelope rose with her. "Thank you for coming. I appreciate your support and guidance more than I can say."

But after Leah left, she resumed her seat and stared into the empty fireplace for long minutes, contemplating her next steps.

He had followed through on sponsoring a student. And Leah wondered why I love him. I need that nest egg to invest in a business, but more, for freedom. They were right when they said not everyone is suited to this profession. Even the pragmatists have their limits.

As the room darkened with shadows, she reached a decision. Impossible to imagine as it was, if Michael was nearing a marriage contract before the end of the Season, she would attend a Cyprian ball. She preferred to have someone else paying for her housing for the long winter months.

If he remained single, mayhap they could continue their association until the mini-Season at the holidays. As much as she'd like to go home and save her money and start fresh next year, to have time to recover from this first intense relationship, it was best to get back on the horse, so to speak.

When Mrs. Thorpe indicated that dinner was ready, she returned to the present and took Leah's advice to move forward with her routine again, Michael or no.

Chapter Seventeen

The theatre was busier than ever. The new show that had begun while she was away was still early in its run, and the cast and crew were working out the kinks in the scene changes.

Penelope helped with run-throughs all day. At long last, she plopped into a seat with some food from the buffet backstage, readying to return home.

Will Michael be here with a date this evening? Will it be the same girl I saw him with twice before?

She rose and meandered toward the costume closet. Flipping through the costumes, she remained uninspired. She had used several, and others had gone in trades to other theatres as productions changed. Toward the back, she unearthed a young girl's dress. She touched her pocket. She had made a batch of ginger sticks two days before—her favored recipe to uplift her spirits—and she had wrapped one and brought it as a snack. But the day had been too busy today to even think of it, much less eat it. Recalling her naïve approach to the auction, she eyed the girlish dress. That and the ginger stick should strike a chord for Michael.

With a snap decision, she whipped out of her dress and into the girlish high-necked dress with a smock and no waist and grabbed low-heeled ankle boots. A dark wavy-haired wig for disguise went over her hair, the wig left down. Adding a tinge of pink to her cheeks, she checked to ensure she looked several years younger. Realizing her breasts in her stays were not those of a younger girl, she removed the dress and stays and grabbed a light scarf. She wound the fabric around her chest to flatten it as much as possible before redressing without the stays. Candy in hand, she headed out front.

She hovered in the lobby, trailing behind a couple of an age that could support having a daughter of thirteen or fourteen. When they entered the theatre to find their seats, she veered off to trail behind another couple she targeted. The crowd swelled as the performance time neared, more groups entering to greet friends before finding their seats. She inched her way toward the stairs that led to the private boxes.

The air around her stirred, and she knew without turning that Michael had arrived. Looking around, everyone else appeared oblivious. Only she was so attuned to him.

She stepped back into the curtain by the stairs to his box and watched.

His favorite hat made its way through the crowd, along with a wake of plumes from women's millinery behind him.

She caught glimpses of his face as he neared and raised the ginger candy to her mouth, licking it so it would not stick to her lips.

One last person shifted, and he was striding toward her.

Her tongue ran up the other side of the stick before it disappeared between her lips, her cheeks hollowing as she sucked it, staring into his eyes.

His gaze caught hers, his eyes widening as he recognized her. He took in the costume and the candy and the pose. His abrupt stop caused the woman behind him to bump into him. His lips parted, a quiet groan emerging before the woman said something to him.

Stepping aside, he muttered, "My apologies, Mother. You know the way. Please go ahead."

Penelope spared the woman another quick glance, curious about this person Michael spoke of so much. She refocused on him as she drew the savory treat out of her mouth, her lips fighting the motion of her hand the whole way. Then, dropping her gaze, she brushed by him as he stood statue-like, making sure to skim her hip along his.

His hand dropped as though to grab her or adjust his length in his breeches. She wasn't sure which, but she did not intend to stay and find out.

She forged her path past the others in his party to see who accompanied him. Sure enough, the same young lady was there for a third time—Lady Grace, if Penelope remembered correctly.

Something cracked wide open inside her. She was pretty sure it was her heart, despite her assurances to Leah. She was almost out of time.

****

Michael climbed the stairs, still trying to talk himself out of visiting Penelope even as he gained the upper floor of her house.

You must stop this. You are going to offer for Lady Grace any day. You must wean yourself off this, this, paramour*!*

He winced as his subconscious used his mother's label for members of the demi-monde. Then he told his subconscious to go to hell and snicked open the door to Penelope's bedroom.

A single glance at her sleeping form, one candle still lit as was her habit on nights he might visit, and his cock rose. His throat tightened at the thought of not having this view, this woman in his life. Shaking his head to avoid any more thinking, he slipped his cravat free and sat on a footstool to remove his boots. After shucking the rest of his clothes in seconds, he climbed into bed behind her and scooted her form back against him. She mumbled something, snuggling in, before waking a bit more and trying to turn around for him.

"Ssshhh, sleep," he whispered, tightening his grip to keep her in the curve of his body. She reached for his hand, nestling it with hers under her breast, effectively wrapping him around her as a blanket. Her head relaxed into the pillow, and she murmured his name as she fell back asleep.

Michael lay awake. Smelling her hair and a lingering scent of ginger, he freed his hand with a slow tug, groaning as it slid against her breast. He raised it to stroke the softness of her long ebony strands, then the skin of her arm. His fingers ran over the curve of her waist, her hip, her thigh, only to start at the top again.

The candle gutted out some time later. He stilled, staring into the darkness for hours. His brain circled from his mother's pleas to marry appropriately and quickly, to Edward's words, to Penelope's portrayal of financial concerns for anyone without a sizeable estate and her dream of a bakery.

He sorted through ideas. He could choose never to marry and remain with Penelope, but then the estate would go to a distant cousin unprepared to handle the responsibilities. He hated that idea for his tenants' sake almost as much as his parents did. He could keep

Penelope after marriage and deal with his conscience. But even if he could silence that and ignore his parents, she would be miserable. And she preferred to do this only until she had enough to start a bakery. Mayhap he could give her the money now for the bakery, so she would not need a new patron. But that did not guarantee she would not marry, as he must.

The idea of her with another man in any kind of relationship tortured him.

Why is that so galling? And why have I been dragging my feet to ask for Lady Grace's hand? He stewed. *For the same reason, I cannot picture myself with anyone other than Penelope. I have not been able to admit to myself that I love her. Blast it! Damn Peterborough and his ideas. Why could my parents choose love and I cannot? This was hard enough before Edward pointed out the unfairness. Before I admitted the depth of my affection.*

No matter how many ideas he dug through, 'twas impossible to make everyone happy. He was bound to satisfy everyone's demands except his own—and Penelope's, if she had ever made any on him.

****

Michael's sleep was fitful, and he left at first light. Determined to refocus on his family obligations, he returned to his parents' London house rather than his bachelor quarters. Ordering breakfast to his father's study he had shared these past two years, he sat at the desk to pore over Parliamentary bills. His father prioritized what he wanted Michael to review, ensuring he was up to snuff with the current issues on the floor of the House of Lords.

He checked correspondence from the estates and

set a few things aside to summarize with the earl.

After three hours, he stood and stretched, then rang for more tea. He circled the desk and paced the floor to get the blood flowing in his muscles again after sitting for so long. Hearing his father's voice in the hall, he turned toward the door.

The older man stepped into the room and exclaimed, "Michael! I was glad to hear that you were here when I came down to breakfast. Have you eaten?"

"Yes, thank you, Father." Michael strode over and hugged his father, squeezing his shoulders in affection. "Come. I've rung for tea. Let's go over a few notes I have outlined."

"Excellent. I wish to discuss the Poor Laws with you again. Did you see the draft of the Workhouse Act currently in the House of Commons?"

"Yes." Michael's lips flattened.

The Poor Laws, in effect for the past few decades, allowed each local parish to set the parameters of punishment for a person's inability to pay their debts. The result was significant inequities across the country and, in many instances, no solution to alleviate poverty. Throwing the old and infirm into workhouses did not produce viable output or offer them a livable wage. Penelope's comment about mothers with young children exiting their shift in Gressenhall made that clear. No education meant the cycle would continue, in addition to the dangers for the children.

"They are forming a Special Committee," his father said. "I should like to join, but I am worried I do not have the energy for the extra hours and travel to perform discovery on the issue. Unfortunately, as you are not a member, you cannot join the Committee.

Mayhap you could volunteer as an adjunct?"

"I can. But I am unsure whether they will accept that. And I worry they shan't listen to a non-member of Parliament for the final decision. There may be another way. How well do you know the Earl of Suffolk and the Earl of Peterborough?"

"Young bucks, are they not? About your age? They have been allies in a few of the bills I've pushed for votes this Session."

He nodded. "Yes, you've got it. Peterborough is returning from his honeymoon to finish the Session, and Suffolk is his cousin-in-law. Peterborough is of a like mind. I will pay a visit to Suffolk House and see if we can coordinate as a group."

"Excellent, my dear boy. I am grateful. I only wish I could be the flag-bearer for this important reform needed. Now, do you have time to visit with your mother, or might you have other appointments?"

A second later, his mother's voice filtered in from the hall. Blast, she'd want to know progress on his betrothal, especially after another outing with Lady Grace with both mothers in attendance. He replayed his father's question in his head. His father was giving him an out.

He smiled at the earl, who winked. "I must get to my club to see if I can catch other members of our group there and to send round a note to Suffolk." He finished speaking and stood as his mother rounded the doorway.

"Michael! So lovely to see you, my favorite son!"

"Mother." He kissed each cheek as she presented them to him, holding her outstretched hands, and replied with his usual, "I am your only son."

"Yes, you are lucky the bar is low." She squeezed him and chuckled at their standard greeting, as did he.

"So—" she began.

"I am afraid I was just leaving for my club, Mama. I'd love to catch up, but I have"—he glanced at his father—"appointments. I shall return as soon as I can."

His mother frowned at her husband, showing her suspicion about who had voiced concern over appointments.

His father contrived to look innocent.

Michael fought a snicker and kissed his mother's cheeks again. He bowed his excuses and stepped into the hall for his coat, hat, and gloves.

****

After nursing her cracked and probably irrevocably broken heart for a day, Penelope renewed her decision to see more of the demi-monde. As a student, she had learned of this shadow world whose parties mimicked the Ton's formal balls but with a much shorter set of rules. Gentlemen attended these with their mistresses, sometimes in the same night after a visit to Almack's with their wives.

She wrote a quick message to Leah and planned to discuss the idea with Michael when she saw him next.

But for a fortnight, Michael sent notes round saying that there was an important project for Parliamentary reform he was working on with his father and some allies, and he was too busy to visit during the day. He sent small gifts as well—gourmet treats that she'd dissect to see if she could emulate, if the urge to cook ever returned, garden plants that saddened her as she'd likely only have them for a month more; and a gorgeous necklace with a daisy pendant, each leaf and the center a small diamond that caught the light and glittered with every movement. But none were a substitute for seeing him.

She helped at the theatre, ensuring she left an hour before the performance began, even if she took costume mending home with her. Most nights that was not necessary. The productions did not have enough funding for extra costumes, so most had to be worn every night in whatever condition they could be brought to before showtime. Then she wandered her house, trying to sew while there was light, scribbling recipe ideas in the hope they would incite her to venture back to the kitchen.

Each night she carried a glass of sherry up to bed after a light meal and read by candlelight, listening for a key in the lock or a tread on the stairs. Sometimes, she'd awake late in the darkness, the candles gutted, to a silent house.

A number of nights Michael slipped in late, she never asked from where. She preferred to assume he had been at his club talking politics.

He would climb to her room, murmuring instructions if she was awake. "Ah good, come undress me." "What, you are not naked yet?" "Kneel, my lovely girl, I need you." Gathering her hair in one hand, unfastening his breeches with the other.

He always ensured her pleasure, either before or after his, then he'd hold her until she slept. He was always gone by the time she awoke.

The whole routine discouraged her as much as waking alone did. She needn't even bother acting happy or sensuous for him. He did not stay long enough, but she did as she was told.

As I am paid to do. Her lips twisted with bitterness each time her mood devolved. Then she chastised herself for thinking that way. Hers was an honest living, and one she had chosen, one that she had been warned not to risk by falling in love with the man paying her.

'Tis one of the better alternatives women have for gainful occupation. Think of Mary's experience as a much-lower-paid governess. I need to treasure any time I have with him, even as he is pulling away. With that reminder, she shook off her melancholy and moved on with her day.

She daren't ask where he had been, nor did she question the status of his betrothal. Her Lady Grace sightings made it clear that it was imminent. She trusted his moral choice from their past conversations. He would inform her when it happened, so given the lack of updates, she cherished each additional evening she had with him.

She hoarded her money, her conversation with Lord Cheltenham and the research he had left with her telling her how much she needed for her bakery. She needed at least one more benefactor if Michael married this year. Each scenario had been calculated and recalculated—going back to her stepfather's, contributing to their household expenses for the winter before finding her next relationship, or finding a new patron before the Season ended.

The smart choice was to expedite her savings and search for a new relationship. To that end, she must see the choices available to her and how she would react when faced with them. Therefore, she had to broach the subject with Michael. Her best chance at a safe, profitable, and happy placement was for him to help arrange it, ideally by introducing her and helping coordinate the transition. She worried about his reaction to this idea, given his concern about decorum for both his parents' sake and his own as a future earl. Demimonde parties and masquerade balls were a poorly-kept secret among the Ton.

Had he ever even attended one? He'd never mentioned them, even when they spoke of his wilder years after university.

Well, I shan't know unless I bloody well ask. But she hadn't had the chance to ask, given his late-night visits.

He'd avoided any deep conversation these past days after their trip. It could be Parliament work, but she suspected it was more than that.

Nevertheless, school had taught her to make her own opportunity.

****

That night, Michael arrived very late again. When he entered the bedroom, he was surprised to see Penelope up and still dressed. He strode to her. "You are wearing too many clothes, Pen." He reached for her.

"My lord, can I offer you a whisky? I am quite refreshed tonight and wanted us to spend more time together." She gestured to her desk, where a small decanter of his favorite Scotch sat.

He growled. "I need you more than whisky, sweeting." *And I can't bear to think about the end of us.*

"Ah, but you may have both." She smiled. Turning, she twisted out of his grip and poured them each a finger of whisky. Handing it to him, she nudged him in the direction of a small armchair.

He sighed, feeling bone-weary. "Pen, I'm not up

for talking, sweet. I have been talking all day, much of the time to no avail. I might be out of words."

She chuckled.

"I understand. I shan't demand more of your verbal energy, my lord." She sent him an impudent look through her upper lashes. "However, I have missed your face. I wish to look at you in the light for a minute. I can speak for the both of us."

"Hmm, I have a better idea. How about you look at my face and whatever else you wish as you rid your delectable body of some of those clothes?" He threw his jacket on the bed and settled into the chair. His spine melted into the chair back, and he propped one ankle on his other knee, bringing the glass of whisky to his lap with both hands loose around it.

"I suspect I could do that." Penelope made an exaggerated thinking face, tilting her head with a finger to her chin and gazing at the ceiling.

Approaching him, she placed her hands on the chair arms, leaning over him. Her bosom, lifted by stays, swayed close to his lips but not quite within their reach. When he shifted to raise a hand, she covered his hands with hers, pressing them around his glass. "I will ask you to sit still then, my lord."

He growled again but subsided, nodding once. He knew he was being grumpy, but the fight over the Workhouse Act had already begun in Commons, involving his father's cronies. Between that, wooing Miss Lud, and Edward's words lingering in the back of his mind, he was tired, emotionally as well as physically. Annoyance at being put off gave way to curiosity about Penelope's actions, and he sat back to watch her.

She arched her back and leaned forward as she rose, so her chest brushed his face before she pulled back to upright. Placing a foot beside his propped leg on the edge of the chair, she bent to slide her slipper off, her décolletage still on display. His gaze obligingly took in the view. She repeated the motion with the other foot then stepped back.

Spinning around, she unlaced the front of her gown, keeping her back to him. She loosened it, allowing it to drop down her arms and sit around her hips, and looked over her shoulder at him.

His muscles locked, his hands gripping his glass with white knuckles. Enthralled, he panted as he watched every step of her seduction.

How does she always know what will excite me the most? And so often with something new, something different. School can't have taught that. I could spend forever and not have enough of her sensual greetings.

He groaned. Reality had crept into his consciousness. He shoved it back.

Facing away again, she lifted her hands to her hair. She removed one, two, three pins, and it cascaded down her back in a dark satiny curtain. Shaking it out, she grabbed a hank in each hand to tug forward before turning to him. It played peekaboo with her nipples as they poked through the fine muslin and lace of her chemise above her stays.

She reached behind her to unfasten the tapes of her petticoat. Raising her hands, she smoothed them over her breasts to her stomach, then to her sides, to give a little push to her petticoats and dress. They dropped to the floor in a heap around her with a gentle thump.

Stepping over them, she sashayed toward him.

Chapter Eighteen

A girl in the advanced classes had taught a few classmates a sexy walk, and they practiced for one another until they strutted with confidence. As Penelope stepped, she crossed one foot to land directly in front of the other one, causing her hips to twist. When she brought her rear foot forward to do the same, her hips would twist back the other way. If she added an extra bounce to her step, her breasts shimmied.

Of course, she had never used it on a man, but the girl had promised her it was a sure success.

Michael's mouth hung open, his gaze darting up and down her body as he took it all in. He licked his lips and leaned forward, dropping his crossed foot to the floor.

Gor. I owe my classmate a gift, or at least a heartfelt thank you card.

Nearing him, she pivoted on the balls of her feet to face away. With him still seated, he'd have to reach the full length of his arms to touch her back. She looked over her shoulder. "Would you be so kind as to help me with my stays, Michael?"

Gulping, he closed his mouth and tugged on the ribbon tying her stays before adding the other hand to unlace the length of the crisscross.

She let the stays loosen and drop, pulling her chemise out of them and over her head.

Clothing rustled.

She stopped Michael when he started to stand to reach around her body to grab her now-naked breasts.

"Thank you, Michael. Sit back, please."

More rustling and a deep-voiced rumble reached her ears as he sat back. She hoped it was a rumble of impatience, not exhaustion.

Twirling to face him, she dropped the chemise and stepped closer. She was left in stockings and garters she had made, with decorative ribbons on them. Gliding her hands up the sides of her body, she lifted them to her hair. She bent her head back to shake it, knowing her raised arms lifted her breasts and tossing her hair made them jiggle.

Michael braced his hands on the chair to stand.

She dropped her head forward to look at him and wagged a finger. "Ah, ah, my lord. I will come to you."

Sauntering near, she stopped between his legs and reached to unbutton his waistcoat.

"Pen…" He seemed unsure what he wished to ask.

"Let me take care of you." *At least he looks less tired and more interested now.*

She leaned over him to reach the last few buttons of the waistcoat, her knuckles brushing back and forth against the fabric-covered ridge below. His hips bucked, and she shivered in pleasure as his lips skidded along the skin of her shoulder.

When his mouth met her skin, he lost control and dragged her onto his lap to straddle him. His hips thrust against her nether lips, and one hand lifted to pinch a hardened tip between finger and thumb.

Her breath caught at the dual assault on her senses.

His other fingers went between her thighs,

feathering over her wet entrance and the swollen nub peeking between her lips.

The fleeting stroke made Pen arch into him then sag back when his hands left her. Her desire to beg for more clashed with her goal of directing this interaction.

He drew her back a few inches, and she opened eyelids she hadn't realized she had closed to see why he was pressing her away. He had opened his breeches without bothering to remove his shirt or even his cravat and raised then yanked her downward, impaling her on him.

Ah. Even in his urgency, he is careful with me.

The glance of his fingers had been to check she was ready for him so he would not hurt her. He shoved his hips forward in the chair to meet her, but the carved chair arms pushed at her thighs, not allowing his full length inside her. He leaned her back with one hand behind her back and lifted one of her legs, then the other to drape them over the arms of the Hepplewhite chair.

Pen gasped at how wide she was spread open, with no leverage. He was deeper than he had ever been.

Truly a part of me.

His hands returned to her hips, his mouth to a nipple, and he lifted and lowered her on him.

She struggled with his neckcloth for a moment before dragging it free. She left it around the back of his neck and held each end for leverage. Surrendering to the eroticism of the moment, she pulled his head to her breast. Her head fell back, and her eyes closed to focus her other senses on his deliciousness.

His hot wet mouth warm on her skin. The air cool over her damp flesh when he paused. The slick sounds of his cock as it slid out of her channel then plunged back in. His small grunts as he bottomed out each time. Even the swish of her hair against her back and his fingers spiked her pleasure. Sparks from the point of impact of his thrusts curled outward through her limbs and fed her hunger.

Her fervor morphed to a different passion, that of adoration, as she imagined this life, this man, every night. She did not care what the circumstances would be, what moral code, even what house or apartment.

She desired *him*. His drive, his love for his parents that conflicted with his wish for other choices, his sentimental purchase of the theatre, his enjoyment of cooking. All of him. These thoughts took her over the edge as much as the friction of their bodies' movements.

"Michael!" Her back arched, and her arms dropped the cravat to clutch his head to her. His teeth clamped down on her nipple. The small bite of pain whipped the froth of her orgasm into jagged points that scraped every inch of her skin. The explosion rippled through her, and her inner muscles contracted, milking him as she shuddered in pleasurable release for a long moment.

"Pen…" He moaned and shoved up into her one last time before his body echoed the shudders of hers. His hands released her hips to slip around her back and clutch her close as his mouth went slack against her chest.

After a short time, their breathing calmed. Pen felt the chafe of his shirt against her skin, the armrests digging into her thighs, and the folds of his opened breeches beneath her.

As though they both realized the intensity of their

post-coital hold, they disengaged, and Michael helped her stand.

He offered a handkerchief to clean her before tending to himself. He stood, and she half expected him to flee and establish a safe distance from their intimacy.

She must speak to him. But how could she discuss finding her next benefactor after such a visceral experience? On the other hand, that very subject might give him relief, allow him the space he needed. Steeling herself, she reminded her soft heart that he had a home—many homes, in fact—and all the money he could want. She, on the other hand, needed to secure her future, and he was not keeping her informed.

In the next moment, she was once again angry at him. *How could he be so lov—ah,* caring—*in some ways but not tell me what is happening?*

She squared her shoulders and slipped her robe over her nakedness, handing him his glass of whisky. "Michael, may I ask you something, please?"

****

Michael was still in a fog of sensual and emotional repletion.

This…this was home. Not his townhouse or even Mansfield Manor. Penelope's mere presence soothed him, her body enthralled him, and her lov—*no, caring* support infused him with strength.

He was contemplating taking Penelope and his whisky to bed and ignoring the rest of his world for the night. At her question, he frowned, not quite ready to return to reality and a little afraid of what she would ask.

She took his silence as consent. "We were told before the auction about ways to find subsequent benefactors. I know you are likely going to be affianced soon. And the Season is coming to an end, which means I will have fewer opportunities to meet someone before my lease ends."

He waited. What was she asking for? An extension on the lease? He needed to talk to Bags about his plan.

"Would you consider mayhap escorting me to a masquerade ball or other party of the demi-monde so I can consider my options in plenty of time? Please?"

His gut clenched. *No! I need more time.*

He frowned and stiffened his spine. *Over my dead body,* he wanted to shout. *I cannot even picture you with someone else like this, much less help you interview them and wax poetic about your many charms. No!*

His shoulders slumped. He had no right to any of those thoughts. He had been squiring Lady Grace and other young ladies of the Ton around London for more than a month. Blast it. He was working on a betrothal contract to present to Lady Grace's father.

He gulped the contents of his glass and stood. She was still waiting for his response. He had no choice in what he could say. "Agh, Pen. I hate thinking about that, but I would never leave you in the lurch. If you wish to attend an event, I will see what I can do, although you know we must be very discreet. I will also ensure you have a generous settlement and are safe."

"Thank you, Michael. I wanted to look into them but desired to discuss it with you first. I will let you know what I learn."

He nodded, needing to hold her now more than ever. He shucked his clothes and slid into bed. Holding the bed covers aloft, he gestured. "Come here, and let me hold you, sweeting."

She flinched at the endearment, and his heart turned over with an echoing twist. After laying her robe over the foot of the bed, she slipped in with him. He reveled in her softness, her smell, her smooth skin as she curled into him.

Home. His exhaustion returned full force with the new task set before him. His arms circled her, and he rolled, draping her over him in a sexless mimicry of their pose earlier. "I cannot think about aught else tonight, please, Pen. Just let me hold you."

"Always, Michael."

He sank into blissful oblivion.

****

Pen visited with Leah at the theatre the next day to reassure her friend she was being smart and to ask her guidance in finding Cyprian balls.

As she made her way to the manager's office, a tall, lithe young man sauntered down the hall toward her. He walked with the grace of a dancer, his hips canting for each step more like a woman's than a man's. His gaze remained on hers even as he neared, and she was taken aback at his forthright stare.

Did she know him? She scanned his clothes, no different than any of the crew's daytime working togs of black, except he wore a cap. He ducked his head at her in a deferential nod, his hair almost the exact red-brown of Michael's.

She shook her head as she passed. There were sometimes new faces. Mayhap he was simply evaluating her as she was him.

After knocking on the open door, she entered and Leah looked up. As she stepped inside, she caught a flash of black in the corner of her eye as the youth slowed in the hall a few feet away.

Then her entire focus narrowed to the topic at hand—her unfortunate need for another benefactor.

"I asked Michael to accompany me to a Cyprian ball or comparable event."

Leah's eyebrows rose. "And how did that go?"

"As well as can be expected, I suppose." She raised one shoulder in a quick shrug. "He agreed, in any case."

"Good. As he should. Now, I organize some events for that purpose, but—" She broke off at Penelope's look. "What?"

"Nothing." Pen shook her head. She should have expected that, given the older woman's involvement with the school and the auction.

However, Penelope, or rather, Michael, had one imperative. "We need one that is particularly discreet. Michael's family does not know of my existence, and he needs to keep it that way."

"One in particular might work, then," Leah told her. "Most balls are in private homes, but then we don't know how well the attendee list will be vetted. You can wait until late summer after the season when Parliament is out. House parties that last a week or longer are excellent ways to test"—she wiggled her brows— "potential partners. While they are more raucous and some are even near-orgies, they attract many would-be patrons and are away from the London gossip circles. Cheltenham's is one of the wildest but also one of the most selective and secret."

Penelope was not shocked in the least by that statement. Certainly, she might enjoy a rout with the right partner, someone she trusted. *With Michael.* A quick spurt of excitement shot through her before she ruthlessly dismissed the last thought. But a rout might set the wrong expectation when looking for a new benefactor. And even with her house paid through the year, she wanted to plan her future.

"I'd prefer something sooner, please. Are there discreet options in Town?"

"I'll ask. Sarah sometimes hosts one. That is the one I think might work best if 'tis scheduled."

Sure enough, within a sennight, Leah had an answer. Sarah Potter's Spanking Club had a masquerade ball planned. It was always well-attended, but by an exclusive, vetted list of invitees, ensuring the event remained somewhat tamer. It sounded promising and was in a fortnight, unlike the house parties.

She asked Leah to obtain invitations, but she needed to confirm with Michael.

She grew impatient every evening, bathing and dressing in the hope that he'd arrive, even late, but 'twas several nights before Michael visited again.

****

The days continued to be busy, drawing Michael ever closer to having to make a decision regarding Lady Grace. Estate work, meetings at the club, pouring over Parliamentary bills with his father, or social commitments in the evening, followed by late nights with Pen when he could.

These normal activities had begun to feel like a suit of clothes that did not fit. They constrained him, and he twitched against the limits and rules of his position. His conversations with Penelope from the start had cemented his understanding of how few restrictions he lived with, but that reminder from his conscience did not help.

She never asked about his looming betrothal. As he was leaving her house one night, she handed him a scrap of foolscap with a name, place, and date on it, indicating the event she wished to attend. He glanced at it, assuming he'd need to vet the host, but it was to be held at Mrs. Potter's Spanking Club.

Ah, good. With Sarah and Leah involved, I know the attendees will have been scrutinized as much as those for the auction.

Trying not to frown—this whole dilemma was his doing, after all—he leaned in and kissed Pen, promising to ensure he was free that night to accompany her. He left in a dismal mood, slamming the carriage door, then the front door of his townhouse.

He found a reminder from his mother waiting for him. He'd agreed to attend a ball with her the following night. There, etiquette dictated that he dance twice with Lady Grace, an implicit declaration of his intent after three outings and a handful of balls.

Even more frustrated, he banged back out and headed for White's, ignoring the paperwork and his father waiting for him at the family's London home.

That evening he shrugged on whatever his valet laid out for him. It could have been yellow and pink satin for all he noticed, although in actuality, the plum waistcoat turned his blue eyes indigo. He joined his mother in the crested carriage, kissing her on the cheek before settling back on the bench seat across from her.

"How have you been, Mama?"

"Well, thank you. I've caught up with almost all my friends and have visited Matilda several times. I know you saw her at a dinner at our house, but you really should make an effort to see her more." She grinned mischievously. "'Tis not every day one's sister is enceinte. And for all we know, she may be carrying a future earl, given the speed you've been moving."

He laughed, knowing she was teasing. "Mother, you cannot have it both ways. Either I need to work harder on finding a wife, or I can spend more time with Matilda." He scrunched his nose at her before he changed the subject. "And how is Father doing?"

"Ah, 'tis always good days and bad days. Yesterday was a good day, thankfully, and I forced him away from all that Parliament drudgery to go see Matilda. If ever priorities could be clear, I think 'tis under these circumstances, but the blasted man nearly didn't go." She turned away, and Michael caught the sheen of tears in her eyes.

Damn, he wanted that depth of feeling for his lifelong mate. When he realized Penelope's face floated in his mind rather than Lady Grace's, he sat forward.

"Father went, didn't he?" Michael reached for his mother's hand and squeezed it. "He knows who makes the rules." It was a lame attempt at humor, but his mother sniffed, smiled, and returned his hand squeeze.

The carriage slowed, and he realized they'd arrived. Alighting, he handed her out and escorted her inside. As they separated to find their cronies, he heard her voice.

"Michael."

He turned back. He saw from her countenance that she was fully recovered from the emotional moment in the carriage and was in full Mama mode now.

"Don't go straight over to the penguins and peacocks"—she nodded to the cluster of suits with white stockings and dark shoes flocking together like earthbound birds—"and bury yourself in Lords nonsense. Find Lady Grace and request a dance or two."

Michael firmed his lips but nodded, and his mother sent him a last smile before strolling toward a group of women her age in a corner of the vast room.

With lowered brows and a jutting lip, he scanned the ballroom for his potential betrothed. She stood with her mother and a few other girls in pastel gowns, serene as she watched and waited.

How comfortable it must be to know your place in society. No concerns regarding the laws of the land, the state of the poor, the taxes on grains, food on the table. Only the color gown you'll wear to the next party, who you'll dance with, and who might call on you.

He scowled. That wasn't fair to the young lady. She had spoken intelligently to him about books and plays and even their impact on society. It was normal for titled ladies not to read the news. After all, as Pen pointed out, they could do little to change it.

Gah, do not think of Pen right now. Focus.

Sighing, he steeled himself to approach her and mark her dance card, but he could not force his body across the floor. He was in a foul mood. He'd worn his polite façade when necessary in the past, but this was more.

He was, quite simply, done. He could not fathom being married to Lady Grace. Or anyone else in this room, for that matter.

Edward's questions kept ringing in his ears. He needed to have a frank conversation with his mother and father. He'd never wished to disappoint his parents or lose sight of his responsibilities to the earldom. But his parents had always had each other through those obligations.

He needed a partner he could turn to in good times and bad, in happiness and sadness, someone who would care for him like he protected and supported her. And he could think of only one person he wanted in that position—the woman he loved. His shoulders lowered a fraction with the admission, despite the insurmountable hurdles.

After lurking in the card room as long as possible, he found his mother with her cronies. He could not begin to fathom what they had to discuss as they gathered at these events at least once a sennight. Regardless, he was determined to leave before speculation on his lack of dancing became too much.

He leaned down by his mother's ear. "Would you mind departing after this hand, please, Mama?"

She turned to stare at him in surprise, mouth agape. Whatever she saw in his face must have convinced her of his need, because she turned to make her excuses to the group.

"Michael? Are you quite all right?" she asked as they navigated the crowd to the entryway.

"Yes, Mother. I simply cannot bear to be here any longer."

"Mmm, 'tis a bit of a crush." She nodded as if agreeing. Then she came to an abrupt halt. "Oh, but you did not dance with the Lud girl. Not even once." She tugged on his arm as though to turn him.

"Nor am I going to," he replied, surreptitiously pulling her toward the front door. "We can talk about it in the carriage."

He clenched his jaw, a muscle ticking in his cheek. His mother's gaze flicked over his face, and she allowed him to pull her out to the carriage without further comment.

Once they were underway, the barrage of questions began.

"Michael, whatever has gotten into you? You did not dance with Lady Grace, and now you are rushing away? What will people think? Did you talk to her, at least? When are you going to offer for her? You cannot lead her on much longer."

"Mother, please. I can only answer one question at a time," he said and proceeded not to answer any. His fingers tapped against his leg.

His mother watched him as he fidgeted. Her expression changed from confusion to concern. "What is it, my boy?"

"I cannot marry Lady Grace, Mother. I am sorry. I hate disappointing you."

"Well. I guess 'tis a good thing you did not dance with her tonight then. That might have been awkward." She sat back against the carriage seat.

"Quite."

"Michael, you could never disappoint me." She reached a hand forward, laying it on his where it rested on his knee. "I do hope you shall marry soon. I desire that as much or more for you as for your father and me. Of course, we'd like to see you settled. But we also wish to see you happy. We would adore grandchildren, especially whilst we—well, I—am healthy enough to be involved in their lives, but that is secondary." She cocked her head. "Mayhap we have pushed too hard. We did not intend to drive you into a marriage not based in love."

He stared at her, surprised at these revelations. He appreciated understanding more of their reasons, but he still had one concern. "Er, I believe I could in fact disappoint you. What if I choose not to marry? Or marry someone from outside the Ton?"

"Oh, favorite son of mine. You know my reasons for wanting you to marry someone in our set. You will be the next earl, and I hope that you will carry on our line rather than the title going to your cousin in Bristol. He did not have the opportunity to learn how to support the households and all the people who depend on us. As for who you marry, I do not know if you shall ever understand the struggles your father and I had—his positions on bills in Parliament being called into question because of the scandal of my acting and protecting you children from gossip. We had to dismiss several servants for disrespect, which I hated doing. I always hoped for a better life for you, as all parents do."

She'd told him this before. But Edward's question came back to him. Would his mother or father make a different choice, knowing all the struggles their marriage brought them? Before he had a chance to ask, they arrived at his parents' townhouse. Alighting to hand his mother out of the carriage, he tucked her hand through his arm and walked her inside.

"Will you visit with us, since the night is young?"

He shook his head. "I have somewhere to be." He quirked his brows in a quick frown at his mother's smug smile, confused as to why that entertained her. "But, Mama." He unconsciously reverted to the affectionate moniker of his childhood. "What if a better life is facing it with someone you love, no matter the challenges? You and Father managed all of it. What if the scandal and struggles and disrespect feel like a better option than your choices in the Ton?"

"Are you telling me you think you're in love? With someone outside our set? Not Lady Grace?" The countess grew teary-eyed.

He held her gaze, straightening and taking both her hands. He nodded slowly. "Yes, Mama."

"Then be certain, Michael. Be very sure. 'Tis not a path to tread lightly, and there is no coming back once you start down it."

He nodded again. "I will."

"You know why I wanted an easier path for you. But you also know I love you. As I said before, we always wanted you to love the person you choose as your wife. And we will support that no matter who you choose."

He heaved a big sigh, and his shoulders loosened. "Thank you. I needed to hear that."

"I did not realize… I beg your pardon for not being more clear."

"There's no need to apologize. I simply needed to ask the right questions." He leaned in and kissed her on each cheek.

As he drew back, she tightened her grip on his hands and pulled him to her. Wrapping her arms around him, she squeezed tight for a minute then released him. "Now go to your 'somewhere to be.' And think hard, my favorite son."

Flashing her a grin, he didn't even bother with his hat as he rushed back out to the carriage.

Chapter Nineteen

Penelope finished dinner in quick bites. She wanted to try her hand at new dessert pastries she had been playing with, using the various size Nailsea rolling pins to gauge how varying the pastry thickness worked for individual miniature pies.

As she finished cleaning up, sounds of Michael entering surprised her, as it was earlier than his recent visits. When cooking, she did not wear stays, only a chemise and one petticoat and softer, older frocks. She looked down at the apron she wore to protect her clothes, and her costume work at the theatre jolted an idea. It had provocative detailing—a heart-shaped neckline, wide straps, matching wide trim around the skirt, and ties of the same fabric.

Michael's footsteps headed upstairs, as she was usually in her bedroom at this hour.

Making a quick decision, she drew everything off and then re-donned the apron alone, with nothing under it. From the front, it covered all the essentials, aside from her shoulders. The cut was no lower than an evening gown and higher than many she had seen at the theatre Friday night. She twisted and turned and grabbed a pan scrubbed to a shine from a hook to see her back view. The straps crisscrossed, the ties from the waist covering the crack of her bottom if she stood motionless but providing a tantalizing view of her cheeks in the gap between the sides of the apron skirt.

She wanted to face the door for Michael's arrival, to ease into this game. But she also wished to get the new pie recipe she was testing into the oven. She bent to slide the peel under the two small tins.

A shoe scuffed at the door.

"What in damnation are you wearing?" he roared.

Oops! Unable to tell if he was mad or simply surprised, Penelope stayed stock still.

"Er…an apron, my lord. I did not wish to get messy." She recovered her courage and turned to slide the personal pies, as she liked to think of them, into the baking oven. He breathed an aborted grunt as her apron fell forward, and the ties covered only the seam of her bottom.

"Did not wish to get messy? What did you think would happen by flaunting that derriere in front of me, eh?" He stalked forward, his furrowed brow like a mock frown. His growl had sex in it rather than anger.

Phew. It seemed he, too, was in the mood to play, bringing theatre to the kitchen again.

"I have made you a new fruit pie to try, and I did not dirty my clothes," she retorted cheekily.

"Excellent. As it appears you have finished, you can take off the apron." His response was bold, and he watched for her reaction.

"My lord and master, that ain't fair. You are wearing far more clothing." Allowing her working-class upbringing to leak into her words, she reached out to tug on one end of his cravat. Undoing it an inch at a time, her hand brushed his chest and stomach before falling away.

Michael made an exaggerated stern face as he

shrugged out of his waistcoat, cravat, and shirt. "Right, then. Apparently, it falls to me to keep this house in order."

Reaching for her and twirling her, he yanked the apron ties, and they fell away from the globes of her bottom and legs to her dainty slippers. Unbuttoning the crisscross straps rather than drawing it over her head, he tossed the straps forward and the apron fell to the kitchen floor unheeded.

She began to turn, but he continued in role-play mode.

"Well, well, if 'tisn't a very naughty kitchen wench here. Parading around naked, flaunting her bits and tormenting the honorable master of the house. Seems to me, she is looking for trouble. I think she needs a punishment to remember her place. This is a moral household, and this behavior shan't pass undisciplined."

Turning her, he bent her forward over the kitchen table.

Did he measure various tables before selecting this as the perfect height for my hips? If so, 'tis a good thing, given how often I end up on the bloody thing.

He stepped away, and she shifted to watch.

"Naughty wenches may not peek, or their punishment gets worse," he admonished.

Turning back around, she twitched in anticipation.

****

His hand smoothed over her back, from a shoulder down, skimmed her inner thigh as he passed over her bottom to cup her leg, then started again on the other shoulder. The hand returned to her lower back and remained there, palm holding her down.

A dull, heavy *thud* struck her as Michael swung at

her bottom. She tried to place the sensation. It was not broad like the peel, not even the width of her arm. It could not be metal or flat, or it would make a different sound.

Thud, thud, thud.

More impacts hit over her cheeks and thighs, her flesh warming but not hurting. What other materials did the kitchen have? Wood? It could be. Marble? The heaviness could be either of those. But what implement?

The thuds halted.

"Well, wench, what do you have to say to your master?"

"Gor, sir. What are you using to spank me?" She was dying of curiosity. The spanking did not hurt, and she desired more. Twitching her bottom as he liked, she tormented him more.

"That is what you ask? Truly?" Mock outrage colored his tone. "It appears you need more."

The blows came harder but still a duller impact than instruments he had wielded in the past.

She moaned, the warmth moving from back to front, making her crave his hand—in a spank, a caress, a pinch, anything. Heat pulsed, swelling her sensitive breasts and nether lips. She imagined bread leavening, needing a warm, wet environment. And wet she was. Spreading her legs a bit farther, she stuck out her bottom.

"Oh, I see you are not penitent in the least, wench. This goes beyond naughty. I shall need a fresh approach to gain your penitence."

Penelope licked her lips eagerly, guessing he might put her on her knees to suck him. That would give her the intimate touch she craved.

Then he did touch her. One hand stayed on her back, the other dropping between her legs. She heard his fingers slick over sensitive flesh and moaned as they rubbed her nub. With the lubricant her body provided, there wasn't enough friction. She needed *more*. Her muscles quivered, reaching for that next touch, that next curl of heat to plump her breasts, her nub, her lips further.

He cleared his throat, and when he spoke, his voice was a growl. "Do not think that I will reward you for this wanton behavior. Oh no, I have the perfect penalty for wayward kitchen wenches. The very tools that you use will be used on you."

Was the gruffness him still fully in character? Or was he as aroused as she was from the play? She dearly wanted to turn around and find out, even if it risked further punishment. But she was pinned in place by his hand on her back.

A cold, hard cylindrical shape slid between her legs.

She shivered, unsure whether it was from the temperature of the rod touching her hot delicate flesh or the sensations it sparked as it brushed her sensitive knot. The hard points of her breasts scraped against the table with the shudder, igniting more sparks that raced toward her core.

What was it, though?

The rod rubbed forward and backward, gliding along her nerve endings, waking them. Her fingers gripped the far edge of the table, knowing Michael would never let her touch herself to ease this ache he was working so hard to build. The heat magnified, her flesh swelled more, little bread rolls fully risen and ready to eat.

Please, eat them. Devour them. Pound them back into unleavened dough. Something!

Then the pressure became firmer, dragging the protective hood back and exposing her most responsive bit of flesh. Back and forth.

Yes, yes, there. But the object, whatever it was, was too smooth, too unspecific a touch to propel her past this excruciating hill of pained pleasure.

She alternated rising on tiptoe and dropping to shove against it to try to find a better angle. But that tantalizing tease of a smooth glide over the nub remained at a pace designed to drive her mad. She rubbed sideways on the table, dragging her breasts across the wood, craving friction of any kind. She twitched her hips sideways but then lost contact with the rod at her most sensitive spot. She breathed heavily, trying to think. Maybe if he spanked her, or she could provoke him to use his cock.

Struggling to remember her role, she managed to find words. "Oh, la, sir. That feels bloody good. Please punish this naughty wench more."

He chuckled, then bit off the sound and took a step away from her, reaching for something.

Gor, what, now? Dare I peek? Knowing better, she remained as still as her arousal allowed, hips shimmying back an inch to seek his touch.

His hand returned to the base of her spine, gripping her to stillness. Something clacked on the table near her, and his other hand smacked each cheek once, very hard. "Be still, wench! We have not even started the punishment yet. You should not be so eager."

I beg to differ, sir. But she bit her cheek to not say the words aloud. She knew he was aware of her arousal and was enjoying prolonging it as a part of this faux-punishment.

The hand on her back slid lower, pulling one bottom cheek sideways, baring her so he could see all of her secret places.

Pen clenched her rear muscles in unease. Would he put his finger in her bottom again? Would she like it again?

Smack! His hand came down.

"Naughty wench. Stop tensing and take your punishment, or it shall be worse for you. You need only an apron to wear? That can be arranged." He may have muttered, "But it will be the death of me."

She was not certain. Wiggling one last time, she tried to relax.

A bit of liquid spilled down the crack of her exposed bottom. He'd grabbed the crucible of cooking oil. A finger smoothed the trail of oil until it reached her rear entrance, where he circled, pressing harder each time. She moaned as a new rush of heat flushed through her.

His hands withdrew for a minute, then the crucible clacked on the table and a hand pulled her cheek aside again. This time it was not his finger prodding at her. The cold, hard rod he had slid back and forth over her nub pushed against her.

She reared up, and his hand moved to her upper back, giving her a carefully rougher shove back down. "If you fight me, we shall change this out to a larger one."

She froze, confused.

What had he said? *The very tools that you use will be used on you.*

He would not dare! Her beautiful Nailsea rolling pin? He was going to put that in—there? *Oh. Ohh...*

For a fleeting moment, Pen imagined them in this kitchen—or any kitchen—together, night after night, cooking together, playing together, and engaging in crazy sexual games.

Only Michael could spark the trust to be naughty and see where it took her. Or rather, only Michael and her love for him.

She was brought back to the present as the object probed at her flesh. The beating must have been with her larger, heavier marble rolling pin. The glass rod sank a short way into her bottom. She gave a strangled groan. 'Twas larger than a finger. *Gor, 'tis a good thing I'm not a molly boy. Michael's cock would never fit there. Wait, do men do that to women, too?*

Her thoughts stalled as he twisted the rod, lighting up nerve endings she remembered from his finger. Her body was on fire, her front channel begged for invasion, and her back channel already felt stuffed. But she waited, knowing he wasn't done with this pleasure/torture. He drizzled a bit more oil in her crack right above the rod and pushed another inch.

"Mmmphh."

"Does it hurt, wench?"

She smiled. Even in play, he toed the line between concerned lover and his role. "No, master, but your serving wench is feeling more penitent. Mayhap we could move on from the punishment part of the evening?" *Not quite please fuck me, but sassy enough he'll likely use it.*

Sure enough. "I think not." He pushed in smoothly and quickly.

"Ahh." The pin felt huge inside her. She shifted her weight from foot to foot, trying to process the sensations. She dared not turn and check what size he'd chosen. Her inner muscles spasmed around the foreign object, trying to reject it or accommodate it.

He tapped the end. "You won't get it out easily. The indentation before the hand knob at the end will keep it in place."

Her core muscles tensed and untensed, her front passage still craving its own insertion. Her nipples were poking into the table, and lightning ricocheted through her from the edge of pain and pleasure in her rear hole and from her heated bottom, forward and up and around and down. She sweated and panted, dangling over that cliff of pleasure the way only Michael could hold her.

Her brain short-circuited, her hips made small cants forward and back, looking for more here, less there, any touch. Why did something in her bottom make her feel emptier in front? Her juices ran onto her thighs. She was close enough to her peak even a strong breeze might send her over.

"Now we can start the punishment."

The rod, likely the smallest, only about an inch in diameter despite how huge it felt and about six inches long, slid back out and then in again, allowing her to ease into the sensation.

"Please, my lord. Ah! Gah!" She heard her own voice begging through the tingling haze, although her requests were unclear. "Please, touch me. Take it out. Ooohh, faster. Take me! Let me touch you. Please!"

"Now, that is more like it. Finally, you wish to

please the master of the house, wench. Yet still, I do not hear penitence. We shall try a different tact then if you cannot find the words to apologize. You will use your mouth for better purpose."

Leaving the rolling pin embedded, Michael grabbed her hair and tugged her up, then urged her to her knees.

"Wait a moment, naughty wench. There's no sense in you catching cold." He strode over to where his jacket hung on a peg by the hall door and folded it as he returned. He laid it down and gestured for her to drag it under her as his other hand unfastened the fall of his trousers. Reclaiming a hunk of hair at the back of her head, he held his cock in one hand and drew her head to it. "Lick me, wet me. And I'd best not hear that rod hit the ground. Keep that in you."

She shuddered in surrender. She loved being surrounded by him, tugged to and fro for his pleasure and hers. Life without him, not being at his command, was unimaginable. She licked and licked, then sucked his length into her mouth as he pushed on the back of her head until her nose touched the coarse hair at the base of him. Relaxing her throat, she let him direct her as he wished, playing the penitent—*adoring*—servant to her master.

He grew harder, and the hand on her head drove her faster and faster until he yanked her off him. He lifted her and shoved her back down on the table in her previous position. When he tapped the rod to ensure it was still embedded, she groaned, and her hips twitched.

****

One of Michael's favorite acts was to have Pen suck him while he controlled her head. It smacked of the power in their relationship, yes, but that was not why he loved it. He loved her overt expression of trust inherent in allowing him to thrust into her as far as he could, knowing he would not choke her or hurt her.

The Nailsea rolling pin set had been so convenient, and Pen had enjoyed his finger in her arse when he had added that to their play. He needed to be in her, but more, he craved seeing that decorative plug in her bottom.

He eyed the others in the set. Mayhap he could ease Pen into taking him that way over time. In his lust-induced haze, he conveniently ignored the fact that he did not have time.

Despite his cock's need to be in its favorite place, Michael paused. Looking down at Penelope spread across this perfectly placed and proportioned table, he tried to imagine finding a "drab" Ton wife dressed only in an apron or role playing or any of the other activities Pen reveled in. They were so comfortable together, even after such a short time, allowing them to let down their walls. His need to find a way to keep her became an imperative.

Channeling the compulsion, he lined up his shaft at the heat of her opening and slid into her. With the rod still embedded, the fit was almost impossibly tight.

Pen groaned as his cock forced its way inside her, his heavy bollocks smacking her bundle of nerves.

Withdrawing, he drove back in, not fast or rough, but not slow either. He slid in in one smooth drive. Then, knowing he would not last long, he grabbed the rod in her bottom and began thrusting it in counterpoint. His other hand squeezed her hip to hold her in place or maybe to anchor himself.

Still in character, she panted out, "Master, your serving wench is quite contrite. Please, I will wear what you tell me. Have I been punished enough? May I have pleasure now?"

He swore under his breath and sped his movements, his hand on her side likely to leave bruises with its grip. "Yes, wench. Pen, come with me." He groaned as his hips pistoned in a punishingly fast rhythm.

He shoved both his cock and the rod into her, his hips jerking against her. The slaps of his bollocks against her sensitive nub sent both of them into a vortex of bliss, and his cock leaped and spasmed inside her for long moments.

Her walls contracted around him. She screamed a wordless cry and pulsed around him for longer than ever before.

After a quiet moment of lying over her on the table bonelessly, he straightened. Withdrawing the rod slowly and then his cock, he grabbed a cloth to wrap around the rolling pin and another to clean her before attending to himself. Lifting her and his jacket, he wrapped her in it for warmth and sat in a chair with her on his lap. He buried his head in her hair where her neck met her shoulder and held her tight.

Pen looped her arms around his neck, putting her face to his hair and raining light kisses on him.

She seemed content to remain silent in the aftermath of intensity again, but his mind raced. He needed to take the time his mother had suggested and be certain of the path he wanted. And he should take Peterborough's suggestion and talk to his father. But the demi-monde ball was approaching, and nausea threatened at the idea of her role-playing like this with anyone else.

For now, though, he simply wished to hold her.

"All right, sweeting?" he asked. When she nodded against him, he teased, "Right, then. What pie have you made me?"

Pen gasped and shot up. She raced to the baking oven to check that the miniature pies were not overcooked. He sat back and admired her derriere again, without benefit of even apron ties.

Chapter Twenty

The next day Penelope received a card from Sophia, inviting her to call upon the countess at her home in Mayfair. Penelope asked the young man who had delivered the missive to wait, and she scrawled a quick note on the back of the card in reply.

She was happy to hear Sophia was in Town, but she declined to call on a titled lady in her home and risk Sophia's reputation. Could they please meet somewhere away from Mayfair, mayhap for an ice or a stroll in a quiet park?

She changed dresses, eager to see her friend if she was willing to meet somewhere out of the way that afternoon. When the knock came, she hurried forward, shooing away Mr. Thorpe. She opened the door and shifted forward to reach for the return message she expected but stopped short at the sight of Sophia standing there.

Her friend stood well back from the door and was half turned, gazing around the street as though evaluating the neighborhood.

Penelope gasped and half-stepped through the door, grabbing Sophia's arm to yank her inside before someone saw her there and caused a scandal. As Sophia cleared the doorway, almost overset by her forceful pull, she dropped her arm. She was tempted to shove her friend back out and shut the door on her, she was so furious at the blatant disregard for society rules.

Sophia opened her mouth to question her on being manhandled, but Penelope superseded her friend with her own tirade.

"The crested coach, Sophia? Was that truly necessary?" She placed her hands on her hips. "Do you have no sense of decorum or concern for your reputation? Or did you forget what I told you of my situation?"

One side of Sophia's mouth tilted in a lopsided smirk, and she tugged her gloves off, finger by finger. "Ah, so that is what has you in a huff. Pen, you are my friend. And—this is part of the reason for my visit— you have more friends and allies than I think you realize."

Realizing she was not going to preserve Sophia's reputation without her cooperation, which was not forthcoming, Penelope ushered her into the parlor. She called to Mrs. Thorpe in the kitchen for tea and pastries she'd made earlier.

"Sophia, 'tis a lovely surprise to see you." She tripped out in a monotone, grimacing as Sophia smirked. "To what do I owe this pleasure?"

"Edward had to come to London to coordinate work on the Poor Laws with his cronies in Lords. I came along as I must speak with you. After you left, I visited with Leah Godwin, who offered me a bit of information I wish I'd known sooner." Sophia darted a slight frown at her friend.

Penelope frowned. What had she had done wrong? "I was not aware you knew Leah. Did you meet her in Peterborough then?"

"In a way." Sophia grinned, bouncing a little on the

settee in her excitement.

Penelope pressed her lips together, annoyed. Her friend should have gone on the stage. She had a knack for building drama.

"Leah had been informed of my move there when I married Edward."

"Er…why? By whom?" She still was not following and could not avoid playing into her friend's slow unraveling of the story.

"It seems she is a recruiter and something of a matron of the School of Enlightenment—"

Penelope straightened in shock. *Sophia?* She thought back to their discussion in Peterborough. She supposed it made sense, but a countess?

"—which I attended early in my marriage."

"Oh. My."

She had glossed over her training and even the auction when she told her friend how she and Michael had met, saying only that he chose her from a line of women at the theatre and made arrangements. Now, she could share much more, and get Sophia's opinions on next steps.

How tempting.

But Sophia might not have the perspective to help, having led a very different life than Penelope. Even her curriculum had been unique.

"Indeed. Imagine my surprise when Leah sought me out at home and authorized me to discuss this with you. Normally, even if two friends have attended separately, the matrons do not disclose that to them. However, she said your current circumstances and our history allowed some leeway in the rules." Sophia grinned and bounced again. "Oh, Pen, I am so excited to share this adventure with you and have someone close I can confide in!"

"Mmm, so you must have been in the Marriage Preparatory course." She tilted her head, knowing her friend's marriage date. "Mayhap even when I was there, although in a separate building."

"Yes. In fact, I swore I saw you one day but dismissed it. Oh, if only I had pursued it, you could have been at my wedding, and we could have had more time together again."

"Sophia." Her voice was soft but firm. "You are forgetting something. I could not have attended your wedding. 'Twould not have been appropriate."

Sophia frowned. "Well, be that as it may, I shan't allow the Ton to dictate my friendships. Besides, I need you. Roslynn—my cousin Nicholas's wife, Lady Suffolk—and I talk when we can, but Edward and I are out in the country much of the time. I am hoping you shall come back to Peterborough after the Season. Do you know yet where you and Slade shall winter?"

"Ahh, we shan't be wintering together." The tea arrived, and she had a reprieve from her friend's questions to pour and hand the plate of pastries to Sophia.

"What?" Sophia looked dazed as she took the plate. "Why ever not? You appeared so happy together. Do I need to blacklist him or something? Did he treat you poorly?"

Penelope briefly outlined Michael's family's expectations.

"That does not seem fair at all." Sophia lounged back against the settee cushions and flung a hand wide. "His father may choose who he wants to marry, gossip be damned, and then expects his son to toe the line?"

"No, 'tis actually his mother who is so focused on avoiding talk and marrying appropriately."

"Oh."

"Besides which, Michael has already identified the young lady he plans to ask for. They have attended the theatre thrice now and danced at several balls, which I understand is a tacit betrothal." Her lips twisted in bitterness before she subdued the emotion that would get her nowhere. "I have asked Michael to attend a private ball with me, one frequented by the demi-monde for those looking to forge a new partnership."

"Hmm." Sophia looked pensive. "When is this event?"

"In a few days. I keep expecting Michael to tell me he has signed a marriage contract, but mayhap he is waiting. He has been very good to me. I knew from the start most relationships would be short-term. I was very lucky to have such a kind, young, generous benefactor." She hoped Leah would be proud of her for putting that forth.

"Yes, not to mention handsome." Sophia smiled. "Do you really believe he will offer for the chit he has been squiring around, then? I could have sworn he was in love with you."

Penelope cringed. Hearing that did not help her state of mind.

"I do." Her voice was short as she rose. Rude or not, she could not bear to discuss this any longer.

Sophia rose graciously, making her way toward the door. "Oh! I also wished to tell you about a group of alumnae from the school. And you and Roslynn will get along capitally. Would you come visit me tomorrow then?"

At the shake of Penelope's head, she sighed. "Fine. Then I shall return around the same time." Triumphant, she grinned, adding, "One more question. Who hosts these private balls? I have not heard of them."

"Various members of the Ton who are, shall we say, a bit less discerning about the company they keep. This one is at Sarah Potter's Club."

Sophia nodded as though unsurprised. She knew of her husband's past then.

"Thank you for having me. I look forward to seeing you tomorrow." Sophia kissed her cheek and whisked out the door. Showing all the boldness Penelope lacked, she swept down the walk to her carriage then turned to wave again.

Penelope shook her head at the audacity but could not help laughing as she waved back.

****

Michael stepped into White's and shook the rain off his hat and cloak. Handing them to the servant standing nearby for just such a service, he asked the host where to find his father. He was directed to a private room on the second floor.

Stepping into the chamber, he surveyed the men circling the round table. His father and the Earl of Peterborough to one side, the Earl of Suffolk farther on. Evan and two other men he recognized but could not name. As he was not yet a member of Lords but rather his father's steward and unofficial proxy, he worked outside the official Parliamentary capacity and sometimes saw names written more than in person.

He poured a Scotch from the decanters on the sideboard and claimed a seat at the table. The men were discussing the recent formation of the Parliamentary Select Committee to analyze the Poor Laws and their implementation in different parishes and shires.

These men had grown increasingly alarmed at reports of the wide range of treatment of the poor, and especially the impotent poor, those whose age or infirmities did not allow them to work off their debts. Some of the Poor Laws were over a century old, and the prevailing belief of this faction was that they needed updates.

Outlines of various ideas sat on the table, each man having been asked to bring thoughts on reforms for review by the group. The author of one began summarizing his.

Michael pulled his small sheaf of notes out of his pocket and laid them down as he focused on the discussion.

The group made significant progress over the next few hours. Many of the ideas overlapped, in part because the members were friends and relatives and had evaluated this in smaller conversations between meetings.

One of the unfamiliar men turned out to be William Sturges-Bourne, chair of the newly-formed Select Committee. Once the group agreed on the best combination of necessary, politically prudent, and most cost-saving measures, the chairman collected the final notes and promised to take them for consideration by the Committee. The meeting broke, and everyone stood. A few of the men wandered toward the couches to wait for the post-meeting supper Michael's father had arranged. A few refilled their drinks.

He ended up between Peterborough and his father,

with Evan completing the circle.

Evan turned to Edward. "Peterborough. Good to see you again. I am sorry for your loss. How is the Dowager Countess?"

Edward's eyebrows rose. "Lady Charlotte?"

Evan nodded.

"She is well, thank you, as far as I know. She resides here in Town full time whilst Sophia and I are at Peterborough as often as Parliament allows. How do you know her?"

"I knew both of them. She is amazing at money management and investing. We are partners in a few things."

"I learned that when she began handing off information about the estate," Edward replied, nodding. "'Tis good to know your opinion as well. I dare say I'd do well to keep that in mind."

"You know I'm happy to talk investments any time as well. I'm at White's as much as anywhere. Or you could attend a party again…" Evan leered at Edward.

Michael ducked his head, knowing that even the tamer Cheltenham parties were somewhat notorious.

"Do not, whatever you do, mention your parties to my wife." He glared at Evan. "I'm serious."

Evan threw his hands up in defeat and walked away.

Edward turned to Michael. "Have you given my suggestion more thought?"

He looked at Edward agape. Out of the corner of his eyes, he saw his father tilt his head in question.

Does he mean asking my father if he would make a different decision on marriage given the Ton's retribution? Is he trying to force my hand by asking here? But why? What could be his motivation?

"Er, yes, thank you, my lord. I am still considering it," he said quellingly.

"Hmm." Edward appeared pensive, sliding a glance at his father, mayhap to gauge interest.

"What are you considering, son?" his father asked.

"Ah, the same thing you and Mother are considering for me—marriage." Flapping a wrist once, he tried for lightness in his tone but feared he fell short.

"Oh? And Peterborough had a suggestion? Well, good." His father chuckled. "Mayhap you will listen to him more than you do us."

He sighed, thinking it might be left there. But no.

"What was the suggestion, if I may ask?" The earl turned to Edward.

Edward watched him, ready to defer to him if he wished to address the question. But both men's expressions told Michael it would not remain unaddressed.

He stared at Edward, willing him to silence, as Evan rejoined their group.

Edward wagged his head once. Summarizing obliquely, he answered the older earl, "I wondered if he had asked you how you came to marry your lovely countess and whether you recommended that approach for him."

"He knows that." Michael's father frowned.

Edward nodded. "I understand you married for love, as I did. Is that correct?"

"Indeed I did. Never regretted it for a moment."

"I feel the same. And hopefully will after as many years of marriage as you, my lord. If I may broach a sensitive subject, I believe that like mine, your wife was not a titled lady when you met her? But having fallen in love, you did not consider forsaking her and marrying someone from your set?"

"Not for a second. There were some sticking points along the way—"

Michael smirked at the typical understated description.

"—but love and family are most important in this world. King, country, duties of a title—all come after that, although I would appreciate you not repeating that to anyone." They were all aware that such statements could be considered treason.

"I understand." Edward nodded again and leaned forward. "And I completely agree."

Evan watched the conversation like a cricket match, head swiveling back and forth with each statement thrown.

"Michael? Your mother said you'd decided not to offer for Lady Grace. What is all this about your marriage then?" His brow furrowed as he considered Edward's statements. "Are you considering someone else?"

Edward arched a dark brow at him but excused himself to pull Suffolk aside for a private conversation.

He turned to his father. "Yes, I am. I did not love Lady Grace. I'm not sure I even liked her all that much. And you and Mother have always stated that you wanted your children to marry for love."

"Who is it, then?"

"There's the rub. She's not a member of society. So Mother encouraged me to think it through before proceeding."

"Ah. Your mother is very protective. I went along

with that 'drab' postulate when you were both young. But there comes a time when you must make up your own mind and forge your own way. I knew the first time I saw your mother, she was mine. I needed a little while to convince her of that. But every consequence, however ugly, was worth the love and joy we found in each other, and later, you and your sister. You know this. I must say, I am surprised and a bit disappointed you needed to hear it from Peterborough as well." He raised a brow at his son.

"I did not want to disappoint you or Mother." Michael barely managed to stop from scuffing a foot on the floor. As it was, he hung his head, one hand at his side fidgeting.

"You could never."

As he looked up at his father, the man grabbed his arm, patting it and squeezing. Michael reached up with his other hand to hold his father's hand against him. "Thank you."

The earl strode over to sit with Sturges-Bourne.

Evan raised his eyebrows, taking breath as if to speak, then looked past him.

Michael turned and glared at Edward as he paced closer.

"Apologies for putting you on the spot there, old man." Edward's lips turned up in a small smile. "I admit I should like to see our women spend more time together now that they have reunited. Mayhap I was a tad over-zealous."

Michael silently agreed, although Edward did not appear all that penitent.

He realized that, as a result of the man's meddling, he had been able to give both his parents warning that his marriage might not be as "drab" as planned.

****

The next day, Michael's trousers barely touched the chair seat at White's before Evan's questions started. "What was that about with Peterborough, eh?"

"What was what?" Robert sat up from his casual slump.

"Peterborough practically asked Lord Mansfield whether Michael should marry for love or for prestige."

Robert turned to Michael. "Why? Do you have someone in mind? You've always been so focused on keeping your parents happy with a 'drab' girl. I confess to surprise."

"It appears our friend is missing a piece." Evan raised his brows at Michael.

Robert's eyes narrowed at them.

"I bought Penelope's house." Michael sighed and rubbed his hand over his lips.

"So?"

"I had leased it before. Now, I've bought it." He gestured at Bags. "With his help negotiating, of course."

Evan chimed in, impatient with the prevarication. "And put it in her name."

"I see." Robert's eyebrows shot up.

"Exactly. Then he races off to Peterborough with Penelope like a hound on a fox's scent. The next thing you know, the earl is discussing marrying for love with Slade's father." Evan lowered his chin and raised an eyebrow, casting an arch look at Robert.

"No. You don't say. I mean, I can see him buying the house for her as a settlement for when he marries someone else. But after all these years of his mama drilling 'decorum—'"

Here the other two joined in, as they had since Michael had first told his friends about his mother's favorite saying. "—'respectable, acceptable behavior.'"

"I could see him marrying an untitled lady, but…a courtesan?" Robert turned a palm up.

"No one is marrying anyone." Michael's teeth clenched so hard his jaw hurt.

"Look, I think you should marry who you please. If it pleases you to marry someone from the Spanking Club, so you always have a bare bottom handy, you should. Or a titled lady. Or Pen. She's lovely. I like her."

"How did Peterborough get involved?" Robert asked.

"His bride and Penelope grew up together. Apparently, they were best friends until Penelope moved to Peterborough six years ago when her mother remarried."

"Huh. I had wondered that part, myself." Bags was nodding. "As he said last night, Peterborough's wife wasn't a member of the Ton either. And Lord Mansfield agreed that marrying for love was more important than marrying for pedigree."

"Does this mean you are in love with Penelope?"

Michael stayed silent.

Robert tried again. "You must have said something to Peterborough for him to ask that."

"My parents—" he began, but Evan cut him off.

"Your father as much as gave you his blessing last night, old chap. Your mother loves you to pieces. She'll get over it. Besides, she can hardly complain when she was in a similar position, can she?" He grinned at

Michael. "I for one think 'tis a grand idea, and wonderfully romantic. Besides, if you leave her free to pursue other benefactors, I might be tempted."

Michael narrowed his eyes at his friend.

"'Tis a jest! Of course I jest! I would never break our rules of friendship." Evan threw his hands up, palms out, in surrender.

Back in university, they had established that once one of them had been with a woman, she was off-limits to the other two. The exceptions were pub wenches, and later, Spanking Club employees.

Michael's conversation with his mother replayed in his head.

Between her comments after the ball and Father's response the night before, and now Bags...could I actually... He shook his head. "I worry 'tis easier for them to speak in the hypothetical than when faced with reality. Why else would they have held me to the stricture of a Ton wife all these years? That and how difficult the blasted gossipmongers made life for our family."

"What if they were speaking in the hypothetical when they held you to that?" Evan threw out. "For example, life being easier with a Ton wife when they held you to that?"

But Michael dropped his head into his hands, shaking it. "'Twas never a hardship, until now. And even an actress is a step more acceptable than a mistress. Blast. I need more time to be sure. And there is the stupid Cyprian ball Pen wants to attend, because she thinks I'm offering for Lady Grace any day now."

Robert's brow furrowed. "Hmm."

"Please. You'll both come to the club for the ball,

still, right?" Michael looked up without raising his head.

His friends nodded, their faces solemn.

Chapter Twenty-One

Penelope finished pinching the edges of a pie crust. She and Mrs. Thorpe had prepared a few meat pies for her, Michael, and the Thorpes. They had chosen different versions so the pies could be eaten hot or cold over the next two days, as the Thorpes were off the next day.

As she laid the crust on the last pie, a knock sounded at the front door. Dusting her hands on her apron, she passed the pie to Mrs. Thorpe to finish and slipped the apron over her head.

"Miss Penelope, a lady here to see you." Mr. Thorpe entered the kitchen with a heavy-looking embossed card on a salver.

Surprised, she plucked the card, turning it around to read the name.

"Countess of Mansfield." Her hand dropped as though the card weighed it down.

Michael's mother? Why is Michael's mother calling on me? Blast, I am covered in flour. And I am not even wearing stays.

She growled in frustration. Then, taking a deep breath, she called on her schooling and her pride. She had naught to be ashamed of. She had chosen her profession, and she'd stand by it. And she was doing nothing different than the woman's son and at *his* instigation. This was her house, at least for now. The countess could respect it, or Penelope would decline her company, son be damned.

Head high, she swiped at her face for traces of flour before ordering tea to the parlor and sailing out of the kitchen.

"My lady." She entered and executed a quick curtsy before rising again. "I do not believe I've had the pleasure?"

"We have not been formally introduced, although I have seen you several times," the countess replied.

Penelope frowned in confusion but was distracted by the differences in their appearance. In stark contrast to her once-pink-now-more-gray dress, the tall older woman was in a shade of forest green that highlighted her hair, the same chestnut color as her son's. The dress was clearly new, with a tiny white ruffled border along the square neckline and on the capped sleeves. The white provided even more contrast to the warm tones of her skin and hair.

She took in everything from the perfect coiffure to the matching shoes and was suddenly conscious of her own scuffed slippers. She could not fathom where she and the countess had crossed paths, even in public.

"'Tis lovely to meet you, Miss Wood. Thank you for allowing me to call uninvited and with no notice, however rude it might have been of me. I am Barbara Slade, Countess of Mansfield." She pressed her lips together before continuing, "And as you likely know, Michael's mother."

Penelope lowered her gaze before recovering her courage and raising it again.

"Yes. Please have a seat. I have asked Mrs. Thorpe to bring tea." As they settled, the countess on the settee,

Penelope in Michael's favorite chair, she said, "My lady, if I may ask…to what do I owe this pleasure?"

The countess chuckled. "No polite discussion of the weather then? We shall get right to it? I like you. First, please call me Barbara. I hope we can be friends."

Friends?

"Ahh…certainly, ahh…Barbara." Her mouth struggled to form the words. The whole exchange felt surreal. "Oh, and of course, I am Penelope."

Unsure where to go from there or whether the countess would answer her question, she stayed quiet. It had worked the first time she and Michael sat in this room. Mayhap it would work with his mother.

Friends? We shall see.

"Of course you are wondering why I am here. 'Tis true I should like us to be friends. But I recognize this comes out of the blue and that you will need time to trust me and my intentions. Beyond that, our future is not wholly within our control—a common thing for us women, no?—and will depend on my son."

Penelope remained silent, gaze steady on her visitor.

It behooves me to imitate Ann or Leah now rather than Rachel. Her internal giggle was tinged with hysteria.

"It came to my attention recently that you are in a relationship with my son." The countess flicked a glance at her, but she was not going to confirm or deny anything until she understood more of the woman's motivations. The woman arched a brow at her silence. "Right, then. Anyway, his father and I have been hoping he will marry. Admittedly, we preferred he find happiness with a member of the Ton. Our society being what it is, things are difficult when you marry outside your…" She seemed unsure of what word suited best.

"Class." Penelope's voice was flat.

"Ah, set, class, you get the general idea." The older woman waved a hand. "Do you know his father is ill?"

Penelope stared.

"Right," the countess repeated, fidgeting her hands in her lap, plucking her skirt, then smoothing it. "His father is ill. Thus there is the question of an heir, you see. Michael seemed willing, even pleased with the idea of marriage and a family. Content to attend the balls and theatre with me and various young ladies."

Penelope nodded, wondering if mayhap the countess had seen her at the theatre then. Yet she had not been visible at performance times when theatre-goers arrived, aside from in costume.

"Then he focused on one young lady in particular. Pretty."

Penelope flinched, and her guest shot her an apologetic look.

"Quiet. The perfect future countess for him, perfect mother for his children, I thought." Sighing a breath so deep it heaved her whole torso, she continued. "I was looking at her as his mother, desiring acquiescence. Not as a wife, a partner, for someone I love and want to be happy. George and I, we are partners. Oh, he manages the estate and Parliament, but he talks things through with me. He vents his frustrations, especially about Parliament," she said with a quick laugh, "to me. He relied on me to raise the children and involve him where possible and to run the household and oversee our social calendar. And mayhap Lady Grace could do the same, but where would the laughter be?"

Penelope flinched again at the name, and Lady Mansfield raised a hand as though asking for patience.

"Where would the deeper affection come from? When I considered their relationship again this sennight, I could not see it. She did not seem to have laughter or other powerful emotions. Then I realized nor did Michael around her."

"He does with us. And he has always adored the theatre. I suppose you know something of my background." She cast Penelope another glance but had clearly recognized her disinclination to acknowledge any damaging information. "So he comes by his love of the theatre honestly from both his father and me. But he did not...*engage* with her."

"Lady Mansfield—Barbara," Penelope amended when the countess shot her a reproving look. "My apology, but I am still unclear as to the purpose of your visit?" She was not at all certain she could bear hearing any more about the lady Michael was to marry.

"Oh, dear, 'tis I who should apologize! Here I am going on and on without getting to the point. George and Michael are constantly reminding me to try for succinctness. I do try..."

Penelope almost laughed at Lady Mansfield's similarity to Rachel but was too unnerved trying to guess her visitor's point.

"Your existence was brought to my attention—and no, a countess never shares her sources, that is the one area I shall use my title to my benefit—and I had a few chances to observe you."

Penelope's eyebrows rose in surprise.

The older woman leaned back with a small smile playing about her lips.

"I am not sure if you're aware of this, but Michael holds himself a certain way in public. He is always conscious of his responsibilities, both current and future, but his hands betray him. He tends to fidget with them, as though playing scales on an invisible piano at his sides or shoving them into pockets to avoid doing that. 'Tis something only a mother or lover might notice. On recent visits to the theatre, he met a few people with whom he did not fidget. When I looked closer, I realized that those 'few people' were actually one—you."

Penelope's eyes widened. Even Michael had not discovered her disguises, and yet this woman saw through them without knowing the person beneath.

"Let me see, there was the young fop, the slightly heavier older woman... Shall I go on?" The countess was grinning now.

Penelope shook her head once, still fixated on where the woman was leading with this.

"I so admired the idea, I visited the theatre during the day. 'Twas easy enough to arrange, as I know Prudence."

Penelope frowned. She had not seen the countess and Prudence touring the facility.

"Oh, no, dear. You do recall I was an actress?" Her guest seemed to read her mind. "I, too, was in costume."

She stared, squinting a little. The puzzle piece fell into place. "The young man outside Leah's office a sennight ago?"

"Ah ha! Very good." Lady Mansfield nodded, smiling. "I was on my way out from the costume room, where the staff lauded your sewing skills and hard work."

"But…er, why?" She was still confused.

"To get to know you, of course. Once I ascertained who calmed my son's hands and made him grin and caused him to lose track of the second acts of plays that he has always loved, I was intrigued. I wanted to know more. At the start, I was not sure whether you were a man or a woman," she added matter-of-factly.

The countess was ready to accept a relationship with a man, but Michael did not think she'd accept a non-aristocrat? It seems as though Michael does not know his mother as well as he believes. She'd ponder that more later.

"Ah…well done, my lady," she managed with a nod. "But what did you think to gain by spying on me?"

Lady Mansfield winced at the term but recovered. "I wanted to understand if it was mayhap an infatuation for him, one that we could wait out."

It was Penelope's turn to wince.

Michael's mother shrugged. "'Tis true. I quickly discovered, from Prudence's comments and Leah's, as well as my own observation, that you were more. I found—find—you a delightful young lady, someone who could be a true partner to my son."

Penelope's mouth dropped open. *Bloody hell. I cannot be a countess. And what of Michael's insistence that his parents want him to marry within his—*another internal wince—*class?*

"Right. As I suspected." Her guest was nodding at her alarm. "The other evening, Michael told me that he could not marry the young lady he had been courting. And my acceptance of that surprised him. It seems our encouragement to find a suitable wife within his *set,*" she accented, overriding Penelope's inclination to substitute *class*, "to make his life easier, was taken to heart mayhap more than we intended. Of course, we'd prefer our son have an easier time of it than we did. But more than any other factor, love makes for an easier time."

Penelope took a deep breath. "My lady, Barbara, I appreciate you sharing all this with me. I admit that Michael did indeed give me a different impression of your wishes. Or, shall we say, he understood them to a different degree as you suggested. All that is between you and Michael, however. I do not have any say in his decisions."

The countess snorted.

Penelope barely stifled her surprise at the less-than-genteel sound.

"If you do not recognize that you are in a position of power when a man is in love with you, then you are not well-suited to the aristocracy, my dear. And before you think it, I firmly believe you are quite suited to it. So I came to give you my blessing. What you do with that is up to you."

Lady Mansfield rose, shaking out her skirts, and made her way to the front entryway where she pulled on her gloves. "It was lovely to meet you. I do so hope to see you again soon. Mayhap become friends. I shall send you an invitation to visit me next time rather than come here and invade your space unannounced."

Penelope dithered, unable to fathom calling at Mansfield House, unable to form a response to the older woman's parting words.

Before she could disentangle her thoughts, the countess was out the door and whisking down the path to her—crested, blast it—carriage.

Gor, the neighbors must all be hanging out their windows.

****

Penelope dressed for the demi-monde ball with care. She'd had a pale cream gown made to resemble the original sheer shift she had worn for the auction.

If it worked once, mayhap it will work again. There must be someone *engaging enough to take my mind off Michael, whether or not he marries.*

She shuddered, frustrated she had not been able to follow Leah's and the school's advice.

For propriety's sake, she wore a petticoat and low-cut chemise, then added stays that pushed her breasts up on display in the deep scoop neckline. Her hair was up, as she was uncertain of the typical dress for these balls. Leah had said only that they contained a wide assortment of formal and risqué. The last item she donned was the diamond daisy necklace from Michael, hoping the sparkling flower nestling at the top of her cleavage would draw men's—*his*—focus.

She was waiting when Michael arrived. He had not come by the night before, for which she was both sad and grateful. She still had not determined whether or how to inform him of his mother's visit. He had sent flowers in the morning with a card to cheer her, but her mood remained gloomy, hating the task before her of choosing someone to replace him.

Other than thanking him for the flowers, they were both quiet on the ride to the club.

After queuing in a line of carriages, they alighted and made their way to the ballroom, used as a theatre for the regular club events. A small orchestra sat on the stage, allowing for an open dance floor, surrounded by small tables with chairs.

Michael grabbed two glasses of champagne from another servant and handed one to her as she gazed around the room. Her lips twisted at the irony of starting and ending their relationship with that particular beverage. It might be ruined for her forever.

There was a wide variety of dress present, every color of the rainbow creating a feast for the eyes. Some women and men wore masks, although their partners did not all have the same inclination. A few of the women appeared to have rouged their nipples and lips, and one had foregone undergarments beneath her dress. Penelope caught a shadow at the vee of her thighs and a seam of her bottom through the yellow muslin.

Michael seemed comfortable, if not happy, raising his glass to a few men who caught his eye across the room. He stayed by her side, her hand linked through his elbow, steadying her while she acclimated.

She glanced up at him, still unable to read his thoughts through the silent demeanor he'd worn since he arrived at her cottage. Shrugging, she reminded herself that she could not make his decisions for him, but she must make some of her own.

She gulped her champagne for courage. "Would you like to greet those gentlemen, then?"

He nodded, his face impassive, his voice still silent, and guided her toward them.

Several women were slow to shift out of their way, running their gaze greedily up and down Michael's form, lingering on the bulge below the points of his waistcoat.

One licked her lips, and Penelope stifled a gasp.

Her hand tightened on Michael's arm before she forced her grip to loosen.

A few men eyed her, and she leaned in toward Michael's side.

I ain't ready to give him up. Then countered. *I bloody well have to be. Whether 'tis to Lady Grace or someone else, he will marry. I have barely enough funds to live for a year without working, and if I did that, I'd be no closer to a bakery with no savings.*

The realization that her nerves were showing in her lapse into vulgarity, albeit silently, forced steel into her spine. She rolled her shoulders back and raised her chin.

Michael caught the movement and peered at the pendant resting on the mounds of her breasts above the dress. He stopped and reached a finger to trace the chain along her skin and down to the daisy to lift it. His knuckles rested against her flesh, causing her breath to stutter and speed up, creating more friction of skin to skin. His stare, hot with lust, met hers as he rubbed his thumb over the pendant and dropped it back to her chest after a beat.

'Tis a bloody strange party.

She knew an action like that could only happen in the darkness of a garden at a Ton ball without incurring scandal.

He greeted the men, introducing her to them and the woman accompanying one of them.

She heard the names Cheltenham and Orford and realized Michael's closest friends were among the group, although her nerves had precluded her putting the names with masked faces.

She swapped her empty glass for a full one but was

careful to sip rather than risk a replay of the first night Michael visited the cottage.

One gentleman asked Michael how they came to be here, seeming surprised at his attendance.

"Penelope desired a night out, and this crowd is as discreet as any," he replied.

She frowned. Was he not going to help introduce her to possible partners? She would need to take the initiative.

"Would you care to dance, then, Miss Wood?" Another gentleman preempted her need to do so.

"Thank you, my lord." She studied his mask. This might be Cheltenham. She glanced at Michael, not quite for permission.

He was frowning but remained silent.

"I should love to dance."

Having learned several dances for just such occasions, she set her half-full glass down and glided onto the floor with the man.

The orchestra had been playing waltzes, and people were dancing rather closely. The gentleman tugged her to him, wrapping his arm around her. Her breasts grazed his coat, and his arm rested in the middle of her back. If either of them turned, her hip would graze his groin, and his hers, she realized with alarm.

"My lord—" She caught her breath as he swung her into the dance.

"Interesting. Michael is glaring at us," he hissed toward her ear, his head almost close enough to whisper, despite the music. "He did not stop you, but he does not like it, either." 'Twas definitely Evan, the troublemaker.

As they turned, she spied Michael, arms folded.

Definitely glaring. A flame of hope flared only to be ruthlessly tamped down by her practicality.

"I think we shall end this dance on the other side of the floor, and I'll introduce you to a few more people, yes?" he asked with a cheeky grin.

"My Lord Cheltenham, I am not sure you want Michael to be angry with you."

His response was a silent smirk.

She tried a different tack. "I am not sure I want Michael to be angry with me."

"Right. Then why did you wish to come?"

Knowing that open conversation was acceptable with this audience, she replied, "Michael is going to marry soon. I need to secure my future."

"Then introductions are exactly what you need. It seems as though you should worry about that more than Michael's anger. He did bring you here for that very purpose, did he not?"

With that, the earl turned her one last time to ensure they ended the dance on the opposite side of the dance floor from Michael.

"Cheltenham, I can't say I am surprised to find you here," a rather block-shaped man said, leaning back on his heels. "And who do you have here? Is she yours? I had not heard you had an understanding? Or are you considering one?"

Evan smiled and nodded his head to acknowledge the gentleman.

"North, allow me to present Miss Penelope Wood. Penelope, the Earl of Northumberland, or North to some of us." Turning to the earl, he said, "She is here with Slade. But she is always interested in meeting new people."

She flashed him a look, recognizing how well versed he was in the protocol of these parties. He was a good choice to help her navigate these waters for the first time, no matter how sorry she was at the need to do so.

"Lass, good to meet you. You are lovely." His accent was almost a Scottish brogue, which made sense if she remembered Northumberland's location.

"Thank you, my lord. I am delighted to make your acquaintance."

Evan tugged her arm, moving them along. "Ah, Dartmouth, how have you been?" he asked as he reached another gentleman, this one with a woman on his arm.

Penelope had glimpsed the woman when she first arrived and been riveted. Dark hair gleamed against a deep vee of creamy skin in her décolletage. She wondered how the dress stayed put over the slopes of the woman's breasts as the neckline centered just below them. For that matter, normal stays would show under that dress, so either the woman did not wear any or wore a modified corset. *Her bust* must *have help staying up and visible like that.*

Closer now, the woman's age was older than she'd first guessed. Makeup helped the creaminess, and given her dress, most eyes would not be on her face as much as other places. Regardless of age, the woman was beautiful.

"Cheltenham. Lovely gala here, don't you think? I've not been to one of these in years, but Isabella wished to come. You remember Cheltenham, right, my dear?" Lord Dartmouth smiled down at his escort and patted her hand.

"Why yes. 'Tis lovely to see you again, Cheltie. And who is your friend?"

"Allow me to introduce you to Miss Penelope Wood, Slade's companion for the evening. I am helping him introduce her to a few other guests. Let me know if you see anyone you think she should meet, won't you?"

"I shall. And 'tis a joy to meet you as well, Miss Wood. Enjoy your evening." This came from Lord Dartmouth, but Isabella was smiling and nodding.

They continued around the room in this manner. She continued to slant quick looks at Michael who stood glowering in the same spot they had left him.

As they neared him again, Evan leaned down to her and said, "You would not be here now if I had won you at that auction. But my hands are tied now. Michael is my friend. I dare not risk the friendship after knowing his feelings for you."

She looked up at him in question, but they were within hearing distance again.

Michael stepped forward, reaching for her and pulling her away from Evan's arm.

"Dance with me," he muttered crossly, not asking.

He led her onto the floor and stepped one foot even closer between her legs than Evan had done.

"You seem to like a closer hold," he grouched, leading them off.

"Mmm, I do with you." She pressed against him wantonly, for once not having to consider the public venue.

"Gehhh." A non-word emanated from him as her hip pressed his cock, her breasts against his chest and the inside of his arm.

They twirled in silence for a few moments until he

tugged her out of the path of other dancers near the veranda doors. Keeping her hand in his, he wrapped it over his other arm and propelled them out to the veranda.

Other couples stood in dark corners, many very close together. She would swear that at least two couples were kissing. A third, in the farthest corner, were in an even closer clinch, the woman leaning against the townhouse wall, her skirts up above the one knee hooked around her escort's shin. His hands were not visible, and Penelope imagined where they might be.

Michael turned her to him, clutching her shoulders and smoothing his hands down her arms, then up to cup her head. He stared at her, silent again.

Penelope understood. She, too, had an endless stream of words going through her head, none of which she could utter.

Take me home. Don't make me choose this. Stay with me. Keep me. And the worst, *Marry me.*

"Pen…" he began.

She could not bear it if he asked who she preferred, so he could help her negotiate her next contract. Going up on tiptoe, she used her hands on his triceps for balance as she leaned up and slanted her mouth over his.

Chapter Twenty-Two

"Umph," Michael groaned into Pen's mouth, yanking her closer and returning the kiss. After long moments, he pulled his mouth from hers and wrapped his arms around her. He buried his face into the side of her hair, whispering, "Please," uncertain what he was asking for. His throat was too tight for more anyway.

He had spent the last two days attempting to determine a clear path forward. It was easy enough to admit he wanted to marry Penelope, given that he already loved her. But could he put someone he loved through the struggles they were bound to face? And his future children?

On the other hand, they had Edward and Sophia, and mayhap other close allies such as Suffolk, on their side. Mayhap most surprising, his parents were also supportive, which meant their friends and associates as well.

He needed more time to think through it. To buy that time, he had landed on an approach of telling her he was not marrying this Season and extending her contract. Then the Poor Laws issue had remained contentious and had taken all his focus these past days, so he had to attend tonight. He still had not found the right words. His thoughts kept jumping ahead to marriage rather than the contract.

He felt out of control. His life had been so easy,

with clear rules and roles. Even when he broke them, most of it was at Bags' instigation. Come to think of it, Bags was provoking conflict again tonight.

"Ahem."

Michael looked up at Evan, realizing that his friend was reminding him there were limits to the discretion allowed in the public area of these parties and they'd been gone for some time.

Taking a step back, he offered his arm to Penelope, following Evan back into the ballroom. As they entered, one of the first men Michael had introduced Penelope to approached, a young blonde woman on his arm.

"Ah, Slade, there you are. I have been thinking about making a change. And my lady here assures me she likes variety. Any interest in swapping for a month and seeing how it goes?"

Michael growled, fisting his free hand, seeing a red haze surround the man. He could not believe it. He'd literally growled.

Penelope stared, aghast, and Evan burst out laughing.

"Well! I say. Not quite sure why you are here then, old chum. Cheltenham here gave me the impression that you might be making a change soon."

He should be helping Penelope. That was their reason for attending. Clearing his throat, he said, "Er, not yet. Apologies, you surprised me."

The man nodded and moved on, the woman on his arm still eyeing Michael from head to toe with hunger.

Evan sighed and rolled his eyes. Standing to her free side, he ran his gaze over the room. "Hmm. I see several good candidates, my dear."

"Define 'good,'" Pen declared.

He grinned. "Don't you worry. I know good. They are considerate of their partners, flush, and generous. And neither too old nor ugly for you."

Nodding, she gestured for him to continue.

He named a few but then turned. "Truly, I think North is the best of the lot. And honest as the day is long."

"Northumberland? Are you kidding?" Michael jumped in, frowning. "He's almost two decades her senior, and if he doesn't crush her with his size, he'll kill her dream of the bakery. How would she find the spices she needs so far from London? No. He won't do at all."

"Then who would you—"

Penelope laid her free hand on Evan's arm and turned to him.

"He sounds lovely, and he was nice enough. Mayhap we can go talk to him a bit more?" She dropped her other hand from Michael's arm.

Michael stood frozen as they strolled away, his mouth agape.

No! Don't let her go! What are you waiting for? You know your decision. You're dithering. You'll lose your chance.

****

After Evan facilitated a second conversation with North, Penelope excused herself, needing a minute to ponder all that she had seen and heard. She ricocheted between heartbreak at the need for this choice and attempts at focusing on the fact that she was only a year away from her dream of financial independence.

She made her way to the ladies' retiring room but froze inside the door.

A woman a little older than she stood over someone sitting on a hardbacked chair, curly brown hair obscuring the seated girl's bowed face.

"What did I tell you, Beth? No touching men without permission! We won't attend events like this if you cannot behave."

Looking up, she spotted Penelope staring at them. "I beg your pardon, miss." She returned her attention to her cowed companion, "We will leave immediately if it happens again."

The girl jerked her head up. "Please, no! I'll be good, Althea."

Penelope frowned for a moment. She recognized that voice and the glimpse she caught of the girl's face past the other woman. Trying to place it, she cast her mind back. Theatre? School? Peterborough?

School. And the auction. Gor—Beth?

She gasped.

Both women looked up.

"Ahh, Beth? Beth Jenkins?" she asked.

The girl peered around Althea. "Penelope? Lud, Pen, 'tis that you? How are you?"

Althea murmured to Beth, and she subsided.

"I'm, ah, sorry to intrude. Mayhap you can find me downstairs or call on me." She rattled off her address and excused herself. It made sense that she would see others from the advanced classes here.

Mayhap if Beth did—was allowed to?—search her out, she might have another path to finding her next position. She laughed, realizing that she had recognized the voice because she had heard Beth apologize so many times. That girl was always up to mischief.

What other students might be here? This could be

fun.

The sight of Michael brought her melancholy rushing back.

"Oh no," she breathed, dejection turning to dismay.

Edward and Sophia stood conversing with Michael. Sophia was dressed somewhat more conservatively than most but had taken a similar approach to Penelope's. Her sheer dress showed her stays cut below the breast, and Penelope suspected she had rouged her nipples to show through, given her fair complexion. Penelope's own darker skin had not needed that to show hints of flesh through the gown.

Edward's hand was on his wife's lower back, keeping her close.

Proprietary or preventative? Mayhap both, given her friend's lack of regard for rules.

Sophia was scanning the room, taking everything in that she could as the men chatted. Catching sight of Penelope, she started toward her, but Edward tightened his grip on the side of her waist and held her in place. Succumbing, she sent Pen a little wave.

"What are you doing here?" Penelope hissed at her friend as she neared.

"Why, helping you, of course." Sophia's tone was as blithe as when she'd turned up on Penelope's doorstep.

"What? You are risking your reputation—*again*, I might add—*my lady.*"

"Nonsense. The men here know Edward was a member of Sarah Potter's. I am going to lean on Leah to see if she will tell me, but my guess is that several of the women are involved with the school in some way."

Given how Edward and Sophia had united and

what Leah had said about the vetting for this party, Pen supposed this was the least risky action she'd seen from Sophia.

Then Sophia's second statement registered. As she had encountered Beth moments ago, her laughing thought after the retiring room was a real possibility. A wider school representation was indeed likely here tonight.

"Edward is telling Michael who he knows is safe, supposedly. Really, we are both here to get Michael to see that you are the best candidate for a wife. I am here as a perfect example." Sophia giggled, and her husband squeezed her waist.

"Hmph," came from Edward at the words "perfect example," at which Sophia elbowed him.

Penelope rolled her eyes at her friend as Beth and the older woman re-entered the ballroom. Sophia saw them over Penelope's shoulder and squealed. "Beth!"

Beth turned, finding them across the room, and squealed. "Oh my gosh, 'tis a reunion," she said, dragging the other woman toward them.

"You and I should compare Beth's stories at some point…" Penelope muttered under her breath at Sophia as they approached.

Sophia snickered as Beth and her companion stopped in front of them.

Beth began introductions. "May I present my cousin, Lady Althea Egerton. Althea, Miss Penelope Wood and Miss Sophia—"

Sophia was shaking her head. "Delighted. I am now the Countess of Peterborough, here with my husband." She gestured.

Beth blinked and nodded. "That's right.

Congratulations, my lady." She curtsied.

"Come now. We shall always be Sophia and Beth and Pen." Sophia laughed and waved a dismissive hand.

Michael and Edward had noticed the commotion and turned to the women as Evan rejoined them. Introductions were made, Evan bowing low over Althea's hand, his grip lingering.

The ladies asked for a few moments to sit and catch up in the corner. Evan volunteered to bring them refreshment, and the men strode toward a long table.

Penelope's gaze lingered on Michael until her friends pulled her toward some empty chairs.

****

"Peterborough. Why are you really here?" Michael's foul mood had not improved with the earl's entrance. He suspected the couple was here to support Penelope, but he was unsure what direction that stand would take.

"Well, now, chap, I should think you'd know, after our conversation with your father at the club. Being single, you may not yet realize that once a wife sees a cause to champion, the best course of action for the husband is to do everything he can to help. I am not going to dissuade Sophia from this need to look out for her friend. Besides which, I enjoy showing Sophia off in all settings. I am hoping to take a stroll through the house with her, in fact."

It was common knowledge that couples could borrow upstairs rooms for further intimacies. If they left the door ajar, it signaled they did not mind being watched. Some were looking to show their prowess if they were hunting for a new partner. Others simply enjoyed an audience. Either way, for anyone with voyeuristic tendencies or looking for new inspiration, it was a perfect opportunity for some titillation.

They reached the women, carrying champagne for their ladies. Evan had glasses for both Althea and Beth.

After Althea thanked him and slid a look at Beth that Michael could not interpret, the two ladies excused themselves to circle the edge of the dance floor.

Evan stood with Penelope, murmuring with her as they cast glances at different men around the room.

Michael's hand tightened on his glass stem. He'd expected Edward to stay single forever, because he'd been so adamantly against marriage. Between that and his previous interest in the Spanking Club, Michael was surprised at how easily Edward spoke of capitulating to his wife's wishes. The world was upside down, and he was lost. He looked for his anchor, his calming influence, chatting blithely about a new relationship with Bags.

Edward stood to one side, arms folded, eyebrow arched, watching them.

Sophia slid her arm through Penelope's, chattering as though at tea rather than a demi-monde ball. "Pen, we need to discuss an outing to your milliner. I am still pining for that hat you wore the other day."

He frowned. An outing? A countess and his mistress? No countess he knew would risk such a thing, friend or no.

His father's words returned to him, along with his mother's. So that was why Sophia referenced an outing, and that was why Lord and Lady Peterborough were here. She and Edward were offering public support, even at a cost to their reputation.

Edward nodded to a woman in a low-cut red gown

being escorted upstairs by gentlemen on either side.

Were they going to observe or be observed?

"Just think. In a few months, that will be Penelope with her new benefactor or two." Edward leaned over to hiss. "Do you think you shall bring your wife here?"

After the haze of anger cleared, his thoughts clicked into place.

The only way I can see bringing my wife here or seeing Penelope here in future is if Penelope is that wife. The repercussions we can sort out together.

He shot Edward an irate glare and stomped off, interrupting Penelope's conversation with Sophia and dragging her with him.

"Michael?" she questioned at his abruptness.

Turning down a hall past the stairs, he tried the door to a salon he remembered. It was open but occupied. Closing the door, he continued on. Another door was locked, but Sarah was coming out of her office at the far back of the hallway.

He gestured. "Sarah, may we have a few minutes in the library? Please?"

Penelope sent him a side glance, looking miffed. Mayhap the abstract knowledge of his club membership and the stark reality of his familiarity with the rooms sat differently in her mind.

Good. That's not even a tenth of how I have felt watching her interview men to replace me. He unclenched his jaw and gave a small quick shake of his head to loosen his muscles.

Sarah unlocked the door for them, and Michael stepped into the book-lined room, pulling Penelope with him. Turning to close the door, he saw Edward and Sophia framed in the doorway.

319

He opened his mouth, but Edward reached for the doorknob. "We'll be out here to ensure no one disturbs you."

The door clicked shut.

His mind was racing. 'Twas all fine and good to bemoan struggles and society and their poor fictional—at least now—children. But just as his parents would not trade one aspect of their relationship, nor could he fathom a life without Penelope in the center of it with him.

I cannot lose her, blast it. I at least have to try. If she hates the idea of society's backlash, she can say no. I might die alone if she does, but she can say it. I could ponder the pros and cons forever, but I've seen tonight that I'll lose her if I wait too long. And she is scared, too. If I simply tell her I am not marrying, she still might decide she has too much to lose by staying with me.

Fear gripped him still. He stared at her, gathering his courage.

Penelope watched him quietly, patient as ever.

No more. She should not have to wait on any man. She deserves everything I have to offer and more. Now.

He dropped to a knee.

"Michael?" Her voice rose at the end, shock coloring it. Her hands clutched at his shoulders to lift him.

"Pen, I am begging your forgiveness."

Her hands dropped for a moment. "What? Whatever for?" She tugged again. "My lord, please get up."

He shook his head, catching her hands and remaining in place. "I have been so caught up in pleasing my parents, until they disabused me of my notions of their hopes. I have been so focused on society's views, until I saw what true friendship looked like." He gestured back toward the door where Edward and Sophia had stood.

Penelope stopped pulling at him, her hands going slack in his, her eyes wide. Her head cocked to one side as she watched him.

"Penelope, please. Don't do this. Don't go to another man. Stay with me. Please."

****

Penelope's forehead creased in confusion. "But Michael, we discussed this. Neither of us are comfortable continuing if you marry. What of Lady Grace?" She wanted to hear it from him.

"Forget her. I will not offer for her. I did not dance with her, or anyone, at the last ball. You are all I can think of, Pen."

"Michael, I care for you. I should like naught else than to stay with you." Unsure of what he wanted, she ventured a guess. "But there will come a day when you marry, and I do not want my heart to be broken irrevocably. I must protect myself."

He shot to his feet. "No, Pen, you misunderstand me."

"Oh?" Now she was more confused than ever.

"I wish to marry *you*."

Penelope's knees liquified, the settee behind her catching her as she threw out a hand.

"Michael?" Mouth agape, she tugged her other hand from his to press against her chest.

"Penelope, I am asking you, nay, begging you, as I said." He reclaimed her hand, pressing it between his

321

and frowning in consternation and earnestness. "Please, stay with me. Marry me and save me from settling for a life with some boring miss from a well-heeled family. Share your laughter with me, your delicious recipes, and"—he leaned in—"keep me guessing what will be on the menu each night."

"But, your parents…" She hadn't yet shared his mother's visit with him. "And…and I cannot be a countess. The scandal!"

"Society be damned. My parents dealt with it for love, and so can we. A good number of the Ton attended the auction. And look at the people here. For many of us, there is an understanding of the threat of mutual destruction. Look at Sophia and Edward's attitude."

He'd referenced love, but only indirectly. Dare she hope?

"Pen, please. I am begging here. What do I need to do?" He gripped both her hands again, raising them to his lips.

She straightened, her back stiff. He hadn't told her what she needed to hear. Every particle of her cried out to say, *"Yes, a thousand bloody yeses!"* But his mother's words came back to her. She was in a position of power, and she had to be sure.

Her voice was strong and serene when she answered him. "Very well, my lord. Here is what you need to do. First, putting the offer in light of what I can do for you does not make it attractive. Tell me what I shall get out of this. Second, there was no mention of any motivation for begging. Was it only for the scones? And the sex?"

Michael blinked, then laughed. "Damn me, I love

322

you, Penelope. Any other woman would have leapt at the chance to be a countess. But no, you ask what is in it for you."

"Aha!" She nodded decisively. *There, he'd said it!*

His laughter died, his head tilting as he quirked his brows.

"Yes, yes, I will," she said with a last nod.

He shook his head, confused. "Wait. What did you say?"

"Michael, I simply needed to hear you say you love me. I am in love with you, and I should like to leave this ball right now and forget I ever had to think about attending. I wish to show you exactly how much I adore you. Likely in the carriage, as I do not know that I can wait until we gain the house." She sprang into his arms and planted her lips on his for a long kiss.

A moment later, he raised his head, staring at her in wonder. "You're certain? You love me?"

"Of course, you silly man! Now take me home, please." She could hardly believe it. Everything she had dreamed of and more.

She gulped. *A countess.* Challenges lay ahead with the Ton, but together they'd have strong allies to help them—his parents, Sophia and Edward, and other school alumnae.

She breathed a quiet snort. Even Leah could not be mad that she had fallen in love now.

Epilogue

As Penelope cleared the door of the bakery, Michael aimed for his usual table and took a seat to watch his wife cross to the display counter.

She chattered with the woman behind it about the day's offerings, pointing and gesturing at various items. The manageress, Fanny, had been there almost from the opening.

He looked toward the rear kitchen, envisioning the fireplace with its baking ovens and racks, the piles of tins of various sizes, and the line of hooks holding various sized peels. He'd helped Penelope choose them, along with the metal rack beside them. Two vertical rows of graduating metal hooks aligned and, held together with a few crossbars, it boasted various sized rolling pins. These were sturdier than her still-treasured and oft-used Nailsea set in their kitchen at home.

Ah, what I could do to my little baker here. He snickered.

He inhaled, enjoying the scents of cinnamon, cardamom, and ginger mixed with the yeasty smell of flour.

He was so proud of Penelope. Not one to give up her dream, she had instead expanded it. If she could form a bakery with unique offerings for financial independence, why couldn't it help other working-class graduates of the school?

She would not allow either Bags or Michael to fund the enterprise, so Evan had put them in touch with the woman-friendly investor he had mentioned to them, the Dowager Countess of Peterborough, Edward's sister-in-law. She had closed the gap between Penelope's savings from the auction and the funds necessary to start the business, based on Evan's analysis. They had not needed quite the full amount planned, as Lady Peterborough's negotiating skills rivaled those of Evan. And working with Helen Montague at the School of Enlightenment, they created a successful apprentice program, as Fanny could attest.

Penelope's dream had evolved and blossomed as their love had evolved and blossomed.

His wife turned back, plate piled high with pastries in one hand and a cup of tea for him in the other.

He smiled at the sight, her protruding middle leading the way. His smile turned wistful, wishing as he often did that his father could have fought off illness long enough to meet this baby. But he knew Father was watching. And they had joked that Mama Mansfield, now the Dowager Countess, would be enough of a force in this child's life to cover his father's part.

He laughed at his beautiful wife as she sat across from him and sorted the pastries, hoarding anything with ginger and allowing him only the fig tea cake.

"Really, Pen? Not even one fruit tart or scone? Pretty please?" He shook his head at her pregnancy cravings.

"But Michael…" She offered him her innocent puppy eyes look. "…they're for the baby."

"There is no way that child can eat five pastries."

But he let it go. They both knew he would give her whatever she wanted.

He changed the subject. "How is Fanny doing?"

The bakery's apprenticeships featured several areas of study. The introductory course taught baking. Girls must learn the recipes offered and create them uniformly for three months. Then, students who were creative or preferred to remain separate from customers could pursue advanced baking and decoration skills while others learned the selling and management sides of the business. All were paid a decent wage to be able to live and even save if they were careful.

"Excellent, thank you." She picked up one of the pastries. "She has two new girls arriving in a week to start in the back. And that means she'll have one more person to help out front."

"Only one?"

"Yes." Penelope bounced on her chair once in her excitement. "Nancy has already begun fiddling with some recipes and trying her hand at new creations. It will be lovely to have someone other than myself to spark new offerings, as they make the customers return more often."

"Hmm. I suppose you encouraged her to play with ginger?"

She grinned. "Of course."

"I am happy to help you play with ginger, too, my pretty." He wiggled his eyebrows at her, referencing the figging he had given her during a late-night baking encounter in their kitchen.

Her eyes had gone round as he shaped the ginger into a wedge, with a narrow neck and a flange below it. It had taken her a week to eat ginger again after, although she had eventually admitted she was not averse to trying the exercise again.

For now though, during her pregnancy, he was teasing her simply to watch her squirm. He would bet her bottom was clenching at the memory.

"Husband! Oh, please, hush," she whispered the admonishment.

"I am trying to help my beautiful wife satisfy her cravings." He was laughing openly.

"Not here, please?" She looked around, scrutinizing the patrons.

Realizing what she was doing, he gazed around as well. As soon as Penelope had agreed to marry him, he brought her home to meet his parents over dinner. He had been surprisingly unsurprised to learn that his mother was already aware of her existence and had befriended Penelope. However, he was shocked to learn she had brought her acting skills into the mix.

Since then, he and Penelope had kept watch for strangers with her build, paying attention to them when they were out. One never knew with his mother, as much as he loved her. And 'twas a fun game.

"Right, then. Is all ready at home for David and Matthew's visit?"

"Oh, yes. I cannot wait. I haven't seen them since—well, this." She gestured to what was left of her lap.

Her family had attended the wedding, and a few months later, Michael and Pen had made a trip to Peterborough to visit them as well as Sophia and Edward.

At the wedding, he had encouraged David to take on an apprentice to enable more frequent visits to Pen and Michael. Creating a future earl was important for the Mansfield lineage, and Michael wanted all available grandparents to have as much time as possible with their family. He assured David that any education or training that interested Matthew would be funded, as well as a retirement cottage for David in the location of his choice, to free his time for grandchildren.

He hoped his father-in-law chose somewhere closer to Mansfield Manor than Peterborough, and Matthew would eventually choose Oxford rather than Cambridge, but either way, they were family and he'd support them.

And whether this baby was a boy or a girl, Michael planned to give him or her the same treatment as Penelope—whatever he or she wanted.

A word about the author…

Maggie Sims began her love affair with romance before her teen years, drawn to the Regency by her mum's British influence. In her twenties, she did her best to live the Carrie Bradshaw life in New York City, albeit with less expensive shoes and more books.

Despite reading hundreds of romance novels in her life, she was still blown away when she met the love of her life, an ex-Marine cinnamon roll with creative woodworking and culinary skills.

Having retired from corporate life, they live in Central Texas and are parents to a varying number of dogs and cats. When not writing, Maggie is a wine enthusiast, a travel junkie, and a romance reading fiend. She also sporadically crochets for KnotsofLove.org and does just enough exercise for that second glass of wine at night.

To find out more about Maggie's latest reads, favorite wines, and travel destinations, sign up for her newsletter here.

~*~

Contact Maggie at
www.MaggieSims.com
and sign up for her newsletter

Thank you for purchasing
this publication of The Wild Rose Press, Inc.

For questions or more information
contact us at
info@thewildrosepress.com.

CPSIA information can be obtained
at www.ICGtesting.com
Printed in the USA
LVHW080509290922
729514LV00012B/410

9 781509 245956